# HOT ~~SEX~~—
# A COMPUTER PROJECT
# CALLED *SOCRATES*

Tomasso shook his head, staring off into the darker recesses of the little cocktail lounge. "You are," he said finally, very softly, "a twenty-four-karat son of a bitch."

Mathias ignored the comment. "Vincent," he said, "without people like me, pushing people like you, nothing would ever get done."

"Burt," Tomasso said abruptly, "SOCRATES could really screw up."

"I don't think that will happen," Mathias said. "We're supporting this one hundred percent, we'll put all of our technical people behind you, we'll essentially give you an unlimited budget to make this thing go."

Tomasso closed his eyes. "Burt," he said, "I've never seen anybody who was in a hurry like you. Don't you ever do anything slow?"

"Why?" Mathias asked, raising his eyebrows in feigned surprise. "Slow is good," he said, "only in bed."

**"SUPERHEATED MINDS . . . TALENTED
ECCENTRICS . . .
BIG BUSINESS WHEELING AND DEALING."**

—*Publishers Weekly*

# SILICON VALLEY

## Michael Rogers

PUBLISHED BY POCKET BOOKS NEW YORK

This novel is a work of fiction. Names, characters, places and incidents are either the product of the author's imagination or are used fictitiously. Any resemblance to actual events or locales or persons, living or dead, is entirely coincidental.

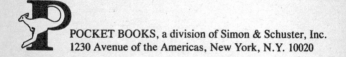

POCKET BOOKS, a division of Simon & Schuster, Inc.
1230 Avenue of the Americas, New York, N.Y. 10020

Copyright © 1982 by Michael Rogers

Published by arrangement with Simon and Schuster
Library of Congress Catalog Card Number: 82-3207

ISBN: 0-671-46692-5

First Pocket Books printing January, 1984

10 9 8 7 6 5 4 3 2 1

POCKET and colophon are registered trademarks
of Simon & Schuster, Inc.

Printed in the U.S.A.

For my father and mother,
who taught me to love both
science and stories

# SILICON VALLEY

A novel of the near future

This is not a fable, even though it is about merchant princes, and magic, and the power to transform lives. It's about fortunes beyond most imagining, and about mortals who attempt to duplicate nature's most mysterious creation. It's about pride and revenge, and avarice, and the sour fruit of excessive ambition. But even for all the apparent magic, this is not a fable. It is, quite simply, the shape of the future: a future that began where apricot trees once bloomed, in the heart of Silicon Valley.

# one

THE TORITRON LABORATORY WAS MADE OF RED-
wood, smoked glass and gray reinforced concrete,
perched on a hilltop pasture above Silicon Valley like a
small round spaceship. And like a spaceship, it was
bringing an utterly new technology to the planet: indeed, the greatest change since the Industrial Revolution.

Burt Mathias, the president of Toritron, was short
and balding, but at thirty-four he still maintained the
taut, broad-shouldered build of an Olympic wrestler.
Just past eight o'clock, one April morning, he walked
into Alan Steinberg's private Toritron laboratory.
Mathias had wakened at six, had taken his daily swim
and sauna, and was dressed flawlessly in a tan three-
piece suit of light wool, ideal for a Silicon Valley
springtime.

Steinberg, Toritron's research director, had been in
his lab since midnight, troubleshooting a circuit, so
engrossed that the sunrise over the broad Santa Clara
Valley to the east had actually startled him. His tattered work shirt and well-worn jeans made him look
more like a displaced panhandler than a millionaire
several times over.

When Mathias pushed open the hermetically sealed
laboratory door, the soft sigh of the mechanism caused
Steinberg to look up in surprise, running his fingers
through his shaggy black hair. "Isn't this a little early
for you?"

Mathias, who tended to enter a room as if he were

7

thinking of buying it, glanced around the apparatus-filled little lab. "Board of directors' lunch today," he said. "You forgot."

Steinberg shrugged. It was true. "I thought we had one of those three months ago."

"That was a full meeting," Mathias said. "This is just a little lunch. With a surprise." Mathias looked around some more. "That's why I'm here so early. We need privacy." His uneasy gaze finally settled on a large blueprint tacked to a wall of corkboard. The blueprint looked as complex as the road map of a large city. "How is Ultrachip?"

Steinberg returned his eyes to the little green circuit board in his hand. "Still a great idea. But we're so damn far from having this thing in production."

Mathias nodded, said nothing, locked his hands behind his back. "But the prototypes are still solid?"

Steinberg sighed, his long night of troubleshooting finally catching up with him. "Sure. Maybe a thousand units, checked out and running."

Mathias walked over to the big tinted picture window on the east side of the laboratory, scrutinizing the view over Stanford University and Palo Alto and the San Francisco Bay. Directly below the window, the newly green hillside dropped away steeply, dotted with bright-orange California poppies. The view ran all the way from the red tile roofs of Stanford—where, decades earlier, a few farsighted electrical engineers had planted the seeds of this silicon orchard—down to San Jose, once a sleepy agricultural town, now on its way to becoming one of the largest cities in the nation. Its own orchards were now long gone, to provide space for electronics plants, and the acres of ragtag shacks built for dustbowl refugees in the thirties were newly covered with stucco apartment houses.

After a moment, Mathias turned back to Steinberg, his small silver-and-turquoise cuff links briefly flashing in the slanted morning light. "Ah," he said, with uncharacteristic tentativeness, "I don't want to sound like a stand-up comic . . ."

"Feel free," Steinberg said. "We could use one."

"Okay," Mathias said. "I've got good news and bad news. The good news is that we're going to prototype another ten thousand Ultrachips, and we're going to run SOCRATES. By fall. The first public test of whether computers can show human intelligence. We might even get a satellite TV feed."

Steinberg continued to scrutinize the little circuit board. "Why the hell now?" he asked softly. "We're not ready. It doesn't make sense."

"Okay," Mathias said. "That's the bad news. Ever since we sold the connector division, we've had problems. Toritron is in trouble. We can't get a damn penny out of the banks, and the SL-100 is already six months back-ordered." Mathias stepped over to Steinberg's bench and pulled the circuit board out of his hand. "*Listen* to me, dammit," he said.

Steinberg looked up and blinked, once, twice, and listened.

"You don't even pay attention to this stuff anymore," Mathias said. "The Japs are knocking us out of the box on one side, IBM is doing it on the other, and you're spending half your time hiding in the damn redwoods."

"I haven't washed the etching acid off that board yet," Steinberg said quietly. "Could you give it back to me, carefully?"

Mathias stared momentarily at the little plastic sheet and then cautiously set it back on Steinberg's solder-scarred workbench. "Lord," he said, shaking his head slowly. "For a guy who started an industry, you're awfully slow to pick up on realities."

Steinberg looked away. "I didn't start any industry."

Mathias snorted involuntarily and squeezed Steinberg's shoulder, as the disheveled scientist started to clean the etchant off the circuit board. Mathias stuck his hands in his pockets and circled the little lab once and then stopped. "I want to sell Toritron," he said.

"As soon as possible, and even that probably won't be soon enough."

This time, Steinberg dropped the circuit board and simply stared, stunned. "But . . ."

"No buts," Mathias said, turning his back and gazing out over the soft early-morning vista of the Santa Clara Valley. "Do you remember," he said, "four years ago, when you started work on Ultrachip? You told me, take care of business, do what you have to, just keep me in the lab." Mathias turned around, deadly serious. "I did that, Alan. I did more for you than you'll ever know." He rubbed his high forehead with the palms of both hands. "But this is it. We can't go on like this. We're cash-poor and our inventory looks like a fire sale. I've never stiffed you on R&D funds—you know that—but the fact is the vulture is home to roost."

Steinberg did not move a muscle. He had not paid much attention to Toritron finances recently, but he did know that Mathias, a perpetual poor-mouther, had never before sounded so serious. "But we're so close," he said.

Mathias took off his suit coat, tossed it on an empty lab bench, and sat down on the stool next to Steinberg. "Have you ever heard of 'jaws'?" he asked.

Steinberg shrugged. "Some movie."

"It's also this," Mathias said. He reached for a sheet of paper and pulled a Cartier fountain pen out of his shirt pocket. "This is what they teach the kids in business school now about developing technology." He quickly sketched a graph:

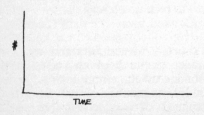

"Pick a curve," Mathias said, "and that's how long it will take to bring a new product to market. You spend a lot of money, it shortens the time. You spend less money, and it takes longer. In both cases, diminishing returns set in." He traced in two curves:

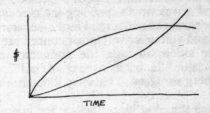

"But," Mathias went on, "you've got to go one way or the other. Either spend a lot, or have plenty of time. We could be spending a hundred K a month less, but then Fujitsu would sure as hell beat us. If you screw up, you end up between these curves." He added a few more details to the picture:

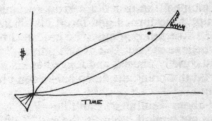

"You end up," Mathias said, "in the jaws."

Steinberg stared at the graph. "And Ultrachip is in the jaws."

"We're already halfway down the goddam gullet," Mathias said flatly. "We're caught in the equity gap. We spent more than it took to get to market. We staffed up for Ultrachip and now we're spending one hundred and fifty thousand a month that's not turning a profit. Frankly," Mathias said, "we're burning."

11

Steinberg stared at his workbench. "It's my fault," he said softly. "If we'd just gotten this damn fabrication—"

"Bullshit," Mathias interrupted. "It's nobody's fault. It was my decision. We're up against Fujitsu and IBM on this. Breaking the ULSI problem is the big time, and it was worth spending the money. But now . . ." He shrugged and turned away, apparently studying a digital voltmeter with great concentration.

"Ever since we sold the connector division," Mathias said, "the banks have been cool."

Steinberg shrugged. "I always thought it was a bad idea."

Mathias stared at him. "Selling the connector division is what paid for your house."

Steinberg shook his head. "But I didn't want to buy a house. It was only because the accountants said I had to."

Mathias rubbed his forehead and deftly segued into an expression of studied pain. "Alan," he said. "Please. No more holier-than-thou today. We have a problem."

For a moment, he paced a narrow rectangle in the lab. Abruptly, he turned and faced his shaggy-haired partner. "Ultrachip is going to be crucial. I believe in it, and I believe in you. But at this point—" Mathias, distracted, briefly paused and tugged at his deep-blue silk tie. "At this point, the damn banks don't believe in us anymore."

"What about Kauffman? Can't he—"

Mathias cut him off. "No. In the end, Kauffman has to go to the bank too."

"So?" Steinberg asked.

"I want to sell Toritron. As soon as possible. It's all we can do."

"But selling Toritron . . ."

Mathias raised one hand. "We'll talk more about it later. It's only a tentative acquisition offer, anyway, and I don't want you to make any decisions right away.

But in the end I think it could be good for both of us. Very good."

Steinberg shifted on the lab stool and looked at Mathias closely. "If you want the company to be acquired, why are we doing SOCRATES? Why are we making more Ultrachip prototypes?"

Mathias was suddenly a thousand miles away. "That's something else we have to talk about later."

Steinberg turned back to the workbench, toying with a handful of tiny electronic components. "We're not ready," he said finally. "The last time I looked at the SOCRATES program, it had real disaster potential."

Mathias' smile disappeared. "So does our next fiscal year."

Steinberg sighed and said nothing for a long time. Then he looked up. "Sure," he said softly. "I'll do whatever you say. I mean, we've been in this thing together since the beginning, right?"

Mathias nodded firmly. "It's going to be fine."

"But look what happened when we sold to Fairchild."

"This time," Mathias said, "trust me. I've got it set up perfectly. We just have to play every step of the game right." He put his hands on Steinberg's thin shoulders. "I know I can count on you."

Steinberg nodded, saying nothing.

"One o'clock," Mathias said. "Don't be late."

Magazine articles about Toritron often speculated on just how two personalities as dissimilar as Burt Mathias and Alan Steinberg had created a multimillion-dollar corporation virtually overnight. The answer was simple, and utterly without romance: pure mutual need.

Steinberg and Mathias first met in the spring of 1970, at Stanford University, in a graduate course called Quantum Electrodynamics. Mathias was twenty-four, Steinberg twenty-three. Mathias was flunking out of the course; Steinberg was bored by it. They made an arrangement: Mathias would tape-record the tedious lectures, so that Steinberg could stay home and read. When Mathias later replayed the tapes, Steinberg would explain them.

This functional relationship germinated a certain odd friendship. Mathias, with the determination of the high school athlete he had been, had worked exceedingly hard to stay in the upper half of increasingly competitive classes. At the Stanford graduate level, he found himself rapidly losing even that ground.

Though Mathias generally disliked his more successful classmates, he was fascinated by Steinberg. The young Chicagoan seemed to move effortlessly through the most technical thickets; unlike the rest of the grad students, Steinberg never seemed to work. Yet he did work, reading voraciously five or six hours a day—everything from abstruse scientific journals to turn-of-the-century German physics texts (which he read in German).

Mathias usually resented such brilliance in others. But Steinberg's efforts seemed remarkably natural. It was as if Steinberg were a scientific animal, perfectly at home in his environment. He seemed to have no particular interest in creating an academic empire, or making money in industry. He was the purest scientist Mathias had ever met—studying nature obsessively simply because that was what his brain demanded.

One day in May, in 1971, in Steinberg's small apartment, ten minutes from the lush Stanford campus, the two students were listening to a particularly boring Quantum Electrodynamics lecture on Mathias' little tape machine. Midway through, Steinberg yawned and mentioned that in one of the journals he had just seen a description of a tiny new electronic component called a microprocessor. It was a remarkable breakthrough in electronics that squeezed most of the basic parts of a computer into a single black plastic chip the size of a postage stamp.

Mathias shut off the droning lecture just in time to hear Steinberg idly observe that using the microprocessor, one could build an entire small computer for only a few hundred dollars. "That's what's going to happen," Steinberg said. "You're going to start to see those things everywhere. If we were smart, we'd join a company like that now."

"If we were smart," Mathias said immediately, "we'd start one."

Mathias thought about it overnight. The next morning he borrowed $10,000 and formed a partnership with Alan Steinberg. Six months later, working out of a Palo Alto garage, they offered for sale the first inexpensive small computer, a desk-sized device that looked like an electric typewriter which had somehow sprouted a television screen. Mathias figured that they needed to sell about a thousand of the units to break even; the first day's mail brought that many orders.

Within three years, Toritron sales were approaching $80 million a year, and the two erstwhile graduate students were wealthy men. Three years after that, Toritron was at the edge of financial ruin—and Burt Mathias and Alan Steinberg were about to accidentally initiate the most spectacular computer disaster in history.

Toritron's assembly plant and executive offices were located a mile down the deep-green hillside from Steinberg's saucer-shaped lab. The building was a massive reinforced-concrete structure, in the center of Silicon Valley's suburban sprawl. The architecture was far more restrained than that of the weathered redwood research center, emphasizing quarry tile and aggregate concrete walkways, broken by high atriums filled with carefully tended plants. It was classic Silicon Valley design: a great deal of open space and interior light, surrounded by accessible green spaces, as if to humanize the abstruse work that went on behind the sheltering concrete walls.

Toritron's executive offices were far less spartan. And the Toritron conference room, just next to Mathias' own office, spared no expense. Mathias' wife, Diane Caswell, tended to redecorate the small chamber every year or so. The most recent scheme had incorporated an entire set of Warhol Mao lithographs, along with an ebony-and-glass conference table produced by a Milan designer who delivered each of his pieces in person. The difficulty with this ambitious decoration was that it all somehow tended to end up in the Mathias home, after just enough time to qualify as a Toritron expenditure. The result was that the Mathias residence was superbly overdecorated, and the Toritron corporate offices were treated to a constantly changing array of furnishings.

Steinberg arrived at the shareholders' lunch fifteen minutes late, after managing to sleep about three hours on the small cot he kept in a storage room at the research center. He had adorned his work shirt with a pale-yellow tie, but retained his blue jeans and moccasins, along with a faintly shaggy brown wool sweater. It was a look that even immaculate dresser Mathias approved. "Tattered genius," he had once termed it. "Early Einstein. Very reassuring for a high-technology firm."

As soon as Steinberg walked into the little conference room, he noticed that the used-brick walls had been stripped of their Warhols, and the Italian ebony had been replaced with an uninspired teak table, now set for lunch for twelve. He wondered briefly if the shareholders ever grew curious about the procession of Toritron furnishings.

Steinberg sat in the cobalt-blue chair to Mathias' right, nodding briefly to the familiar faces around the table. Toritron remained a privately held corporation, with only twelve shareholders, most participants from the beginning.

Across the table sat James Caswell, Mathias' father-in-law, a graying San Francisco patriarch and third-generation Californian with an international law practice. He was, in Steinberg's view, a royal pain in the ass. Directly to Caswell's left was Stanley Kauffman, a Silicon Valley venture capitalist in his mid-forties, who

16

was built like a brown bear but had an inscrutable mind. He had made a small fortune in commodity speculation and had moved from Chicago to Silicon Valley a few years earlier. "Middle-age crisis," he explained it. He had bought into Toritron during a cash crisis in 1979 and promptly prospered.

Two lawyers for Toritron flanked Mathias and Steinberg, and past them sat Frieda Steinberg—Alan's widowed aunt from Evanston, a tiny woman given to bad wigs, who by virtue of marriage had been the only Steinberg with more than a nickel to invest. On the basis of her intuition—which usually walked a fine line between shrewd and batty—she had sunk most of her late husband's estate into the startup of Toritron. As a result, Frieda Steinberg now held 23 percent of Toritron. Mathias constantly prodded Steinberg to remain on "her good side," but the woman was sufficiently eccentric that Steinberg had great difficulty telling one side from the other.

The table was completed with two more lawyers. One was an agreeable older gentleman who represented the Mathias family estate. Burt Mathias' mother had died a year earlier, and the disposition of her Toritron holdings was still being contested by Mathias' younger sister. The last lawyer, a younger man from Los Angeles, represented five smaller shareholders who had invested during Toritron's 1979 crisis. Mathias had for months warned Steinberg to watch this thin, impeccably dressed young Harvard graduate. In total, he represented 15 percent of the shares, and in Mathias' phrase, he had all the heart of a stainless-steel cheese grater.

"Eat!" said Mathias, as Steinberg settled into his chair.

"You might as well," said Steinberg's aunt from across the table. "You boys are obviously softening us up for something."

Indeed, Steinberg thought. As much as he admired Diane Mathias' way with a catered lunch, he admired even more his partner's ability to use food and wine as

17

a business tool. Mathias did it with such obvious pleasure that it seemed almost innocent.

First there was chilled asparagus—"first of the season!" Mathias announced proudly—which absolutely had to be accompanied by a taste of a certain rare white Zinfandel. Then fresh grilled salmon. "First of the season," Mathias repeated.

"Season doesn't open until June," said the young lawyer from Los Angeles.

"In Canada it does," Mathias said. "You've never heard of jet aircraft?" The salmon would be lost, he averred, without a drop of a little-known Monterey Chardonnay. And so it went: a small *salade niçoise,* which would be ruined without a bit of a remarkable Australian rosé; then a light fruit ice, making no sense without a new French/California sparkling wine.

By the end of the meal, the diverse group around the table was thoroughly relaxed. Kauffman, the venture capitalist, had once joked that the best way to do business with Burt Mathias was to take Antabuse before meetings.

Once the catering staff had cleared the dessert dishes, Mathias turned serious, with the abrupt, commanding shift that he had mastered early on. Self-made entrepreneurs, Steinberg had noticed, often retained a certain effective, raw edge over associates whose manners had been smoothed in business or law school; it was an edge that Mathias had, with considerable care, never given up.

"We have very good news and very unsettling news, and, most important," Mathias said without preface, "a very big decision which, for obvious reasons, I could not discuss with you by telephone or mail." He pushed his thin gold pen around the table for a moment. "We may soon—and I tend to say will—receive a very attractive acquisition offer from Technology International. It will be in the form of TI stock, which, I'm sure you're aware, will be an advantageous transaction for a number of reasons."

There was utter silence around the conference table.

It was almost an axiom among Silicon Valley investors that Toritron would always remain the last independent firm in the valley.

Mathias took a deep breath and picked up his nearly empty wineglass, sipping at it several times in quick succession, drinking hardly anything. The characteristic gesture always reminded Steinberg of a toy bobbing bird, and it invariably meant that Mathias was nervous.

Kauffman was the first to speak: "Has the offer been made yet?"

"It hasn't," Mathias said. "I am certain that it will be shortly. And my recommendation is that we accept."

Frieda Steinberg interrupted. "You mean," she said, "you boys are giving up Toritron?"

Mathias leaned back in his chair. "We're not giving up anything. We're simply acting in our best interests. We can no longer compete in the small-computer market, because of the Japanese invasion. We have one piece of innovative technology—primarily developed by Alan—called Ultrachip. Ultrachip will be the computer of the nineties. But we don't have the capital to perfect it. It will be monstrously expensive, but TI can afford that kind of outlay, and they are almost certainly willing to make the investment. It is, frankly, this country's last chance to regain the world computer market."

"This is awfully sudden," said the lawyer for the Mathias estate.

Mathias shrugged. "That's what kind of business this is. But I can assure you that the terms will be worked out carefully." He smiled, in the charming fashion that had led one San Francisco newspaper columnist to dub him the Warren Beatty of microprocessors. "When we're finished—with your agreement, of course—I don't think you'll find an equally advantageous acquisition in the history of high technology."

The lawyers were frantically taking notes. James Caswell was stroking one gray sideburn and staring intently at Mathias. And Frieda Steinberg, as usual, was several steps behind the rest of the conversation.

"Why," she asked, "did the Japanese beat you smart boys so badly? It wasn't that long ago that they used to buy our old tin cans and make little friction cars."

Mathias, all too aware of three different legal minds in silent, simultaneous high gear, was thankful for the diversion. He looked over at Steinberg, who was staring at the ceiling. "Alan," he said, "what's the answer?"

"If we knew that," Steinberg deadpanned, "they wouldn't be beating us."

The remark drew no laughter. Mathias discreetly signaled for coffee to be served.

"Seriously," Steinberg said, "there are reasons. A big one was government policy. Back when the feds were spending millions trying to regulate computer companies, the Japanese were subsidizing research— helping companies get together. The biggest example—the one that hit us the hardest, and blindsided most of the industry—was VLSI."

Caswell interrupted, "Which means?"

"Very large-scale integration. Back in the late seventies, early eighties, it was the next step—putting ten or twenty times more computer on a single chip than we did five years earlier. Everybody knew that the first country to sew up VLSI would also sew up a big piece of the global computer market. So the Japanese set up a government-sponsored research project—seven different firms, working together. They called it their Apollo project. They disbanded in 1980, partly to appease American threats about trade barriers. But the real reason was that they'd finished their work—a new computer generation, down pat." Steinberg— unaccustomed to such lengthy exposition—fell silent.

"We got steam-rollered," Mathias continued. "It's that simple."

"But the SL-100 is still selling," James Caswell said.

"Every new housing development I see has that little plaque next to the doorbell."

" 'An Intelligent House by Toritron'?" Mathias said. "Sure. But that's all hardware we sold two years ago. Next year, those plaques are going to read: 'A More Intelligent House by Fujitsu.' From what we've heard, the new Fujitsu hardware will be trilingual and completely self-repairing. It's hard to compete with something that even if it comes off the line with a flaw promptly fixes itself. But that's the kind of redundancy they have."

Kauffman cleared his throat. "I had no idea it was this serious."

"Serious?" Mathias said. "It's tragic. Maybe IBM can still compete, but that's because they still control all their software. For guys like us, out competing in the vast ocean of hardware, the water's awfully cold. And so there's only one option left: We have to jump two steps ahead of the Japanese. That's the rationale behind Ultrachip. That's also why we're going to need the resources of Technology International."

There was more silence around the table. Faintly, from outside, Mathias could hear workers' cars starting in the parking lot. "I'm sure," he said finally, "after all the faith you've put in Toritron, that this comes as a surprise. There's no reason to make any decision yet. I just want you to know the details from here, before you hear them elsewhere."

Stanley Kauffman put his large hands together and leaned forward, across the table. "What if the TI acquisition falls through?"

"I think it's fairly firm," Mathias said.

"These days," Kauffman said, waving one hand, "nothing is firm. What if there's no deal?"

"Well," Mathias said, briefly touching the knot of his dark-blue tie, "then we'll do as Robert McNamara used to say: retrench and recast."

"Alan," Kauffman said, turning away from Mathias, "what's it going to take to get Ultrachip into production?"

Steinberg's mind had been wandering. He had heard the cars in the employee parking lot as well, and was wondering what the acquisition would mean for the workers. TI would buy Toritron for the Ultrachip technology, not for its small computers. Silicon Valley was following the history of Detroit, only in compressed time. The fifty full-scale automobile makers in the thirties had dwindled to four in forty years. The numerous small-computer firms of Silicon Valley had undergone a similar attrition in only four years. And now Toritron was being shaken out also.

"Alan, I asked what it's going to take to get Ultrachip to market."

Steinberg looked up quickly. "Sorry," he said. "I was thinking."

"Perfectly all right," Kauffman said.

Steinberg smiled. He liked, even respected, Kauffman. This was not his invariable reaction to venture capitalists—even though they had played a pivotal role in Silicon Valley. Venture capitalists financed high-risk new technology—computers and, more recently, genetic engineering. They lent money on ideas, a form of collateral that not even the most liberal bank tends to accept. In turn, if the research was successful—a new computer chip, a modified life form—the venture capitalist owned a piece of it. This occasionally spawned hard feelings—"It was my idea; why is he making money off it forever?" Yet prior to success, nobody was nicer to venture capitalists than the struggling inventor.

Silicon Valley ran on venture capital, and Kauffman typified the combination of shrewd financial judgment and technical intuition that made for success. When he had started to invest in computer firms, he knew little of the science, but he did know the right questions to ask. He had been generous with Toritron during their capital squeeze in 1979, during the hectic months when the SL-100 suddenly became the standard of the small-computer market, and in turn, Toritron had made him far wealthier, in a handful of years, than his previous twenty in commodities.

"Stan," Steinberg said finally, "you're not going to like this."

"Try me."

"Thirty-five million. Maybe forty, over the next twelve months."

Kauffman stared. "Holy shit," he said softly, rubbing his forehead. "That's forty percent of your gross."

"We know," Mathias said wearily. "We know."

"What the hell are you guys *doing?*"

Mathias looked at Steinberg. Steinberg shrugged. "We've got prototypes that work like crazy. We've got so much memory and so much speed on each chip that you've got to slow it down to have a conversation. But the problem is production. And we can't get around the production problems without a lot of money."

Kauffman slowly shook his large head. "I can't get you guys that kind of money, these days. You know that."

"Sure," Mathias said, a bit impatiently. "That's why we've been talking to TI."

"I hate to see you guys give it away," Kauffman said.

Mathias tapped his empty wineglass. "There are realities."

The intense young Los Angeles attorney asked his first question in nearly two hours. "To return to Mr. Kauffman's query, should the TI acquisition fall through, where does that put Toritron?"

"Retrench and recast," Mathias said flatly. "We could even go public."

Kauffman made a face. "You don't want to go public. That's not a good way to attract money right now. We've all done well on the sale of the connector division. But that's also weakened our ability to borrow. We should think about selling another division."

Lockhart, the lawyer from Los Angeles, cleared his

throat. "I disagree. And moreover, I wonder what has happened. You guys," he said, gesturing toward Mathias and Steinberg, "were wunderkinder five years ago."

Mathias sighed. "I'm not sure what you're driving at, Mr. Lockhart."

Lockhart leaned forward, across the long conference table. "Why are you people putting so much into Ultrachip? You can't even make enough SL-100s to meet demand. The shareholders I represent feel that capital should go into a proven money-maker, like the SL-100."

Mathias straightened in his chair, clenched one fist. "Mr. Lockhart," he said softly, "I don't want to embarrass you with a public education in high technology. But let me say this: The SL-100, like every other contemporary system, will be useful only as a doorstop five years from now. This is an incredibly volatile field. If we don't act aggressively and earn a place in the next generation, then a few years from now, your clients are going to have you tarred and feathered."

Lockhart stared impassively at Mathias. "I follow that," he said. "I still think your research-and-development expenditures are totally out of line. It's the feeling of people I represent that you've abused your responsibility to shareholders." He glanced down at his notes for a moment. "You've incurred expenses that simply aren't in the best interest of Toritron."

Kauffman came to the defense. "This is not the appropriate place to be rewording your brief."

Mathias nodded vigorously. "A public suit would destroy the TI acquisition."

Lockhart, now clearly angry, shook his head abruptly. "That's not my problem," he said. "My problem is establishing your responsibility for what's happened to this company.

"I'm serious," the lawyer continued. "My clients will want to know how much has already gone into this Ultrachip."

"Alan?" Mathias said. "You want to answer that?"

Steinberg, puzzled, shook his head. Mathias knew perfectly well that the balance sheet was one form of math he had never tried to master.

Mathias shrugged. "About thirty million."

There was a universal release of breath around the table.

"Sweet Jesus," Kauffman said softly.

"We'll want an immediate accounting," the Los Angeles lawyer said, as he started to gather his papers. "Soonest. I find it hard to believe that two scientists as intelligent as you could have thrown so much money down a technologic rathole."

"You're suggesting it went somewhere else?" Mathias said evenly.

"It's not my place," the young lawyer said, "to suggest anything at all."

The shareholders' lunch was effectively over. The lawyer from Los Angeles left quickly, and the next half hour was strained conversation. Kauffman was conspicuously silent. Steinberg wondered briefly why Mathias had not mentioned the SOCRATES test, but he was growing edgy and eager to get back up the hill to the laboratory. He excused himself after a decent interval, but just before he left the table, Mathias slid him a note across the polished teak: "Dinner tonight at 8. Must come."

# two

JUST PAST DUSK, THE AIR RAPIDLY COOLING, STEIN-
berg drove his small, aging MG up the winding Woodside road that led to Mathias' home. Woodside was the
most exclusive area above Silicon Valley; green,
semirural, horsy—a curious combination of old California money sprinkled with *nouveaux riches* technologic entrepreneurs. The former residents had grown
wealthy on ventures ranging from railroads to banks,
the latter on everything from birth-control pills to
video games.

Mathias' house was modest by local standards, on
two acres of rolling land, dotted by a small pool and
Jacuzzi, surrounded by towering first-growth redwoods. Mathias met Steinberg at the floodlit door and
promptly handed him a vodka martini. "Diane's in the
kitchen," he said. "She and the housekeeper are trying to figure out how to run the pasta machine."

Steinberg stared at the drink. "You know I hate this
stuff."

"We'll get you a beer," said Mathias, and then
ushered Steinberg through the high middle of the
redwood-beamed house, past a large, densely planted
atrium, out onto the elevated brick patio.

Mathias sat on a long rattan bench, and Steinberg
momentarily looked out over the rolling pastureland
below the patio. The pasture, usually dotted with
thoroughbred horseflesh, was often enough to distract

Steinberg from the difficulties of the day. But not this time. He turned back to Mathias.

Mathias held up one hand. "Before you say anything. We don't have an offer from TI. In fact, I'm not sure that the TI people have even thought about it."

"Oh shit," Steinberg said softly, turning again to watch the horses below.

"That," Mathias said, "is why we have to talk."

At that moment, Diane Mathias opened the patio doors and brought out Steinberg's beer. Clad in a clinging purple velour dress, her brown hair lightly frosted, she looked as tall and thin and elegant as when Mathias had married her, seven years earlier. She kissed Steinberg on the cheek. "We never see you these days, Alan," she said.

Steinberg, always uneasy in Diane's presence, shrugged. "Work," he said. "You know."

"How I know," Diane said. "Dinner in about an hour," she said, walking back into the house. "As soon as we debug the pasta machine."

Steinberg thought he sensed a certain chill between Diane and her husband, a conspicuous lack of eye contact. "How is Diane doing as a full-time housewife?" he asked.

Mathias waved one hand. "Don't ask," he said. "I have a feeling this is going to seem like the longest pregnancy in history."


Burt Mathias had married Diane Caswell during the first year of Toritron's success. For nearly two years, he had been working twenty hours a day, and his social life had grown so stunted that he would often tell new employees that joining Toritron was something like becoming a monk. But by the middle of 1976, the company was starting to make not only money but news, and Mathias found himself being asked to speaking engagements. Most he declined, but one fall afternoon he agreed—mostly out of obligation to his alma mater—to speak to a special computer seminar at Stanford.

It proved to be a sharp group—two of the students ended up working for Toritron. And it included just one precocious undergraduate: Diane Caswell. When Mathias had returned to Toritron's small office that afternoon, the first thing he had told Steinberg was: "I'm going to marry her."

Diane Caswell was a remarkable anomaly: a slim brunette who seemed perpetually tan, born and raised in the exclusive community of Hillsborough, ten miles south of San Francisco. She was also a remarkable mathematician.

Her father, James Caswell, was a senior partner in a Montgomery Street law firm. Her mother, perpetually active with civic duties from art museums to scholarship programs, was the sort society columnists dub a "doer." Diane was thus born into the upper stratum of California society, a milieu less formal than its Eastern counterpart, but one which nonetheless clung to its own sense of tradition.

Diane diverged from tradition early on. In retrospect—particularly during the trying months when Burt Mathias came courting—her mother tended to blame it all on mathematics. Diane had been sent to one of the best private girls' schools on the San Francisco peninsula, the kind that regularly turns out polished young women, adept at everything from poetry to equitation, prepared for successful careers at Stanford or Cal.

But sometime in the sixth grade, when her classmates' concerns were turning strongly toward boys, clothes and makeup, Diane discovered math, and was instantly fascinated. Later she would suspect it was because for the first time in her life there were absolutely right answers to any given question—answers that came not from the narrow perspective of parents or teachers, but from the nature of reality itself. At first, however, Diane was simply attracted by the neatness and precision of math.

28

She still read *American Horseman* and *Tiger Beat,* but spent enough time alone with her texts that by seventh grade she had mastered trigonometry—and she requested a popular brand of perfume and a beginning calculus text for her thirteenth birthday. By the time she was fifteen, Diane was a striking young woman—a fetching brunette blend of her father's Scotch-Irish genes and her mother's German. That year, she worked intensively on her tennis, and with her mother's selective permission, she began to date. She also discovered electronics, and before her sixteenth birthday had already built her own stereo system.

Computers came next. Diane Caswell had the first small computer in Hillsborough, and before she finished high school she was fluent in English, German, French, BASIC, FORTRAN and COBOL. Her acceptance at Stanford was almost automatic; her vertical trajectory through the Computer Sciences Department foregone; her attraction to Burt Mathias almost inevitable.

During the early days of Toritron, Diane did everything from typing to debugging game programs for the SL-100. And it was an irony never lost on Burt Mathias that his father-in-law's grudging investment back in 1972 turned out to be the best financial move the old man ever made. Less amusingly, this meant that Caswell, in conjunction with Diane, held 12 percent of Toritron, which resulted in a constant barrage of bad advice from the aging barrister, whose notions of sound fiscal policy seemed rooted somewhere in the late nineteenth century.

Diane's participation in the day-to-day affairs of Toritron gradually diminished as the company became successful and Mathias' concerns turned toward the mass market. In recent months, Diane had been doing work at home, involving the controversial Toritron/Stanford SOCRATES project, an elaborate experiment in artificial intelligence. Her partial retirement was for two reasons. She had grown increasingly uneasy about her husband's technologic empire-building. And in addition, at age thirty-two, she had decided that it was time to have a child.

Steinberg leaned back into his chair at one side of Mathias' broad deck and drank deeply from the cold beer Diane had given him. "You guys are going to be the first parents on the block with a kid whose first words are RUN and PRINT."

Mathias tapped the edge of his glass and shrugged. "I don't know," he said, curiously quiet. "Sometimes you wonder—why does everything have to happen at once? Why don't you ever get a chance to just enjoy one thing at a time?"

This was somewhat deeper water than Steinberg had planned to tread. "Well," he said after a moment, "why don't you just tell me what's going on?"

Mathias shifted on the long bench. "You know most of it already. We're way in the hole on Ultrachip, and if there was ever a time to sell, it's now. I think TI will buy, and it's none too soon to start the rumor."

"Self-fulfilling prophecy," Steinberg said.

"You'd be surprised how often it works."

Steinberg shook his head. "I'm sure. This place is a goldfish bowl."

"But that's not all it's going to take," Mathias continued. "We're not golden boys anymore. And that's why I want to do the SOCRATES test." For the first time that day, Mathias looked positively animated. "Do you realize," he said, "how much publicity that could mean? In terms of acquisition, SOCRATES could literally mean millions. We'd be fools not to do it now."

A faint breeze came up over the green pasture down the hillside, and for a moment, Steinberg thought back to the day in 1977 they had broken ground for the Toritron research center—two guys who owned three neckties between them, suddenly shoveling dirt for a $15 million building. "I don't know," Steinberg said. "SOCRATES could also be a bushel of bad publicity.

30

You could go from golden boy to laughingstock, fully covered by network news, film at eleven."

Mathias smiled and sipped his martini. "That's why I'm glad I've got you on my side."

"Jesus," Steinberg said. "You just stopped lying about your age last year. You're sure you want to take a chance like this?" He gestured over the expanse of Mathias' property. "You're worth enough already to keep you in tennis shorts and turbodiesels for the rest of your natural life."

Mathias was clearly not amused; Steinberg immediately regretted his flippant tone. "Alan," Mathias said, and suddenly his previous warmth evaporated like desert dew, "I don't want to discuss this any further. This is my decision. I want you to talk to that clown Tomasso tomorrow. He owes us, and I expect him to take a leave of absence from Stanford, effective now, and begin the SOCRATES setup."

Steinberg simply stared. "Burt," he said, "for God's sake, Tomasso can't just walk in and say he wants a leave of absence starting tomorrow. Tomasso is the damn *head* of the Artificial Intelligence Center."

"Sure he can," Mathias said. "Let me deal with Stanford. You deal with Tomasso." Mathias sipped his martini several times, quickly. "Tell him he'll get to be on television a lot and he'll do anything."

There was a long silence in the dusk, punctuated when the recessed patio lights automatically switched on, controlled—as were all of the household electronics—by a Toritron SL-100 in a kitchen cabinet. Steinberg concentrated on his beer, and Mathias seemed to be staring several thousand yards into the distance.

"Burt," Steinberg said finally, "what did the guy from Los Angeles mean today at lunch, about the Ultrachip startup costs? Have we really spent thirty million?"

Mathias sighed deeply, in the still Woodside air. "First of all," he said finally, "those figures are very hard to firm up. It's very hard to separate out all these expenditures, and it's not something I want you worrying about. Secondly, this kid from L.A. seems to think he can file an action to remove me as board president. Something about excessive research-and-development costs. He's got a couple of cranked-up clients, he wants to make a name for himself, and—" Mathias' attention was momentarily distracted by a sudden rush of swallows, catching flies in the air over the tile patio. "And anyway, this is something else that I don't want you worrying about."

Steinberg considered this briefly. "Did I ever tell you about my father?" he said finally.

Mathias looked over quickly. "Not really. I know he was an engineer. And that he died while you were in school. That's all."

Steinberg shook his head. "He wasn't exactly an engineer. He started as that, but he ended up as a senior vice-president, back on the old Titan II missile project."

Mathias smiled. "Sounds like us. Out of the lab and into the corporate suites."

"I hope not," Steinberg said softly. "We think he killed himself."

"Jesus," Mathias said, genuinely shocked. "What do you mean 'think'?"

"Remember all the layoffs during the aerospace crash, back in the late sixties? Well, the top management wanted to show they weren't just laying off welders—that they were cutting fat at every level. And Dad got picked. They were generous, but it ruined him. He was fifty-five, and in that business, there was no place to go. He got depressed and one day my little sister came home from school and found him lying on the bottom of the pool. Accidental death, the coroner decided. Severe drug interaction."

There was a long silence as Steinberg finished his beer.

"Another?" Mathias said, somewhat lamely.

Steinberg shook his head. "Anyway, I was a freshman at Stanford when it happened, and I've never been so mad, before or since. I decided right then that I was never going to lose control of my own life, just because of technology. Never trust my existence to a bunch of monkeys whose sole idea of higher wisdom is business school. And so far, dammit, I haven't."

Mathias coughed once, twice. "Oh boy," he said.

"Sure," Steinberg said. "I'll have another beer."

"Listen, Alan," Mathias said. "Do you know how this acquisition would work?"

Steinberg shrugged.

"You'd be paid in shares of TI stock. You wouldn't owe a penny of tax until you sold them. You could defer capital gains over decades. It's the best deal going. There are a thousand entrepreneurs in Silicon Valley who would kill for this kind of deal. Half the companies started here get acquired before they've sold a single product."

"What if I wanted to keep working with Ultra-chip?"

"Well," Mathias said, "that's part of it too. We'll write in consulting positions—five-year, no-cut contracts."

"But it wouldn't be our company anymore."

"That's right," Mathias said. "It would belong to about sixty thousand TI shareholders. But that's business. Toritron's just too big for us to handle by ourselves."

"But that," Steinberg said, "was the only part I liked."

Mathias sipped absentmindedly at his empty glass for a moment and gazed out over the pastureland to the west. "Okay," he said finally. "Listen. You always used to talk about setting up that research facility. What were you calling it? Computers for People? Something like that?"

Steinberg, mildly embarrassed, just shrugged.

Mathias didn't hesitate. "You could transfer the TI stock right into a not-for-profit foundation, to support the facility, and draw your salary off that. You could fund it for life."

Steinberg nodded, looked over at Mathias. "So what's in it for you?"

Mathias toyed with his glass. "Same as you, I guess. Freedom. Something like that." He laughed, in a curious, distant fashion. "Maybe I could go back to school. Finish my education."

Steinberg stood and walked back over to the high redwood railing. The sun had set, and the ubiquitous Pacific Coast fog had started to spill over the coastal range to the west, suddenly lending the air a damp chill. "Okay," he said finally. "Whatever you think best. If it takes SOCRATES, then we'll try it."

"Terrific," Mathias said.

"Even," Steinberg went on, "if it's just a publicity stunt."

Mathias stared at Steinberg. "That's part of it," he said evenly. "Keep in mind: TI is public. And so if they acquire us, they're going to have to explain it to stockholders—mutual funds, insurance companies, God knows who. The explanation will be that much easier if Toritron has been in the headlines."

Steinberg said nothing. "Who the hell knows?" Mathias said finally. "Kauffman still says he'll try to set up another loan. Depending on how that works, maybe we can stick it out, get Ultrachip up and running. But in the meantime I'm assuming we should bail out. And that's not going to be as easy as you'd think." He rubbed his forehead for a moment. "You still want that beer?"

"Ultrachip," Steinberg said softly, "is worth some effort. We've got so much processing power and memory on a single chip that I don't know what its limitations could be."

Mathias held up one hand, stood and walked into the big house. While he was gone, Steinberg gazed around the Mathias property, once again struck by just how successful Silicon Valley tycoons could become. Mathias, a self-described high school "nerd" whose most significant credit was becoming co-captain of the wrestling team, was now living on a dream estate, married to a woman with looks out of French *Vogue* and bloodlines back to the Revolution. He and Steinberg and a handful of others had amassed fortunes and changed society, all on the basis of a few good ideas. Increasingly, Steinberg found himself troubled by just how easy it had been—how their luck and timing had been extraordinary, but their subsequent performance all too ordinary, in the face of social challenges that deserved exceptional people.

Guilt, Steinberg thought. The oldest response in the book to unexpected success. He was glad to hear the patio door slide open and see Mathias appear with fresh drinks.

Steinberg took a long drink of the cold, bitter Mexican beer. After a moment, he said, "Do you remember those old science fiction stories—I think everybody wrote one back in the fifties—about what would happen if all the computers in the country were hooked into a network, and operated as a single mind?"

Mathias made a face as he settled back onto the rattan bench. "I always hated science fiction," he said. "Bunch of amateurs acting like experts."

Steinberg shrugged. "Better than experts acting like amateurs."

Mathias looked puzzled, and Steinberg ignored him. "Anyway," he said, "the idea was that such a system could produce true consciousness. That the whole would be greater than the sum of its parts. Back then, you'd have had to hook every computer in the country together to try it. Now you just need a roomful of Ultrachips."

"If only you smart guys could get Ultrachip to work," Mathias said.

"Screw you," Steinberg said amiably. "The problem is production. We're getting maybe one good chip out of every hundred thousand. After they're burned in, maybe one out of a million."

"Jesus," Mathias said. "Don't ever tell that to the TI guys."

"The combination of multilayer plus the e-beam

35

etcher is just about impossible. Hell," Steinberg said, "at this point, each up-and-running Ultrachip we've got is worth"—he calculated quickly on his fingertips—"maybe a million times its weight in gold."

"Only they're not worth a penny if you can't mass-produce them."

Steinberg was briefly silent. The sleek brown horses in the pasture below Mathias' deck had been taken in, and the single bright point of Jupiter had appeared, high in the northern sky. Mathias concentrated on his martini, and then looked up. "What would you do if I brought you information about a more successful production method?"

Steinberg snorted. "I'd ask where you stole it. Right now our people in chip fabrication are walking on their heels."

"But suppose I did?" Mathias persisted.

Steinberg realized that his partner was serious. "Then you'd have stolen it. Who is it? Fujitsu? I hear they're close on the ULSI problem."

Mathias stared into the distance. "I didn't ask what you'd say. I asked what you'd do."

Steinberg thought about it for a long time. "I want," he said, "to see Ultrachip running. I suppose I'd look at the information and use what was practical."

"Good," said Mathias.

"I'd still want to know where it came from."

Mathias shook his head. "I still wouldn't tell you."

Diane Caswell appeared at the patio door. "Pasta machine up and running," she said cheerfully. "Get yourself in here, so we can discuss why Mr. Steinberg never shows up with a date."

Steinberg looked at Mathias for a moment.

"We'll talk more later," Mathias said softly.

# three

DINNER WAS UNEVENTFUL. DIANE CASWELL HAD indeed debugged the pasta machine, and the *tagliarini al pesto* she served was exemplary. But the dinner itself was curiously quiet; both Mathias and Diane seemed distracted and distant. Afterward, Mathias surprised Steinberg by bringing out a small vial of cocaine; Steinberg hadn't seen his partner use the drug for several years. Steinberg took two lines, more out of a contrived sense of camaraderie than any real desire. But the cocaine only made him feel more uneasy, and after a bit of desultory conversation, he excused himself and drove home.

Home for Steinberg was a small redwood aerie high in the coastal range above Palo Alto. It had only two bedrooms, but commanded such a rare view, from two acres of forest, that it had cost just over $2 million. The previous owner—another young scientist who, having made his fortune in synthetic hormones, had migrated to Manhattan—had furnished the house in hi-tech hedonism. Steinberg, although he felt uncomfortable being anywhere near a hot tub, was no interior decorator, and left the premises as he found them. The place was kept spotless and the numerous large plants green by a young woman who came in three afternoons a week. Somehow Steinberg still didn't feel that he actually lived there; indeed, he occasionally reflected, the house had really been chosen more by his tax attorney and Diane than by himself.

But Steinberg had come to love his view. When

working on a problem, he could sit in the living room for hours, staring blankly at the vast, hazy landscape below him, with the blue of San Francisco Bay behind. Sometimes at sunset, individual puffs of fog, broken off from the immense bank out in the Pacific, would drift over the hills. Caught in the last light of the sun, they would turn salmon at the top, and deep gray below. And then at nightfall, the area would blossom into an incredible spackling of neon and incandescent light, multicolored, like some electronic Jackson Pollock. Silicon Valley was so densely developed that were it not for the dark ribbon of the Bay, the nighttime view could as easily have been Los Angeles from the Hollywood Hills. The Valley, Steinberg had been told, would become the Detroit of the eighties. He hoped not. But then sometimes he suspected it already was.

That night, Steinberg parked his MG on the tree-sheltered asphalt slab next to the small house; the garage was still filled with boxes of books and old electronics. He disarmed the alarm system and walked in, tossing his sweater and briefcase on one of the low chrome-and-leather chairs he had acquired with the property. For a moment, he paced around the dim-lit living room, gazing up at the arched ceiling. The cocaine made him feel antsy, and he wondered how Mathias had cajoled him into it.

"Power on," he called out to the big voice-actuated television screen on the far wall.

"Hello," the tiny, synthesized voice of the television said, as the projection screen filled with the image of a newscaster.

"Sound off, channel up and sample," Steinberg said, over his shoulder.

"Thanks," the television said. The tiny microprocessor inside the tuner ran through Steinberg's favorite channels, pausing five seconds at each. Steinberg was looking for an old movie—any old movie, as long as it was black-and-white—but there was nothing.

"Power off," he said, after a minute or so.

"Thanks," the television said, and went dark. Steinberg sighed; the television had been one of the first voice-controlled models, and was programmed to say thanks after every command. He found it an annoying affectation; why should a machine say thanks? But to reprogram the system would be far more work than it was worth.

He circled the living room once more, then sat on the long leather couch, which faced a wall of windows.

He found himself thinking back to another night, six years earlier, when Toritron had been still literally in a garage. Steinberg and Mathias and Diane were working late, in the small space they had leased in a Sunnyvale industrial park. In a curious twist on Silicon Valley mythology—which held that every successful firm started in a garage—this industrial park actually leased garages, complete with roll-up metal doors; these garages, however, were never intended to hold motor vehicles.

Toritron only briefly occupied the pseudo-garage; business grew so quickly that they could no longer afford to remain, and Mathias sublet the space to a newer semiconductor firm, which, six months later, sublet it itself.

Steinberg still recalled the night. The garage may have been ersatz, but the fact that they had only $5 between them was entirely authentic. It was past ten o'clock, and the twelve young assembly workers they employed (at $4 an hour) had long since gone home to their dope and television. Mathias was delegated to drive to the other side of Silicon Valley—the wrong side of the freeway—and return with barbecued ribs and cole slaw.

The three were staying late to remedy an assembly problem that, at the time, threatened to sink Toritron permanently. The Toritron SL-100, like all small computers, was composed of circuit boards—little green boards of phenolic plastic, five by seven inches, each holding a handful of rectangular black chips for memory or processing. The boards slid like oversize playing cards into racks within the little computers, each board connected to the others by a row of tiny gold-plated pins. The boards in the early SL-100 had an annoying tendency to shift slightly, breaking contact and thus suddenly "dumping"—losing forever—whatever program and memory they contained. The problem had lately earned the SL-100 the nickname "butterfingers" among competitors.

While Mathias was absent on his rib run, Diane seemed unusually quiet. She was wearing her customary costume of the time: blue denim overalls subtly taken in to accentuate her thin waist, and a cream-colored T-shirt she had made up for Toritron. In royal-blue letters, the T-shirt read "Byte My SL-100." A byte is a measure of information in computing, and the pun earned Mathias' stern disapproval. Diane, however, wore it anyway.

Although working together had brought them closer, Steinberg was always a bit shy, slightly in awe of Diane. "So," he asked, after a long moment, "is there something wrong?"

Diane shrugged and looked away, toward the darker recesses of the big garage, where piles of empty SL-100 shells waited to be filled with electronic innards, each soon to be the equivalent of the best computer sold by IBM just twenty years earlier. "Oh," she said finally, "sometimes I wonder what will happen if all this takes off. Toritron, I mean."

"Of course it's going to take off," Steinberg said.

"Well," Diane said, "not unless we get rid of the butterfingers glitch. The price of used SL-100s is already dropping in the hackers' newsletters."

Steinberg nodded. It was an ominous sign. Hackers were the first generation of computer hobbyists, a breed that had started in the suburbs of Silicon Valley. Usually young, male and unmarried, they tended to center their lives around a small computer—one they had built themselves, or one like the SL-100. They changed computers far faster than hot-rod buffs changed cars, and so the market for used hardware was always in flux—and the prices were a good indication of a particular computer's current reputation.

Steinberg scratched his nose. "What the hell do those dilettantes know?" he said.

Diane was silent. To a surprising degree, they tended to know a lot. The first hackers worked with huge computers at their offices—then came home to play with their small computers. It was a bizarre, technologic form of busman's holiday that foreshadowed the addictive nature of computing.

"Well," Steinberg said. "Okay. But we'll debug the boards—that's no real problem."

"I guess that's not what I'm really worried about," Diane said. "I'm worried about what will happen if we're successful."

Steinberg frowned and looked down at his thin hands. "I don't follow."

"I wonder what Burt's going to do."

"Burt's going to be rich, get fat, spend lots of money trying to lose weight," Steinberg said. "He's got that kind of build."

Diane laughed distantly. "I don't know," she said finally. "There's something about business that's changed him, I think. He never seems to be satisfied anymore. What is it they say about business—that it can never remain at a steady level, that it always needs to increase?"

Steinberg shook his head. "Listen," he said, "if I have to explain capitalism to *you* . . ." He stopped. "You sound like half the rich kids I went to school with, as soon as they figured out how their own system worked."

Diane was suddenly cold. "If I was your age," she said reasonably, "I would have been one of the rich kids you went to school with."

"I'm sorry," Steinberg said. "I just meant—"

"Forget it," Diane said, and then she shuddered slightly in the damp cool of the big steel garage. "I suppose everybody would like to know what's going to happen. And I suppose everybody wants to know, because inside they're frightened about it.''

A few minutes later, Mathias returned with dinner, a brown paper bag filled with ribs and hot sauce. And, in all likelihood, Steinberg would have forgotten the evening altogether, except that later that night, after Mathias and Diane had departed for their little apartment in Menlo Park, he had a dream.

Steinberg was sleeping on the floor of the garage, in a sleeping bag, in express violation of their lease, when, in the middle of the night, he dreamed of an army of marching pinecones. He woke straight out of the bizarre image, curiously shaken. But then, as he tried to go back to sleep, he suddenly saw how a principle similar to the helical structure of pinecones could be applied to the connectors on the SL-100 circuit boards.

It was not only the solution to the butterfingers glitch, but better than anything else on the market. Steinberg spent ten minutes sketching what would become Toritron's first patent, and the industry standard, and then went back to sleep. In the morning, however, when Steinberg ate his customary breakfast of canned pineapple, he realized that he had really been dreaming about pineapples, not pinecones.

The take-home lesson, Steinberg later told Mathias, was that you can never trust a dream in the first place.

All that seemed very far in the past, as Steinberg watched the glow of light from his perch high above Silicon Valley. The only part that remained familiar was Diane's odd concern about the future, a concern that Steinberg had come increasingly to share. He had a bad feeling about Mathias' most recent machinations. Early on, the partners had established a symbiosis often seen in Silicon Valley—if you'll handle the money, I'll take care of the science. And the symbiosis had worked better than either would ever have imagined. But now Steinberg was curiously restive, uneasy—like Diane, six years earlier, he was not at all sure what was going to happen next.

Steinberg sighed and reached over to pick up a bluebound technical report describing difficulties encountered in mounting Ultrachip in its tiny case. But the report was so badly written that he rapidly lost interest. He stood and walked briefly around the high-ceilinged living room, staring again at the view spread out below him. His thoughts returned to Toritron, and he suddenly realized that what he really wanted was someone to talk to.

For the most part, Steinberg was happy to be alone. All too often he found the company of others a distinct waste of time. But in recent years, he had become more aware of the painful tradeoff involved in his self-imposed solitude.

Steinberg had come from a fairly reclusive intellectual family; his mother was a philosophy professor at the University of Chicago, and his father was an influential aerospace executive. He had been raised in an atmosphere of extraordinary erudition, where the dinner-table conversations were as quick and witty as any he would subsequently encounter.

Steinberg knew that everyone had trivial memories that somehow characterized their family life—a camping trip, a litter of puppies, a fishing pond behind the barn. His own memory was of the dinner table, when he was age ten, eating a TV dinner and listening first to his mother describe a new journal article about Spinoza, and then his father discuss that year's arms-control negotiations in Geneva. At that moment it seemed to him that he was sitting with the two smartest people in the world, and he was determined to be just as smart himself.

As it turned out, he had a head start. At first grade, his mother enrolled him in the university school. The school had not only a program for identifying gifted children but a flock of doctoral candidates in education, all busily devising "enrichment" programs. Steinberg's IQ and facility for abstraction were identified early on, and he was promptly subjected to positively relentless enrichment. Allowed to proceed at his own pace, Steinberg showed particular aptitude for languages and mathematics. But his real fascination was physics. By the time he was in sixth grade, his bedroom walls were decorated with pictures of Einstein, Maxwell and Newton.

Steinberg, in short, reached his goal: He was, undeniably, smart enough to sit at his parents' dinner table. But the one thing Steinberg hadn't managed was a partner for his own dinner table. The remarkable intellectual communion that he had so admired in his parents had somehow eluded him.

Steinberg was unlucky with women, even though he was, by any conventional definition, an exceedingly eligible bachelor. Diane Caswell had in years past done her best to match Steinberg with her single friends, with generally disastrous results. He was not unattractive; he assiduously kept his lean frame in shape by swimming a half mile several times a week. Yet with women, he was somehow either excessively formal or else oddly off in his own world. He had never, he would say, gotten it quite right.

The longest relationship he had recently maintained was with a twenty-year-old blond hitchhiker he had picked up on El Camino Real, a young woman named Suzanne who had dropped out of college in the Midwest to find herself. Bright, but—in Steinberg's view—typically undereducated. She ended up spending nearly two months at the elegant house in the redwoods.

The first month of having a woman in the house was pure novelty. By the second month, however, the novelty was fading, and Steinberg began to yearn for privacy, or at least less dope smoking and more conversation. He was, he realized, a curious sort of puritan, and he found himself spending more and more nights on his cot at the Research Center. Diane pointed out disapprovingly that only someone like

Steinberg could manage to get himself thrown out of his own home. One morning when he returned home, Suzanne was gone. He was vastly relieved, and entirely happy, to continue the relationship by mail.

Tonight, he realized, he wouldn't mind having Suzanne to talk to. He shook his head. That, quite simply, was not an option. There was plenty of work to do; he should, he thought, begin to design a timetable for constructing the Ultrachip facility.

But instead, he walked into the room adjacent to the big living room. Once it had been a dining room, with glassed-in gardens on two sides. Steinberg, in his only modification of the house, had converted it to a dimlit, cable-strewn computer room.

He decided to check into the hobbyist network and see if Martha the Magnificent had left any more messages.

The computer room was packed with equipment, scattered across the polished oak flooring of the former dining room. Steinberg had one large television monitor, a high-speed printout device, two keyboards, and three tall gray metal cabinets, the size and shape of filing cabinets, containing extremely dense memory units. One leather office chair, on a swivel, faced the beige metal desk that held most of the equipment.

In computer terms, this was a small installation. But its abilities were prodigious. Steinberg was linked by a thick land line, installed at great expense, down the mountainside and directly into the immense main computer at the Toritron Research Center. Past that, Steinberg had installed a small rooftop microwave antenna—a metal dish three feet across—permanently aimed upward and to the east, focused on a communications satellite orbiting thousands of miles above Kansas City.

Toritron leased a transponder on the satellite—a small radio receiver and transmitter similar to the kind that broadcasts pay television programs from coast to coast. Steinberg, however, used his channel for direct computer-to-computer communications with other researchers around the country, thereby escaping the computer clutter that was starting to fill the regular telephone lines as network after network of computer communications sprang up.

Steinberg's use of the expensive transponder made him something of an elitist; ever since the late seventies, computer enthusiasts had been enlarging their own networks, chiefly using regular telephone lines. Most networkers owned computers that could dial the telephone, and carry on a conversation with a computer at the other end, with little or no human intervention.

Steinberg tended to avoid these grass-roots networks. He still remembered the day back in graduate school when he had called up the address of some anonymous East Coast hacker, with whom he had been playing a long-forgotten computer game, only to have the screen light up with a suicide note. But he still patched in occasionally, to see what new sorts of programs and approaches were being passed around. Steinberg was acutely aware that some remarkable programming breakthroughs had come from hobbyists, toiling away in their basements, purely for fun.

Recently, however, Steinberg found himself spending more time leaving messages on one of the oldest Silicon Valley networks—messages addressed to the code name Martha the Magnificent. Many of the networkers chose addresses based on fantasy or science fiction characters, in a technologic update of Citizens Band radio "handles." But Steinberg had never come across anyone who called herself "magnificent" before.

Martha the Magnificent, as it developed, was devising insidiously clever little game programs, which she offered monthly over the network—games with titles like "Seduction" or "Mr. Right" (the latter including instructions for how to convert the program to "Ms. Right").

These games were in the "electronic novel" format that had grown popular with the rise of increasingly dense computer memory. The stories began by typing out a situation, and then plunging the player into the middle of the narrative—as the main character in an unfolding story.

The classic in the genre was a game that opened in a police station. The screen informs the player that he has been arrested for a terrible murder that he actually knows nothing about. After a grueling interrogation, the player is "released," to go out into the world and prove his innocence. The program prints out the different situations he encounters, and, depending on what decisions the player makes, the story itself changes. The "novel" becomes tragedy or comedy, depending entirely on the reactions of the "reader."

The electronic novel was all the rage among the cognoscenti. But for the most part, the narrow narrative skills of the computer hobbyists who could also manage the complex programming tended to limit Steinberg's interest in the genre.

One morning, however, a few months earlier, while idly grazing through the hobbyist network, Steinberg recorded the "Seduction" program, out of pure curiosity. It was another week before he ran it, and he was immediately fascinated. Martha the Magnificent's game was well written, perfectly programmed, with clever twists and turns that ultimately revealed a great deal about not only the complex boy-meets-girl psychology of the eighties, but the player's own psychology as well.

Whoever Martha was, she was at once a fine programmer, a sensitive writer and an astute social observer. She was also severely shy. When Steinberg contacted the computer network coordinator to find this Martha's mailing address, he was told she had requested complete anonymity. Her only address was her computer.

Steinberg had never been so enthralled in his life.

Tonight he checked the network, but there were no

further messages. And then, suddenly, he knew how he would spend the rest of the evening. He sat down to devise a system to track Martha the Magnificent to her lair.

# four

BURT MATHIAS ARRIVED AT HIS OFFICE EARLY THE next morning. His secretary brought him the most important items of the day's mail, and a few telexes received during the night, along with the massive iron-glazed mug of strong French-roast coffee he emptied each morning. There were also a handful of office memoranda, his *Wall Street Journal,* and a daily newsletter on Silicon Valley activity. The last had recently made news by raising its yearly subscription rate to $1,750, and it was a sign of the times—and Silicon Valley—that its circulation had promptly increased.

Mathias was moving slowly, a legacy of last night's cocaine. In a way, it had been an attempt to rekindle a bit of the old relationship he and Steinberg had shared. A few years earlier, both had become briefly enthralled by the drug, perhaps in part because it seemed to distinguish them from the squeaky-clean existence of so many of their colleagues, whose idea of maximally sinful living was red wine, Hawaiian marijuana and hot-tub nudity. Cocaine had a nasty, technologic edge that, in their first surge of success, appealed to them both.

The appeal flickered quickly, out of boredom on Steinberg's part and self-preservation on Mathias', but it remained one of their last shared intimacies. The previous night, Mathias had hoped that it would produce the same intimacy, when the future of Toritron seemed so tenuous. Diane had simply said, "You've got to be kidding," and excused herself to go read. Steinberg at first had said no, then given in. But the late-night jabber Mathias had hoped for had failed to materialize. Steinberg had departed early, leaving Mathias to sit awake until nearly three in the morning.

As the hazy sunlight filtered through the corner windows of his large office, Mathias shuffled desultorily through the stack of open mail. His attention was immediately distracted by a small brown package, postmarked Paris.

Mathias tore the package open, removed a leather presentation case, and opened it. Inside was a gold pen, an uncommon and costly design modeled after a venerable old European engineering pen. Mathias briefly admired the sleek, functional writing instrument, its warm tone glinting in the sun, and then he placed it in his breast pocket. He removed its predecessor—an identical pen, now scratched with use—and put it amid the tattered pieces of package.

His secretary returned with more coffee in a small carafe. "Thank you," Mathias said, not looking up.

"The reporter from the *New York Times* is here," the thin young woman said.

Mathias looked up.

"Maralee Sonderson," the secretary said.

Mathias nodded, rubbed his forehead. "Oh hell," he said mildly. "Give me about five minutes, then send her in. But let her know that we don't have a lot of time today."

The secretary turned to go.

"And oh, Stephanie," Mathias continued. "Could you return this pen to the manufacturer?" He pushed the pile of wrappings across his brown desk blotter.

49

"Something must have gone wrong with the shipping. Probably in Customs. The thing's all scratched to hell."

The secretary stared at Mathias briefly, saying nothing.

"That's all for now," Mathias said, and returned his attention to the mail.

The first time Burt Mathias saw Maralee Sonderson, he suspected that he was in trouble. She was tall and slim, with blond hair and eyes that varied between blue and green. That morning she was wearing a simple beige suit that flattered her willowy figure, and she walked into Mathias' office, leather briefcase under one arm, with a combination of authority and diffidence that Mathias found instantly intriguing. It had been a long time since a woman had taken his breath away; something about Maralee, in fact, reminded him of Diane, when they had first met. She seemed to be a woman at once as smart and as physical as he considered himself to be—and that was a combination he found irresistible.

Maralee was twenty-eight, with degrees in both science and journalism. While Mathias was generally dubious about reporters, she had arrived with the highest recommendations. Her assignment was to do an in-depth series on the new maturity of Silicon Valley, and she had chosen Toritron as the focus of the story.

"A ten-part series on Silicon Valley?" Mathias asked her that morning. "Your readers are going to fall asleep after the first paragraph. There's nothing exciting here. We're all old-time industrialists now." He leaned back, locking his thick hands behind his head, and he sighed, mock solemnly. "You should have been here in '76," he said. "Now *those* were the good old days."

Maralee smiled politely and settled back into the ebony-and-leather chair that Diane had recently placed in the office. She adjusted the collar on her jacket. "I hope," she said, "it won't get too boring. At least, I have a lot to learn."

The morning sun, filtering through the narrow blinds, created delicate highlights in her shoulder-length hair. Mathias realized he had been staring just a bit too long, and he shook his head, still slightly groggy from his late night. "You don't really mean that you know nothing about computers?"

"I use a video display terminal at the paper," Maralee said. "But that's it."

Mathias was puzzled. "So why did you get this assignment?"

"My idea," Maralee said quickly. "You know, they keep sending out these science reporters with Ph.D.s who know everything to start with. When they do a story, they skip basic details. So I came up with this: Send somebody who doesn't know a thing about it. As I learn, the reader learns."

Mathias smiled slightly. "Terrific," he said, with no enthusiasm. "You do have some background in science?"

"Biology," Maralee said. "Emphasis in ornithology."

Mathias stared for a moment. "Bird-watching," he said finally. "That's going to be a big help."

"I'm a fast study, Mr. Mathias," Maralee said.

"Burt," Mathias said. "Call me Burt." He glanced at the paper-thin digital clock on his desk. "I've got about twenty minutes," he said. "It's still lunchtime in New York. Let's take a quick walk around the place."


"This is really only part of Toritron," Mathias said, as he and Maralee walked down one of the high, sunlit corridors that connected the buildings. "Our research facility is about a mile up the hill, and that's where we try to keep the theoretical guys. Down here, we basically only assemble the SL-100 computer. We have our chip fabrication plant about ten miles south of here."

"By 'chip,'" Maralee said, "you mean 'microprocessor.' 'Computer on a chip,' they call it."

51

"Basically yes," Mathias said. "But you can really put almost anything you want on a chip. One big use is for memory. And there are subsidiary chips that do things like control printout devices, or synthesize voices."

"So you make the chips in San Jose, and send them up here?"

Mathias took Maralee's arm to turn her down one corridor that led to the assembly room. "No. Actually, what we do is produce about one hundred chips at a time, on little disks of silicon. Little being from the size of a quarter to maybe the diameter of a saucer, depending on how complex the circuit is."

Maralee hesitated. "I thought computer chips were those little black things with sixteen legs. About the size of postage stamps."

"Those are the cases," Mathias said. "The actual electronics are smaller than a baby's little fingernail. And that's why we don't do it all ourselves. What we do is air-freight the silicon disks to Malaysia. There the workers cut them into separate chips and install them in the plastic cases."

Mathias stopped abruptly. "Damn," he said softly, gazing up at the recessed lights in the acoustic-tiled ceiling. "Half of those fluorescent tubes are supposed to be disconnected."

"Beg pardon?" Maralee said.

"Nothing," Mathias said. "Anyway," he continued, "it's strange. Our main contractor is in Kuala Lumpur. Dreadful city. But there you can hire women straight out of the countryside for a dollar an hour. They're glad for the money, and they have this entire tradition of delicate handwork. There's nobody in this country who would do it. Although a few years ago, one company did try to set up a plant on an Indian reservation in the Southwest. They figured that wiring integrated circuits wasn't that different from weaving blankets, and in a sense, they were right."

"What happened?" Maralee asked.

"Beats me." Mathias shrugged. "I think they discovered oil shale on the reservation. Anyway, the last I heard, they were assembling all their chips in Singapore."

Mathias took a quick right turn, opening a glass door that led out onto a catwalk above the Toritron assembly room. The air was chill, the lighting bright fluorescent, the floorspace not much larger than a high school gymnasium. Except for an undercurrent of quiet talk, the big room was as quiet as a library, even though nearly one hundred people were at work.

Maralee stared down, surprised. "This is it? From this you gross a couple hundred million?"

Mathias shrugged. "This is the heart of it. It takes us about forty minutes to assemble a desktop computer that is basically smarter than your average ten-year-old. Once you hook it into a cable TV/computer feed, it knows a hell of a lot more than both of us put together."

For the first time that morning, Maralee flipped open her notebook.

"You should notice," Mathias said, "that the machines we're building here will change their owners' lives just as much as automobiles did fifty years ago. But this plant is silent, scentless, air-conditioned—as ideal a workplace as we could make it. We offer child care, our plant physician practices holistic health, the cafeteria has a meatless entrée daily . . ."

Mathias suddenly noticed that Maralee was at the edge of silent laughter, and he stared at her.

"If you think all of that is stupid counterculture decoration," he said sharply, "you're missing the point. The next decade is going to make a lot of that counterculture decoration real. Small computers, like the SL-100, will create a complete revolution in information. And that revolution will be, precisely, that we don't have to waste oil, waste steel and copper, waste trees, waste God knows what, to get one piece of information from here to there."

Mathias was briefly silent, then shook his head. "It's too late for humans to turn back now—we're in big trouble, because we got so smart so fast that we used up the whole planet. The only answer is to get even smarter. And that's exactly why we're making these machines."

"Please," Maralee said, touching Mathias' arm. "Don't be upset. I'm really just asking questions."

Mathias gazed down on the assembly area for a moment. "I'm not even sure why you're so interested in Toritron in the first place," he said finally.

"You know what's interesting," Maralee said. "You're the industry leaders. You were the first small-computer company to buy your own chip-producing facility. Everybody else had to buy their chips from some big company, like Texas Instruments, or Fairchild. But you make your own."

Mathias shrugged modestly. "We were lucky. A small chip fabrication firm was going bankrupt—bad management, basically—and we were able to help out by taking over their plant."

Maralee's eyes remained fixed on the assembly work below the catwalk, her expression unchanged. "I've also heard that you signed a four-million-dollar long-term contract with them, six months before they went bankrupt."

Mathias coughed softly. "We had great faith in their capabilities."

"And then," Maralee said evenly, "you canceled the contract after they had expanded their production facilities, which forced them into bankruptcy."

"Let's just say we lost faith in their capabilities."

"Yet then," Maralee said, "you turned around and bought them out for five cents on the dollar."

Mathias tried to smile. "Well," he said slowly, "I guess we felt partially responsible."

"Ah."

Mathias straightened up and leaned back against the steel rail of the catwalk. "Listen. That story has been going around for too long. We asked them to do something they couldn't do, and we were entirely within our rights to cancel the order. It was pure luck we could help save the company."

"I see," Maralee said.

"I thought you said you didn't know anything about computers," Mathias said.

"That's not computers," Maralee said. "That's business."

Mathias nodded slowly. "I sure as hell hope that you're not going to be as much trouble as you sound like," he said finally.

Maralee smiled. "I don't see why I have to be any trouble at all."

Mathias gazed at her for a long moment, then glanced at his watch. "I have to get back," he said. "Tomorrow, come for lunch, and then I'll show you the chip fabrication plant."

"About noon?" Maralee said.

Mathias nodded.

"And when could I meet the famous Alan Steinberg?"

Mathias looked distracted. "Not today. Alan's very busy today."

# five

EVEN THOUGH IT WAS ONLY NINE IN THE MORNING, Dr. Vincent Tomasso was already upset. His day had started with a breakfast-table fight with his live-in womanfriend, which had been interrupted by an early telephone call from New York, indefinitely postponing his upcoming appearance on the *Today Show*. And now, moments after he stalked into the large, spare Stanford building that housed his artificial intelligence project, someone was telling him that during the night, Newton Bray had once again locked himself in the central processing room—the filtered, air-conditioned cubicle that held several million dollars' worth of state-of-the-art computer hardware.

Tomasso was short and stocky, with curly black hair surrounding a premature bald spot. He looked like a cross between a Mafia hit man and a stand-up comic; his customary garb, winter and summer, was blue jeans and a bright Hawaiian shirt draped over his modest potbelly. Without moving, he dropped his briefcase on the tile floor of the computer lab. "Newton goddam Bray," he said softly between his teeth, almost to himself. "Dumbest mistake I ever made." He stared abruptly, fiercely, at the graduate student who had delivered the news.

"Shut down the ventilators in that room," he ordered curtly. "This time we'll suffocate the little rat." He nodded once, decisively. "That'll teach him."

The graduate student stared. Tomasso picked up his briefcase, snorted briefly, and headed into the sanctity of his small office. But even before Tomasso collapsed in his desk chair, his elderly secretary came through the door. "Dr. Tomasso," she said, "I don't mean to—"

"I know," Tomasso said, waving one hand. "I know. Newton Bray. It's all taken care of. We're going to suffocate him." He looked up after a moment. "Just kidding," he said. "Just kidding."

His secretary looked unconvinced. "But that's not what I was going to tell you. Alan Steinberg has been calling here every half hour since seven."

"Oh, shit," Tomasso said. "Any message?"

The small, gray-haired woman shrugged. "He wants to talk to you right away."

Tomasso closed his eyes.

"You've also got an interview with a Maralee Sonderson, from New York, at three."

"See if we can postpone that," Tomasso said. "Call Steinberg back, and let me know when he's on the line." He reached over and punched a button on his desk intercom, then looked up at his departing secretary. "What's the number for the processor room?"

"One thirteen," she said.

Tomasso nodded impatiently, adjusted the collar of his loose, colorful shirt, and tapped out the numbers. The intercom buzzed softly several times, and then the quavery adolescent voice of Newton Bray answered. "Hello?"

"What the hell are you doing, Newton?" Tomasso asked.

"I'm on strike," the thin voice answered through the tiny intercom speaker.

"The hell you are, Newton. You're screwing everything up."

"I'm on strike," the voice repeated, with somewhat less certainty.

"Newton." Tomasso sighed. "What's the problem?"

"Nobody will let me run my program."

Tomasso closed his eyes again. "This is your infinite number series?"

"Yes."

"Newton, running that program would take all of our processing capacity for an hour. We'd have to shut the damn university down. You're talking about thousands of dollars in computer time."

There was a long silence at the other end. "But I *want* to run it."

"Newton," Tomasso said softly, "there are lots of things that people would like to do, but they can't sometimes. You've just got to accept that."

"I'm not coming out," Newton said defiantly.

"Newton, if you're not out of there in two minutes, I'm going to dump every program you've got stored here. And then I'm going to call your probation officer and tell him that you'd be better off in a forestry camp studying chain-saw technology." Tomasso shut off the intercom.

His secretary was watching from the door. "I don't know why you put up with that kid."

Tomasso shook his head. "Sometimes I wonder."

Newton Bray had been fourteen years old when he had first used his parents' telephone, and the Toritron SL-100 he had received for his birthday, to break into the Stanford computer system. In a spectacular feat of pure computer intuition, he managed, via public telephone lines, to gain access to the university's main computer, and then simulated the complex entry codes that even legitimate users were required to use. For nearly a month, Bray's computer presence terrorized the artificial intelligence project. He styled himself the "unknown glitch," popping up unexpectedly in the middle of other programs, often destroying months of work. In addition, he used his access to the big computer to run his own bizarre, home-brew programs.

After weeks of sophisticated electronic detective work, Tomasso and the Palo Alto police department tracked Bray down to his parents' modest tract house in Cupertino. When arrested, the diminutive Bray was sitting in his shorts, in his bedroom, alone with his SL-100 and his telephone—patched directly into the main Stanford computer.

Bray broke into tears when he was arrested, and not without reason. The initial charges against him included not only vandalism (for destroying computer programs), but grand theft as well. In all, Bray had stolen computer time worth well over $100,000.

Neither the juvenile authorities nor his baffled parents knew precisely what to do with Newton Bray. But Vincent Tomasso took something of a liking to the odd, introverted teenager, and had the young genius put on probation in his custody, as an assistant at the artificial intelligence project.

Perhaps it was due to Tomasso's own background. The youngest son of an old San Francisco fishing family, Tomasso had watched his three older brothers follow in the family tradition: One bought a small fishing boat, one became a crab and salmon wholesaler, one went to business school and opened a seafood restaurant.

Tomasso, however, was caught on the hook of science, early on. Partly it was a matter of timing: Vincent Tomasso was educated exactly in the middle of the post-Sputnik science craze in American public schools—the curious panic that resulted when the Soviet Union managed to put a metal basketball in orbit before the United States did. Why Johnny Can't Read became, overnight, Why Johnny Can't Understand Math. Tomasso, only mildly inclined toward science at age ten (he collected minerals), found himself solidly reinforced in that direction. His father—by then in his early sixties, with three sons already in the business—didn't really care one way or the other.

By the time Tomasso was in eighth grade, he had won his first science fair, with a project called "An Investigation of a Simple Electrolytic Cell." The project itself was competently done, but had limited appeal—it was, after all, basically a study of how batteries work. But young Tomasso added one twist: a demonstration that involved half a lemon, a zinc clip and a copper penny, wired to a small electronic oscillator and a loudspeaker. The passerby could press the penny and zinc clip onto the cut surface of the lemon, and the electric current thus generated would create a loud tone from the speaker. "Listen to a Lemon" was a smash—during the fair, Tomasso's mother had to drive him to the exhibit hall twice a day in order to change lemons.

The lesson of "Listen to a Lemon" was not lost on Tomasso. In the years following, he continued to study science—first electronics and then drifting finally into computer science—but he never forgot the importance of having a good act as well.

In 1978, Tomasso wrote a popular book called *Computerfuture*, some speculations on how computers might affect society. Through perseverance on the part of his publisher, Tomasso was booked for the last fifteen minutes of the *Tonight Show,* the position traditionally reserved for authors who will put the audience to sleep. But robust Tomasso bustled out of the curtain in his customary bright Hawaiian shirt, hair tousled, eyes blazing, dangling beads and abacuses from both arms, sat down next to Johnny Carson and proceeded to utterly beguile the audience with a hilarious demonstration of the binary system—involving not only his beads and abacuses, but the upraised fingers of all the show guests seated on the couch next to him.

By the end of the segment, the audience was in stitches and at least under the impression that they understood the on-off, zero-one notation that underlies all computer operation. And, most important, on the air Carson invited Tomasso back—an invitation that was promptly firmed up the next day, when network switchboards were flooded with calls raving about "the crazy computer guy."

Tomasso's career as media scientist was launched. And curiously, his career as serious scientist was proving equally successful. For all his flash and funny shirts, Tomasso was a remarkable scientist, who had, early in his career, fastened on perhaps the most significant and difficult problem remaining in computer science: the simulation of human intelligence.

"I've got Alan Steinberg," Tomasso's secretary said from the doorway. "He's on eleven."

Tomasso punched a button and picked up the ivory telephone receiver.

"Alan," Tomasso said. "I never see you these days. What the hell do you do with yourself? I figured for sure I'd see you at the IEEE meeting in San Francisco."

At the other end of the line, Steinberg was silent for a moment. "Oh," he said finally. "You know me. Conventions give me headaches. I don't drink, I don't smoke, I don't slap backs. So why not just stay home and read the proceedings?"

Tomasso spoke mock seriously. "You know, Alan, if you weren't such a smart guy, you'd be really boring."

Steinberg laughed.

"You didn't miss anything," Tomasso said. "A lot of stuff on how to cut costs on the 256K RAM chips. The upshot was, either lower quality control and have two-for-one sales, or else take over a developing nation and convert its entire economy to tax-free semiconductor production."

Steinberg laughed again, but stopped as Tomasso continued, "Someone also started a betting pool on when you'd announce Ultrachip officially."

Steinberg was silent.

"People are awful damn curious," Tomasso said quietly. "I've never heard so many rumors about one piece of hardware in my life."

"Well," Steinberg said finally, "that's actually what I called about. Burt wants Ultrachip to make its debut."

"It's about time," Tomasso said. "If you guys were public, I'd be on the other line right now, calling my broker."

Steinberg paused. "Burt wants to run SOCRATES on the Ultrachip system. He wants to have a public Turing test."

Now it was Tomasso's turn to be silent. "Impossible," he said finally, staring at the opposite wall of his small office. "Not for at least another year. We've still got so many refinements to make in the program, so much more memory to add—"

"From what I've seen," Steinberg interrupted, "I think it might work. Or else come damn close. We're going to prototype another ten thousand Ultrachips next month."

"Out of the question," Tomasso said firmly. "There's no way."

Steinberg sighed deeply. "Mathias wants to do it in September. That gives us four months to put it together."

"Completely impossible," Tomasso said. "Forget it."

"Vincent," Steinberg said. "I don't like this either, but sometimes you've got to take a chance. Without a push, you could sit on SOCRATES for another five years."

"I don't have the time. I have the center to run, I have my teaching, I have the new book—"

"Burt suggests you take a leave of absence."

Tomasso gazed at the ceiling of his office. "Great. I go to the dean and say, 'I'd like to take a few months off, starting now.' "

"Burt has already talked to Stanford. They're willing to give you a four-month sabbatical, starting immediately. When you return, it will be to an endowed chair."

Tomasso digested this last bit of news. "What?" he said finally, softly.

"Toritron will endow a professorship for the study of artificial intelligence. Five hundred thousand in cash, three hundred thousand in stock, and we're signing over two patents."

"That's outrageous," Tomasso said. "You're goddam buying me from the university."

"I'd say leasing is closer to it," Steinberg said.

"No," Tomasso said. "I've worked on SOCRATES for seven years now, and I'm not about to have it dragged onstage for PR purposes. Forget it. I'm very upset that you'd even suggest it."

"It's not my idea," Steinberg said. "But hell, it might even be fun." There was silence at the other end. Steinberg hesitated, then continued, "I don't need to remind you that Toritron has been a main source of your funding recently."

"That doesn't mean that you own it, or me."

"I don't think Burt is going to back down on this."

"Then you have Burt talk to me, because the answer is no. SOCRATES will run when I think it's ready, not because some megalomaniac wants to promote his goddam company."

"Vincent," Steinberg said, "I'm sorry."

"Aaah," Tomasso said. "It's not your fault. It's just that you've got a completely nuts partner."

"Well."

"Okay," Tomasso said. "All forgiven."

"I think you'll be hearing from Burt."

"I can handle Burt Mathias. Don't worry. And in the meantime, come over and visit. I've got something great for you. The guys in speech synthesis have come up with a new voice for SOCRATES that you're not going to believe. Sends chills down your spine."

Steinberg laughed softly. "Sounds like a perfect guest for the *Tonight Show.*"

Tomasso smiled into the telephone. "Don't think it hasn't occurred to me."

Five minutes after Tomasso hung up the telephone, there was a call from Mathias. And six hours later, Tomasso and Mathias were sitting on opposite sides of a dimly lit, fake-woodgrain table. Mathias, in soft gray suit and silk tie, looked utterly out of place.

"Vincent," Mathias said softly, "I don't think there is any reason for me to talk to you about the relationship between business and the university."

Tomasso shifted slightly in his chair, moving his belly away from the edge of the table. The impromptu meeting had been called, at Mathias' suggestion, at a small cocktail lounge on El Camino Real. Three hundred years earlier, the highway of kings had been a tenuous dirt connection between the Spanish missions strung along the California coast. Now, as it passed through Silicon Valley, it was a highway of neon, punctuated by fast-food restaurants and automotive supply stores. The cocktail lounge attempted an elegant, Spanish atmosphere, but ended up looking like the waiting room of a seat-cover shop.

"However," Mathias continued, "I think you may

have a problem." He shrugged his broad shoulders and looked around the little room. "The work you did for us, the simplified language for the SL-100, was wonderful. I think you deserve every penny you earn in royalties—what was it last year?" Mathias did his absentminded act, and pulled a slip of paper out of his breast pocket, studying it intently. "Ninety-six thousand dollars," he said finally. "Paid quarterly."

"Burt," Tomasso said, "I busted my ass for you on the SL-100, and if you try to screw me—"

"So anyway," Mathias said, without looking up, "it seems to me there could be trouble if Stanford knew that you had done all that work on university time. In fact, that you used your own graduate students to do it."

Tomasso stared fiercely. "The hell if you know that. Everything I've done for Toritron has been my own work."

Mathias shook his head, very slightly. "Stanford might think it was their work. I assume you signed the standard patent agreement when you accepted tenure."

Tomasso ignored the question. "This shit about my graduate students doing the work, that's—"

"That's absolute truth," Mathias interrupted quietly. "I don't have to remind you that Diane Caswell was your student when you were doing most of the work on the Toritron modified language. She was your student, and I tend to trust her word on these things."

Tomasso was silent.

"You want another beer?" Mathias asked mildly.

Tomasso just shook his head, staring off into the darker recesses of the little cocktail lounge. "You are," he said finally, very softly, "a twenty-four-karat son of a bitch."

Mathias ignored the comment. "Vincent," he said, "without people like me, pushing people like you, nothing would ever get done."

"I'm going to run SOCRATES—"

"When you're ready," Mathias said. "Of course.

But science doesn't have any built-in timing, any inherent rhythm. Look at the industrial revolution. Most of the progress there occurred because someone wanted to make some money." Mathias gestured vaguely. "Pump more water out of coal mines, or break Watt's hold on the steam-engine market. If it hadn't been for that kind of pressure, scientists would still be sitting around debating the caloric theory of heat."

Despite himself, Tomasso had to smile at Mathias' earnest hyperbole. "I think maybe you're exaggerating the importance of the market side just a bit."

"Somebody's got to kick you guys in the ass once in a while."

Tomasso shrugged, looked away.

Mathias sighed. He had loosened his necktie earlier, and now he took it off, folding it slowly, absentmindedly running his fingers over the smooth texture of the silk. "I know that this isn't something you planned on doing," he said finally. "But it's awfully damn important for us. And in the end it could be very important for you too."

"Burt," Tomasso said abruptly, "it could really screw up. You and I and Alan could end up looking like the Three Stooges meet computer science."

"I don't think that will happen," Mathias said. "And Alan has more faith in you than you have yourself. And you're going to have facilities like you never dreamed of. We're supporting this one hundred percent, we'll remodel the Research Center, we'll put all of our technical people behind you, we'll essentially give you an unlimited budget to make this thing happen."

Tomasso closed his eyes.

"A lot of researchers would give their right arms for a chance like this," Mathias said.

Tomasso tapped his glass of beer. "When do you need to know?"

"I'm having the initial press release written now. I'd like to send it out tomorrow."

Tomasso laughed softly, shaking his head. "Burt," he said, "I've never seen anybody who was in a hurry like you. Don't you ever do anything slow?"

"Why?" Mathias asked, raising his eyebrows in feigned surprise. "Slow is good," he said, "only in bed."

# six

LESS THAN A MILE FROM WHERE TOMASSO AND Mathias were talking, Maralee Sonderson was sitting in her motel room, inside a massive pseudo-Spanish structure just off the roar and honk of El Camino Real. By New York time, it was well past dinner, but she had no appetite. Maralee kicked off her plain leather shoes, rubbed her feet, and poured a glass of the cold white wine she'd bought half an hour earlier. Lying back on the Holiday Inn bed, she considered the stack of computer books that Burt Mathias had lent her.

"There'll be a pop quiz tomorrow at noon," he'd joked.

"Pop quiz?" she asked.

"No quiz," he relented. "Just lunch."

Mathias, however, had left Maralee with more than just a stack of books. She had a strong sense that his interest in her went past her role as journalist. She recognized this as an occupational hazard—most scientists were men, and when an attractive young woman started asking them questions, they often misconstrued her intent. But this time—as reluctant as she was to admit it—Maralee wasn't certain just where her interest in Burt Mathias stopped. Mathias had an unmistakable virility about him, a physical presence not simply associated with wealth or power.

Maralee knew her feelings were utterly unprofessional. They were also a new kind of feeling, at least for Maralee Sonderson. She was the tall, thin product of Midwestern Norwegian and German parents, with the kind of face called striking, and light, changeable eyes that could be altogether haunting. Yet somehow, during adolescence, her mind had always come between herself and her body; her perpetual fear of appearing gawky and awkward had driven her into books and writing. She married the first boy she dated at college; it was an essentially sexless union that had legally ended two days before she flew from New York to Silicon Valley.

It had been in New York that Maralee had first really developed a life of her own. Following her graduation from journalism school, her unusual background of both science and writing landed her an internship at the *New York Times*. Her husband, however, still working on his doctorate in plant pathology, was bound to his small college for the foreseeable future. Their parting was not precisely tear-stained; their relationship had been primarily intellectual from the outset, and Maralee's husband readily acknowledged the wisdom in her transplantation to Manhattan.

So did Maralee. At age twenty-five, she was truly on her own for the first time in her life. She rented a small studio apartment in the Village, a few blocks from Washington Square. She furnished it exactly as she liked, with rattan and large pillows and Monet posters, and she learned to cook for one. Maralee began to date, casually, and when her escorts asked about the wedding ring she had never quite managed to shed, she would say that it symbolized a marriage being canceled for lack of interest.

Maralee learned a great deal about practical journalism during her first months at the *Times,* and she also learned something about her own sexuality. She slowly came to accept that she was actually a very attractive woman.

On the Fourth of July, after a fireworks show over the Hudson, she spent the night with an apprentice photographer from the paper, and had her first simultaneous orgasm. Three days later, she talked her editor into the Silicon Valley assignment.

"I'll keep it interesting," Maralee promised the editor.

"Also keep it cheap," he told her. But at that point, neither could possibly have guessed just how interesting it would become.

Maralee's reverie was interrupted by the sound of traffic out on the highway. She finished her glass of wine, stood, and walked over to the small motel closet. Abruptly, she realized that she was already planning what she would wear the next day. She shook her head once, quickly, and went back to her notes.

The next morning, Mathias drove Maralee ten miles down El Camino Real to the small cement-block plant where the chips—the actual heart of the small computer—were made.

"It's curious," Mathias said, as he wheeled the dark-brown Mercedes turbodiesel into the big asphalt parking lot, "to think that all of this"—he gestured with one hand, taking in all of the Valley around them—"that it all came from the second most common element on the planet. Silicon. Pick up a rock, a handful of sand, anywhere in the world, and there's silicon in it."

Maralee pulled her thin blue sweater closer around her shoulders. "What's the most common element?"

Mathias frowned. "Oxygen, I think." He shrugged. "I find it difficult to get as excited about oxygen. But *silicon.*" He paused. "In a way, what we do here is almost the old alchemist's dream—the transmutation of elements." He pulled the Mercedes into a reserved parking space next to an unmarked steel door, but did not turn off the engine. The air conditioner continued quietly, and Mathias tapped the steering wheel, oddly distracted. Maralee sat back and said nothing.

"I see that two ways," Mathias said. "One is this: I was at a party the other night, an old friend's house, a guy who did some of the early work designing microprocessors for automobiles."

Maralee looked puzzled.

"You know," Mathias said. "Smart cars—onboard computers, under the hood, that control everything from the fuel mixture to the dashboard display. Anyway, this guy saw it coming, a little earlier than everybody else, and he started prototyping the kind of chips that he figured automobile makers would want. He also designed some software, too—the programming—and copyrighted it. So when the auto manufacturers started to think about small computers in cars, he was already there, with samples. That's how it used to be—"

"Back in the good old days," Maralee said.

"Right. Just one good idea. Just find one market segment and tie down the rights. We used to talk about 'windows'—how wide was the window passing by for getting into a given application; six months, nine months, a year? You got the feeling that if you slept too long one morning, you'd miss something big." Mathias shook his head. "I loved it. You either loved it, or you went nuts."

"So," Maralee said. "Your friend."

"Right," Mathias said. "He did very well. But he didn't know a damn thing about money management, and he wouldn't listen to his lawyer, and he turned gold bug. He really got sort of obsessed, and lost a lot of money he could have tax-sheltered. So anyway, last week, I was at his house, up in Los Altos Hills, and it turned out he's keeping some of the gold at home now. Had a twenty-thousand-dollar vault installed beneath his music room. He took me in and showed me—he had, oh, six or seven hundred ounces, just sitting there, wrapped in muslin cloth. And all I could think was, this guy took sand, and turned it into gold."

Maralee laughed and shook her head. "I'm freezing," she said. "Can you turn the air conditioner off?"

Mathias looked up, surprised, and shut off the engine.

"You said there were two ways you saw it," Maralee prompted.

Mathias blinked, looked straight ahead at the big square building in front of them. "The other," he said, is that in a way, all of this is much more than just turning sand into gold. In a sense—more and more, these days—we're turning sand into intelligence. And that," he said softly, "is true transmutation."

Maralee was silent, and Mathias looked up quickly. "Well," he said. "Let's take a look at the place."

The plant seemed surprisingly small to Maralee— perhaps only the size of a high school gymnasium, holding only fifty or so employees in all. Its security, however, was tight. The building itself was not identified on the outside. Most of the doors had no outside handles, and the single entrance was constantly monitored by a television camera twenty feet off the ground.

As soon as Mathias and Maralee left the car and walked into the camera's field of view, a wall-mounted speaker said, "Hello, Mr. Mathias."

"Forget it," Mathias replied. The lock on the steel door hummed, and Mathias pushed it open.

" 'Forget it'?" Maralee asked quietly.

Mathias, holding the door open, shook his head, slightly embarrassed. "Off the record," he said. "Okay?"

"Okay," she said.

"It's a security thing, for all our executives. If we show up with someone the guard doesn't recognize, we have to say a phrase to indicate it's okay."

"I don't understand."

"Suppose you were holding me hostage, to gain access."

Maralee tilted her head. "That's pretty paranoid."

"I agree," Mathias said. "But we subcontract our security to a company in San Francisco. The contract states that we have to follow their standard protocols, or they're not liable for espionage or terrorism."

"Jesus," Maralee said.

Mathias shrugged. "Modern times. I think it's excessive. It's really more for the genetic engineering firms, and some of the nuclear companies. But these security people do good work. And you've got to follow doctor's orders."

They stepped into a small lobby, all done in dark woods. The air was chill and dry; at the far end of the room, a single security guard sat behind a tan metal desk.

"So security is a problem?"

Mathias waved to the guard, then paused. "There's less real espionage in Silicon Valley than you'd expect. Everybody tends to have a pretty good idea of what everybody else is doing, and there's enough potential that so far, nobody is doing much poaching.

"The two big problems have been pretty conventional. One is counterfeiting—people selling substandard chips in cases with an established manufacturer's trademark. The other is gold theft. We use a lot of gold, mostly for circuit contacts, because it's a great electrical conductor. It's recycled during manufacturing, but some of it still walks out of the plant. Just tiny amounts at a time, but these days, you save a few slivers of gold every week, and at the end of the year, you've got a new videodisc player."

Mathias exchanged a few words with the young guard, and then ushered Maralee into the narrow, fluorescent-lit corridors of the chip plant. And in the corridors they would remain, stopping only at double-thickness windows to gaze at the proceedings within.

Each room of the plant was brightly lit—as intensely as an operating theater—and the workers within were all dressed in blue gowns, their heads covered with white cloths, their feet in paper booties.

"Amazing," Maralee said, after staring silently into one room, where trays covered with freshly etched silicon disks were being removed from a ceiling-high oven. "It looks like a cross between some weird religious temple and a high-technology pizza parlor."

Mathias laughed. "Purity," he said, after a moment. "That's one way to look at it. Silicon Valley runs on pure air, pure water, pure silicon."

"And pure motives?" Maralee asked.

"Absolutely," Mathias said solemnly. "Clean living and regular hours are the only way to the top."

Maralee laughed.

"Actually, the purity thing is true. The great attraction about very pure silicon is that by adding very small amounts of impurities, you can change its electrical properties radically. That's been the heart of semiconductors, ever since the transistor was invented."

"Semiconductor," Maralee said. "That's one of those words that nobody ever bothers to define."

Mathias shrugged. "Some materials, like plastic, don't conduct electricity at all. Others, like gold, conduct it almost perfectly. By varying the impurities in silicon, you can change the way it conducts. It's somewhere between plastic and gold, and so it's a way to control the flow of electricity, whether it's the sound signal in a radio or the binary information in a computer."

On the other side of the double-thick window, another tray of black discs came out of the oven. "What's cooking?" Maralee asked.

Mathias hesitated. "Did you notice the big blueprint hanging on my office wall yesterday?"

"The one that looked like a street map," Maralee said.

"Correct. That was the original design for the integrated circuit we're making here. What we did was shrink it down, using a computer, to a tiny template—

we call it a mask—maybe a quarter inch square. At that point, the lines are about one hundred times thinner than a human hair.

"We set that mask over a chip of pure silicon, and expose it to ultraviolet light, or an electron beam, or X rays—some form of energy that etches away a bit of the silicon. Then the etched lines are filled with tiny, trace amounts of impurities—usually some kind of metal. We bake the chip, to set the impurities, and then we start the process again. Sometimes twenty times, for a single chip, depending on how complex the circuit is."

Mathias absentmindedly traced a complex pattern on the window of the fabrication room. "Finally, we test each disk, mark the circuits that don't work, and ship the whole thing off to Malaysia. In about six weeks, the good chips come back, in little black plastic cases, and we plug them into the SL-100. And that's that."

"You make it sound easy," Maralee said.

"I wish," Mathias said. He tapped the window softly. "We've been making this microprocessor for three years now, and we still get about one failure out of every five chips."

"That doesn't sound so good," Maralee said.

"It's actually not that bad," Mathias said, "considering the odds. Take the chip that operates your average pocket calculator. That chip has the equivalent of maybe six thousand individual transistors, all connected together by thin paths of aluminum, deposited on the chip surface."

He looked over at Maralee. "That's more transistors, on that one simple chip, than there are city blocks in all of Manhattan. But if even one of those tiny aluminum paths fractures, the entire calculator is ruined. That's like shutting down Manhattan completely if there is a single crack wider than a foot across any street in town."

Maralee laughed. "I'd approve only if the crack was in front of my apartment."

"Good luck," Mathias said. "Anyway, that's where the purity obsession comes in. When you're working at this scale of miniaturization, you're almost on the level of individual molecules. Anything can screw you up. That's why the plant manager wouldn't let either one of us into a fabrication room without a shower and a change of clothes. Without that, we'd just be shedding all kinds of undesirable particles. Positive walking pigpens."

"Yes?"

"Yes," Mathias said firmly. "When you're making chips, the air can have no more than, say, a hundred particles per cubic foot. And none of those particles can be any larger than a speck one-hundredth the width of a hair." He glanced at Maralee. "That's small," he said. "It costs more just to purify the air and water in this plant than to power it, pay the property taxes and keep it secure."

He looked back into the fabrication room for a moment and then laughed softly. "We had one guy, last year, working in one of the clean rooms, who had dandruff. Our physician tries to help people with dandruff, but this guy was hopeless. He couldn't stop scratching under his cap. Every time he got near a tray of chips, the failure rate would go up about a thousand percent."

"What happened?"

Mathias shrugged. "In Japan, they probably would have given him six months' dermatologic leave. We fired him, and then put a few photomicrographs of ruined chips in the locker rooms. Under a microscope, the chips looked like London after the blitz. His dandruff looked like boulders strewn across country roads."

Maralee said nothing.

"We have to take it seriously," Mathias said. "A few years ago, one company was all set to build a big chip fabrication plant in Washington State. Then the volcano blew, and there were all the ash problems, and

74

it took them about five seconds to cancel everything. No reason to start with dirtier air than you have to. These days, with something like Ultrachip, even a particle the size of the smallest known germ is enough to destroy the entire circuit."

Maralee looked over. "I'd like to know more about Ultrachip," she said.

"So would everyone," Mathias said, and he glanced at his watch. "You ready for some lunch?"

After a short drive, they stopped at a small French-style restaurant off El Camino, the kind of made-over storefront that reflected good intentions in a dubious location.

"Interesting place," Maralee said, as they walked in.

"It's my secret," Mathias whispered. "Mediocre food, exclusively suburban matron patronage. I've never seen anyone from the business here."

"Mr. Mathias," the hostess said, smiling.

"I don't understand," Maralee said softly, as they were led to a small plastic banquette near the back of the restaurant.

Mathias shook his head. "You should have seen the bar I was in yesterday. But these days, you go to any decent restaurant around here and half the people there are watching the other half. Chinese restaurants are the worst. Jobs, information, tips, God knows what is changing hands. The area is a goldfish bowl."

They sat in the booth and took menus. Mathias didn't bother to look at his. "I was once in a restaurant in Sunnyvale when I realized that three tables away, an executive recruiter was interviewing a prospect for me. Very dumb recruiter—we never used him again. Because halfway through lunch, the prospect's present boss walked in and sat three tables on the other side."

"Wasn't that kind of a problem?"

Mathias shrugged. "Not in this case. The other guy

was with his mistress. He actually wasn't very bright either." He gestured at the menu. "I hope you like nice light lunches. This menu is designed for women who should have started worrying about their weight ten years ago." He paused. "Clearly not," he said, "a concern of yours."

Maralee smiled vaguely, said nothing, and there was a brief, awkward silence.

"I'd suggest the crab salad," Mathias said finally.

Maralee nodded, set her menu aside. "May I ask you a very direct question?"

Mathias sat back, squared his shoulders, touched the knot of his tie, as if preparing for television. "Shoot," he said solemnly.

"Why are you paying so much attention to me? I haven't even talked to your PR guy yet."

"He has the brains of a hamster," Mathias said. "You're missing nothing."

"Really," Maralee said.

"I can't say it's because I like your legs," Mathias said.

"No," Maralee said firmly, "you can't."

"Okay," Mathias said. "Then maybe it's because I need some advice. Maybe even some help."

"I'm not necessarily here to help you," Maralee said.

Before Mathias could reply, the waitress came by and they ordered. "All right," he said. "Let me tell you what we're doing. In a few months, we'll be holding the First International Turing Test."

Maralee's expression did not change. "Beg pardon?"

"Turing Test," Mathias repeated. "Named after a British mathematician—Alan Turing, a big name in the early computer scene. He wondered how we would tell when a computer has become truly intelligent. And he came up with this Turing Test. Basically, it involves a situation where people ask questions of an unknown entity—some mysterious mind behind a curtain, so to speak. They can ask anything they want—excluding obvious things like 'What color are your eyes?' "

"Or, 'What are you doing Saturday night?' "

Mathias smiled. "Like that. Anyway, if they can't decide whether they're talking to a smart computer or another human being, and it turns out to be a computer, then Turing decided that such a computer is effectively intelligent."

Maralee was staring now. "You're actually going to try this?"

Mathias nodded, slowly, deliberately. The glass of white wine he'd ordered arrived, and he sipped it quickly.

Maralee leaned back in her chair for a moment, then looked up. "Will it work?"

Mathias shrugged slightly and tapped his fingers against his upper lip. "I think we have a chance," he said finally.

"Who's 'we'?"

Mathias raised one hand. "All of this," he said, "is still off the record. For now. Although I think we'll be able to make it public very soon."

Maralee nodded, smiled. "Understood."

"Okay," he said. "You know that there are two parts to any computer: the hardware and the software. The hardware is the circuitry, the mechanical stuff. The software is the programming—the instructions as to what the hardware should do. It's like the difference between the thoughts in a human brain, and the brain tissue itself."

"Sure," Maralee said.

"All right. Our project has two parts. One is a computer designed around our next product: Ultrachip. It's made with a technique called ultra-large-scale integration, ULSI, and it means we're putting more memory and processing capacity—more smartness, in short—on a single chip than ever before. A single Ultrachip will be smarter than the entire small computer Toritron started with. And we plan to use thousands of Ultrachips for the Turing Test."

"So that leaves the software," Maralee said.

"Correct. Toritron has helped finance a project by Vincent Tomasso at Stanford—"

"Of course," Maralee interrupted. "I'm going to interview him later this week."

"Good," Mathias said. "He's a terrific scientist, who has been working on a project called SOCRATES which stands for—" He paused, thought for a moment, shrugged. "Which stands for something. Anyway, it's an attempt to create an intelligence that can pass the Turing Test. Nobody's saying it will be truly intelligent, because nobody knows what intelligence really is. But the only way to find out is by trying."

"What is SOCRATES?"

"SOCRATES—as much as I understand it—is a self-teaching program. It learns from its mistakes, and then uses those mistakes not only to correct its knowledge of the world, but to actually change the *way* it learns. And as nearly as I can tell, that's a pretty good approximation of intelligence."

Maralee considered this, and toyed briefly with her silverware. "Why hasn't anyone tried it before?"

"That's where Ultrachip comes in. A program like SOCRATES requires a vast memory. Like the human mind, it needs space for trivia—because you never know when a bit of trivia will suddenly make sense of a larger pattern. But it also has to access that memory very quickly. And that's been the problem up until now. Obviously, computers operate at nearly the speed of light, right?"

Maralee frowned.

"More accurately," Mathias said, "the electrons in a computer circuit travel at just about the speed of light. But increasingly, the fact that there is a finite speed involved—even if it's the speed of light—is getting in the way. A very large memory storage involves distances that measurably slow the transfer of information. Ultrachip, however, has an immense information density on each chip. And the chips will be placed as close as possible to each other—and so the entire memory will be accessible far faster than anything previous."

There was a brief silence. Their lunches arrived, and Maralee picked idly at her salad. "It sounds big," she said finally.

"It's very big," Mathias said. "We'll be bringing in a panel of people from around the world—a philosopher, a theologian, a scientist, maybe a poet. We'll see."

Maralee watched him for a moment and then smiled slightly. "You're probably not going to lose out on publicity."

Mathias shrugged innocently. "We expect a fair amount of attention from the press."

"I'll bet," Maralee said.

Mathias laughed, and then grew serious. "It's going to be a major story. A significant story. We want it handled well." He paused. "I'd like you to be in on it from the beginning. It seems to me that there might even be a book in it."

Maralee gazed steadily at him for a moment. "Who are you most interested in?" she asked. "Me or the *Times?*"

Mathias looked surprised. "Pardon?"

Maralee rearranged the napkin on her lap. "I mean," she said, "you don't know much about my writing at all. I can't help but suspect that you mostly want a conduit into the *Times.*"

Mathias watched her carefully. He finished his wine in one swallow. "You're not saying I'm courting you for publicity?"

Maralee considered this. "Yes," she said finally, with a faint smile. "I guess I am."

Mathias shook his head and smiled also. "You know," he said, "I have the oddest feeling that we have a great deal in common."

Maralee looked down at her plate, then glanced back up. "From what I've read, your wife is fairly active in Toritron."

"Was," Mathias said. "She's been phasing herself out over the past two years. She's just not that interested in the market side. She's still doing some work on SOCRATES, though." He paused briefly. "And she's expecting our first child."

Maralee smiled. "Congratulations."

Mathias nodded.

"I'd like to meet her sometime," Maralee said.

"I'm sure you will." Mathias glanced at his watch. "We should eat," he said. "I have to get back."

# seven

LATER THAT MONTH, VINCENT TOMASSO DROVE HIS aging Saab up to the Toritron Research Center for his first official meeting with Alan Steinberg. The Silicon Valley springtime had turned chill; the young researcher was wearing the same odd combination of Hawaiian shirt and down jacket that had once appeared in a *People* photo.

Tomasso cleared himself at the Research Center front desk, wandered through the sprawling redwood building, and walked into Steinberg's small office unannounced.

Steinberg looked up, slightly surprised, from a half-consumed can of pineapple rings.

"Finish your breakfast," Tomasso said, dropping himself into a steel chair in front of Steinberg's desk. He glanced at his watch. "I've got three months."

Steinberg suppressed a smile and looked back down at the can. "It's never taken me more than two months," he said evenly, "to finish one of these."

Tomasso looked sour. "Listen," he said, "I'm on your team now. Stanford did everything but quarantine my office."

"We've got an office for you here," Steinberg said, through a mouthful of pineapple. He tilted his head to the left. "Just next to mine."

Tomasso folded his arms and nodded curtly. "Terrific."

Steinberg looked up again. "Vincent," he said, "don't resent this. Burt's just doing his job. He's producing technology. I'd be happier staying in my lab, you'd be happier staying in yours. But we can't always do that." He speared another ring of pineapple with his plastic fork. "That's business." He considered the piece of fruit. "You're going to like your secretary," Steinberg said. "Five one, brunette, twenty-one, a knockout."

"Please," Tomasso said, closing his eyes. "No sexist sweet talk."

Steinberg shrugged.

Tomasso was briefly silent. "Italian?"

"Is D'Angelo Italian?"

Tomasso groaned. "Just what I need. Another Catholic girl."

"You're impossible to please," Steinberg said, dropping the empty pineapple can into the wastebasket. "Let's talk about something else. How do we get SOCRATES into the Ultrachip system?"

Tomasso suddenly looked interested. "You've already got the system up?"

Steinberg shook his head. "I wish. We're short about ten thousand components. But Burt tells me not to worry, so I don't."

"I wish somebody would worry for me," Tomasso said.

"The entire academic community worries *about* you," Steinberg said. "Where's SOCRATES?"

Tomasso gazed at the acoustic-tiled ceiling. "Right now, SOCRATES is on about three hundred floppy disks, ten thousand feet of half-inch tape, and inside about ten thousand 64K RAMs. There's another five hundred written pages of programming I'd like to put in too."

Steinberg was taken aback. "That's kind of messy," he said.

Tomasso shrugged. "You know how it is. It just growed."

"So how much permanent memory do you need?"

Tomasso told him. Steinberg jabbed briefly at the keys on his desk terminal, then watched the CRT readout. "Well," he said after a moment, "that's no problem. We can store it all with the Ultrachip system, and still have plenty of empty memory left over for self-teaching functions."

Tomasso straightened up in his chair and, for the first time that day, looked impressed. "No kidding?"

"No kidding," Steinberg said, as he switched off the desk terminal. "While you've been off pondering *a priori* knowledge and the nature of thought, the rest of us have been designing hardware."

Tomasso still looked surprised, and he repeated the figures.

"You bet," Steinberg said.

"That," Tomasso said, "could be really interesting."

Steinberg sighed. "As Burt tells the shareholders, we don't call it Ultrachip for nothing."

For the next few hours, Tomasso and Steinberg went over the details of setting up the Ultrachip system and inserting the SOCRATES program. It would be a mammoth chore, but Mathias had been generous with the Research Center budgeting. "Burt wants this to work," Steinberg said. "Do whatever you have to do."

Tomasso shrugged. "The work is essentially done. All we need to do is get it into the Ultrachip system without any errors." He gazed at Steinberg for a moment. "For the Turing Test," he said, "there's one other thing I'd like to put in. It's something that Diane

Caswell worked on when she was in grad school—the emotion simulation problem.''

A soft tone sounded on Steinberg's terminal, and he punched several keys and glanced at the screen, never taking his attention from Tomasso. ''Was that the simulation of a paranoid personality?''

''Right,'' Tomasso said. ''We have some ideas about how to fine-tune a few other emotional simulations.'' He smiled slightly. ''You know: toss a little personality into SOCRATES.''

Steinberg shut off his terminal and looked up at Tomasso. ''Fine with me,'' he said. ''You're the AI specialist. Anything Diane wants to do is great, in terms of budgeting.''

''I'll talk to her this afternoon,'' Tomasso said.

Steinberg's terminal beeped again, but he ignored it. ''Vincent,'' he said, ''I've got to take care of a few things. We're having a lot of trouble with the Ultrachip fabrication.''

Tomasso nodded, began to stand, then sat down again. ''One other thing,'' he said. ''We need to decide who's going to be the surrogate.''

Steinberg stared blankly.

''The human who provides responses when SOCRATES isn't on line,'' Tomasso explained.

''I never even thought about it.''

Tomasso nodded. ''Turing didn't mention it in his original paper.''

Steinberg thought for a moment. ''What we need,'' he said finally, ''is someone who knows a hell of a lot, but doesn't have any extremely strong personality traits that would give him away.'' He picked up a pencil and tapped it on his desk briefly. ''Not to sandbag the test, but what we need is somebody who thinks as much like a computer as SOCRATES thinks like a human.''

Tomasso gazed at him, and then suddenly smiled. ''Let me take care of it,'' he said.

\* \* \*

That same day, Burt Mathias left his Woodside home quite early; Diane, still slightly morning-sick, remained in bed. He drove down the hill to Palo Alto, then parked the brown Mercedes in front of a downtown beer joint, which opened at eight in the morning and also featured a lo-ball room. The place was one of the last vestiges of the days when Palo Alto was a sleepy college town, rather than one of the most expensive communities in the country.

In his light-gray Brioni suit, Mathias looked utterly out of place among the half-dozen aging VA hospital outpatients who frequented the dingy little bar, and who were already at their stools. Mathias felt extremely uncomfortable. Even the owner of the bar was watching him intently—probably trying to decide, Mathias guessed, whether he was an ABC agent, a lawyer, or a cop. Mathias was distinctly relieved when in a dim corner just past the long, waxed shuffleboard table he spotted the young man.

Mathias sat down on the other side of the Formica table. "Steven?" he asked. "Welcome back."

"Thanks," the young man said, rather nervously. He was wearing a faded blue work shirt and corduroy trousers, and looked to be in his mid-twenties. He was quite thin, and his blond hair just touched his shoulders.

The bartender was still watching them. "You guys want something?" he called.

Mathias turned in his chair and gazed at him for a moment. "Two coffees," he said.

"No coffee."

"Two Cokes," Mathias said.

"You've got it."

Mathias turned back. "So," he said softly, "did you like Japan?"

The young man shrugged. "I liked the food," he said. "I didn't like the attitude."

"The attitude?"

Steven glanced away, looked back. "Well. You know, all the big American firms have research centers there now. Either in Tokyo, the suburbs, or Osaka. We're picking their brains, just the way they picked ours ten years ago, and they know it." He ran his thin hands tentatively across the chipped surface of the table. "It's weird," he said, "to feel like some technologic inferior, when the technology began in your own country."

Mathias' expression did not change. "Well," he said finally. "It's our own fault that we dropped the ball. What we have to do now is pick it up and start running again."

The old bartender brought over two bottles of Coke, and Mathias handed him a $5 bill. "You got smaller?" the bartender asked.

"Keep it," Mathias said, waving him away. The old man ambled off, and Mathias spoke more softly. "I assume," he said, "you've got it."

The young man nodded once, quickly, and indicated the cheap plastic briefcase on the chair next to him. "It's all there," he said. "It's the entire fabrication methodology for the Fujitsu ULSI chips. I've redrawn all the schematics and put everything in English. Most of it was in English to begin with."

Mathias gazed at him. "Nothing to indicate the origin?"

"Not a thing," the young man said. "Everything's been redrawn."

Mathias smiled for the first time that morning. "You did great."

"Wait till you see," Steven said, with so much enthusiasm in his voice that the bartender glanced over. "It's a hell of a clever system for guiding the etching beam. It's all multiple feedback loops, and entirely self-correcting. Very, very smart—the first time you see it, you'll say *of course*. And all you really need to do is build the electronics, and use it with your own etcher." The young man took a quick sip from his bottle of Coke. "Your scientists are going to love this when they see it," he said, with quiet satisfaction.

"Your Ultrachip is way ahead of Fujitsu's. They just figured out the manufacturing first."

Mathias was silent for a moment. "Okay," he said finally. "I gave you five thousand when you left for Tokyo, right?"

The young man nodded.

"And I owe you fifteen more, now?"

He nodded again.

Mathias reached into the inside pocket of his suit coat and pulled out a legal-length envelope about an inch thick. "One hundred and fifty hundreds," Mathias said. The younger scientist appeared slightly dazed by the sight.

"There's a problem?" Mathias asked.

The young man said nothing as he slipped the envelope into his jacket pocket.

"Let me tell you," Mathias said. "Hundreds are really the easiest to deal with." He gazed at Steven for a moment. "You weren't planning to put this all in one bank, were you?"

The young man opened his mouth.

"Don't," Mathias advised. "There's too much computer surveillance of large deposits these days. Break it up into smaller accounts, or keep it out of banks entirely." He shrugged. "That's just free advice."

Mathias glanced around the little beer joint for a moment, then looked back at Steven. "I've always wondered," he said, "how you got access to this stuff in the first place."

The young man blinked a few times. "You really want to know?"

Mathias inclined his head slightly.

"I met a guy."

Mathias frowned. "I don't follow."

"We fell in love."

"Ah," Mathias said, suddenly comprehending.

"You know," the thin young man said, "you read all this stuff about how humanistic the Japanese corporations are. But there are still a few things they just won't tolerate. And being gay is one of them."

Mathias stared at him. "So you blackmailed some-one."

Steven looked shocked. "Absolutely not," he said. "I told you—we fell in love." He tapped the envelope, now in his jacket pocket. "We're going to use this to pay the immigration lawyer. We want him to come to this country."

Oh Jesus, Mathias said to himself, and then he looked up and smiled. "Can I have the briefcase?"

The young computer scientist pushed the briefcase across the chipped Formica. "I don't know if I'll ever get assigned to the Tokyo research facility again, but . . ."

Mathias took the cheap briefcase and stood quickly. "Don't worry about it," he said, almost amiably. "I don't know you, you don't know me, now and forever. Okay?"

"Well . . ." the young man started to say.

"My best wishes," Mathias said, with a smile. He started to walk away, then turned back. "If your friend from Fujitsu ever gets into the country, send him to see me, okay?"

Mathias was in his office well before his ten-o'clock appointment with Stanley Kauffman. The heavyset venture capitalist was clad in his customary rumpled suit—"Robert Hall seconds," as Mathias had once characterized his dress to Diane. In a way, however, Kauffman cultivated his appearance purposely to in-spire trust among young Silicon Valley scientists, some of whom dressed as if they had just stepped out of a time capsule from the sixties. Kauffman's look was reassuringly academic. He maintained an entirely different wardrobe, mostly French, for the days he visited financiers in San Francisco and Los Angeles.

Mathias was at his desk, going over a thick folder of notes that Steinberg had given him, describing produc-tion difficulties with Ultrachip. When his secretary announced Kauffman, he set the folder aside and stood up.

"Stan," Mathias said, as Kauffman was ushered through the door. "It's good to see you."

"I hope you'll still say that in ten minutes," Kauffman said.

Mathias looked slightly concerned. "Sit," he told Kauffman, who promptly dropped his large frame into one of the Italian leather chairs. Mathias sat back down behind his desk. "Coffee?" he asked.

Kauffman just waved one hand. "Burt, we have to talk. We have a problem."

Mathias simply nodded, totally alert.

Kauffman leaned back, exhaled deeply. "The lawyer kid in L.A.—Lockhart—is going to file suit Monday against Toritron, for misappropriation of R&D funds. The shareholders he represents seem to think you've been screwing around with the funding of the Ultrachip program."

Mathias stared briefly. He picked up the gold pen on his desk and made as if to break it in two. His silent anger seemed almost palpable. He dropped the pen loudly onto the teak surface of the desk, stood, and paced to the window. For a moment he played with the narrow beige blinds, squinting out into the smoggy sunlight of Silicon Valley.

Kauffman said, after a long minute, "You don't have anything you want to tell me about, do you?"

Mathias finally sighed and turned back to face the portly financier. "Those goddam pikers," he said softly. "They think just because it's high technology, they can put in a dollar and"—he waved his hands—"whambo-bambo, they get ten dollars back. As if science was some kind of rigged slot machine." He shook his head abruptly and walked over to the wall where the first three Toritron chips had been framed, mounted on green velvet, behind glass, vaguely reminiscent of military medals. Mathias gazed at the little black plastic rectangles for a moment.

He turned back to Kauffman. "These people don't know a damn thing about science," he said, almost sadly. "All these penny-ante tooth-pullers with ten thousand dollars to invest. And these jerks in L.A. know even less."

"Well," Kauffman said, leaning forward, "these shmucks in Los Angeles are out of line. It's a damn shame they ever got involved with Toritron in the first place."

Mathias shrugged. "We needed the money. What can I say?" He rubbed his high forehead for a moment. "It's why I've never wanted to go public. You go public, and everybody wants instant magic. And that's not the way it works." He glanced back at the framed chips. "If we manufactured tractors, say, we could publish a glossy report full of pictures of our new assembly line." He mimicked a radio announcer's voice. "'In the fourth quarter, seven hundred thousand dollars in operating capital went to purchase of a sheet-metal-stamping machine capable of producing twelve thousand widgets per hour.'"

Mathias stared at Kauffman. "That's what those clowns in L.A. want. They don't want to hear about Alan Steinberg poking around in the laboratory at three in the morning. But that's what this business *is*."

"Hey," Kauffman said quietly. "Calm down. I'm on your side, remember? I've been doing this longer than you have. You should have heard the talking I did when a genetic engineering consortium I put together took a bath in interferon. I had fifty angry orthodontists in the San Fernando Valley after my blood." Kauffman leaned back, gently scratched his bald head, then stared at Mathias. "Who ever told you science was going to be easy?"

Mathias was silent for a moment, then nodded.

Kauffman shifted in the big leather chair. "We do have to face realities. And the reality here is that on the basis of this suit—and anybody in the investment community who doesn't know about it is deaf, dumb and broke—on the basis of this suit, I can't raise another nickel for you guys. With pending litigation . . ." He shrugged.

Mathias, still standing, folded his arms and watched

89

Kauffman for a moment. "Nothing more than I expected," he said finally. "I never expected any saving angels."

There was a brief silence. Kauffman finally laughed quietly. "At least you can say you've never been bored."

Mathias smiled wryly. "That's true. I can't even remember what bored feels like."

After another silence, Mathias cleared his throat. "There's one more thing I'd like you to do for us," he said.

"If it's possible," Kauffman said, "I'll try."

"I'd like you to help negotiate the acquisition deal with TI."

Kauffman simply stared, frowning slightly, puzzled. "TI hasn't offered any deal," he said. "You know that." He hesitated. "And now . . ." He spread his large hands.

Mathias looked at Kauffman for a long time. "We've solved the problems with Ultrachip," he said. "A little too late, but we've done it. Ultrachip is up and running, and within a week we're going to announce an international Turing Test, based on Ultrachip hardware. I think we're going to attract a hell of a lot of attention."

Kauffman smiled and nodded. "If TI calls," he said, "I'll be happy to help answer the phone."

"I think I can guarantee you," Mathias said, "that TI will call." He took one more look out of the thin blinds, then turned back to Kauffman. "By the way. Do you get home delivery of the *New York Times?*"

That afternoon, Mathias walked into Steinberg's small office at the Research Center. Steinberg was spending the day just as he had every day for the past two weeks: standing up in front of a brightly lit drafting table, poring over a scatter of blueprints and schematics. He hardly looked up when Mathias walked in.

"Tomasso's here," Steinberg said. "He's next door, carving his initials in his desk or something."

"Fine," Mathias said, glancing absently around the room. "Fine. How's it going?"

"Rotten," Steinberg said softly, still staring at the papers on the drafting table. "I'm sure I'm missing something very obvious here."

"Maybe you need to sleep on it," Mathias said cheerfully. "Have one of those patented dreams."

Steinberg was unamused. In recent days, in fact, he had remained in just about the consistently worst mood that Mathias had ever seen. "No matter what we do," he said, almost to himself, "we can't get the failure rate down. Producing one of these chips is like cutting a diamond." He shook his head and fell silent, leaning to one side, drumming his long fingers on the slick paper surface of the drafting table.

"Hmmm," Mathias said. He pulled out the cardboard tube he carried under his arm. "I have something here I'd like you to look at." He pulled a rolled sheaf of papers from the tube, put the tube on the floor, and spread the sheets out on the drafting table.

"What's this?" Steinberg said, frowning, puzzled, holding the edge of the fresh crisp paper down with one hand.

"A young engineer brought this to me. These are some speculative ideas on how to do ULSI fabrication."

Steinberg, barely listening, was staring at the plans.

"Jeez," he said, after a moment. "This is sophisticated stuff. Who the hell is this guy?"

Mathias, apparently absorbed in the plans, shrugged, not looking up at Steinberg. "Sort of a free-lancer, I guess you could say."

Steinberg raised his head and gazed at Mathias for a long, appraising moment. "That's the most ridiculous thing I've ever heard," he said finally.

Mathias appeared unconcerned. "He's an eccentric. He doesn't want to be bothered. Lives in a cabin above Santa Cruz. I met him at the last IEEE convention."

Steinberg had returned to studying the plans. "This is very interesting," he said. "Very interesting."

"He'll sign over all rights to us," Mathias said. "Flat-fee basis. Is it worth twenty thousand dollars?"

Steinberg was watching Mathias again. "That's a screwy arrangement," he said.

Mathias looked back at the documents. "Damn interesting stuff," he said. "I think it's promising."

Steinberg was briefly silent, and he shifted his weight slightly, cleared his throat. "Burt, tell me straight. This stuff isn't stolen, is it?"

Mathias glanced up suddenly, looking shocked, then hurt, and then his face relaxed and he smiled slightly. "Alan, I can see why you'd ask that. There's a lot at stake here. But I just want to tell you no once, and then I don't want to hear about it again."

Steinberg looked at his partner for a long moment. "Okay," he said finally. "Okay. Just give me an hour to look this stuff over."

Mathias smiled, squeezed Steinberg's shoulder, and silently left the little office.

# eight

"THE BASIC LANGUAGE OF A COMPUTER," VINCENT Tomasso was saying, "is probably the simplest language on earth. It's the binary code—on, off; on, off. Absolutely everything—mathematics, talking, drawing—that any computer does is initially expressed in that form. In other words, whether electricity is flowing or not." He smiled, and made a switch with his hands. "On-off, on-off, on-off," he said, moving his hands around his head, vaguely like a castanet player.

The sight of the mildly rotund Tomasso imitating a Spanish dancer made Maralee Sonderson laugh, precisely as he had intended. After two weeks of telephone calls, she had finally managed to set up an interview with the surprisingly reclusive scientist. It was late afternoon, already nearly six, and Tomasso had said he still had several hours of work ahead and could talk for only a few minutes.

Maralee usually never asked researchers to explain basic science that she could learn from a book. But in this case, she had been curious to see a bit of the famed Tomasso style, and so had asked him about computer languages.

"Okay," Tomasso said, standing now and walking around his desk. "On-off, on-off." In her notebook, Maralee jotted down that part of his effectiveness was a knack for sounding as if he were thinking out loud—just discovering things for himself. "Okay," he repeated. "But suppose *you* want to communicate with a computer."

Maralee nodded. Tomasso tilted his head. "It's going to take forever, if you have to do it in binary code. Pick a number."

Maralee thought for a moment. "Seventy-three," she said.

"All right," Tomasso said, sitting on the edge of his desk. "Just saying seventy-three would take seven separate flips of a switch. In binary code, seventy-three is on-off-off-on-off-off-on. If it takes that long to describe a two-digit number, imagine how long it would take to ask a computer to calculate a reentry trajectory for the space shuttle. Or to say the word 'hello.' "

Maralee nodded again.

"That's why," Tomasso said, "we developed computer languages. Translators, if you will, within each computer, that take our instructions, which are in more efficient language, and then turn them into binary code. The on-off, on-off, which is actually the only true language of computers."

"But I thought there were a bunch of computer languages," Maralee said. "COBOL, FORTRAN, BASIC—"

"Sure," Tomasso said, holding up one hand. "But those are all still just interfaces between us and the computer. When they were first developed, each language was better for one purpose than another. COBOL is better for business; FORTRAN is better for science. It's like Italian is the language of love."

Maralee laughed. "I thought it was French."

"No way," Tomasso said. "But that's off the subject. What a programmer does is translate English into, say, COBOL, and then put that into the computer. Then a portion of the computer translates the COBOL into binary code."

"So when you type instructions into a computer in, say, FORTRAN, you're not really talking directly to the machine."

"In a sense," Tomasso said, "you're talking to an interpreter. But," he went on, with considerable emphasis, "something else has been happening lately. The interpreters are getting smarter. And so we're getting closer and closer to talking to our computers in so-called natural language—that is, straight English. SOCRATES, for example, will understand natural language extremely well—because we've been teaching its interpreter English grammar, vocabulary, and semantics for literally years."

Tomasso paused for a second and leaned back, gazing down at the gray terminal atop his desk. "I remember," he said, "about five years ago, I was at some technical conference, where I met a consultant who works for different computer firms. And she was telling entry-level programmers that they'd be better off learning a trade."

94

"I don't follow," Maralee said.

Tomasso spread his hands wide. "Which would you rather do? Hire some good engineers once, to design a smart system that basically operates in natural language, or else keep paying overpriced programmers forever?"

Maralee frowned. "So where do the programmers go?"

Tomasso shrugged. "I'm no sociologist. But I suppose they either get more sophisticated at what they do, or"—he raised his hands again—"they learn a trade. Computers or not," he said with a slight smile, "we're always going to need plumbers."

Maralee wrote briefly in her notebook, then looked up and smiled. "I'm sure you'll be an inspiration to kids in programming schools all over the country."

Tomasso looked at her with a trace of alarm. "No," he said. "I don't mean there's no future in computers. Not at all. Computers *are* the future. There's a saying you've probably heard—the nation that controls computer technology will control the industrialized world." Tomasso tapped the top of the gray steel CRT terminal. "I believe that the same applies to individuals; that in the future, to control your life, you must understand computers—and not just understand, but keep learning."

He paused for a moment and then shrugged. "I sound like I'm giving a sermon," he said, running one hand across his dark hair. He gazed at Maralee for a moment. "Have you talked to SOCRATES yet?"

She shook her head.

"It's down now," he said. "We're loading more of the program. But later, get Burt to show it to you. Use the voice recognition system, so you can talk to it directly."

"I'm looking forward to it," Maralee said.

Tomasso nodded. "I think you'll be impressed. And when you see it, keep in mind what I said about how important it is to understand that it's just a machine—

that every bit of its operation can be explained, ultimately, in terms of on-off, on-off."

Maralee turned a page in her notebook. "You seem to keep emphasizing that," she said.

Tomasso looked at the floor for a moment, tugged at his shirttails, then looked up. "You know the C. P. Snow essay about the two cultures? His theory that society was separating into two parts, scientific and nonscientific?"

"Sure," Maralee said. "It's a perfect essay for science writers. He was afraid that people would become technologic barbarians, living with miracles they never even tried to understand."

"Exactly," Tomasso said. "And when Snow wrote that essay, he was talking about 'miracles' like—I don't know, television, or thermostats, or something like that. But now"—Tomasso stood and walked back behind his desk—"we're looking at machines that talk, and listen, and draw pictures and write music." He shook his head. "Those really seem like miracles. But they're not—they're just tools. In evolutionary terms, smart computers were invented by essentially the same brain that invented the wheel."

Maralee smiled. "Did anyone ever tell you that for a scientist, you're very quotable?"

Tomasso nodded solemnly. "It's been one of my worst problems," he said, straight-faced. "I was lucky to get tenure."

Maralee laughed quietly.

"Seriously," Tomasso said, "my biggest fear is that in years to come, a whole segment of society will give up trying to understand computers. They'll slip into an almost magical way of thinking about intelligent machines—even as those machines have more and more effect on their daily lives. And ultimately, those people *will* be technologic barbarians."

"Won't something like the Turing Test just make that worse? Make people think that machines truly are intelligent?"

Tomasso was briefly silent as he fidgeted with the

loose collar of his shirt. He leaned forward on his desk, glanced at the terminal display, then leaned back. "Off the record?" he said softly. "At least for a while?"

Maralee nodded.

"If SOCRATES passes the Turing Test," he said, "then I'll be doing both a book and a short television series on how it works. My agent in Los Angeles is already in negotiation."

Maralee stared. "Media tie-ins for a scientific experiment?"

Tomasso shrugged, raised his hands palm upward, and then smiled. "What can I say? If it works, it could be the greatest teaching opportunity of my life."

A minute or so later, a soft tone sounded on Tomasso's desk terminal, and he excused himself, promising that they could continue the interview sometime later in the week. Maralee was slightly surprised that, given Tomasso's reputation as a media hound, he had spent so little time with her. It was only after she had left his office and was standing in the fluorescent-lit corridor of the Research Center that it occurred to her that Tomasso was probably saving his best material for himself.

It was already well past six; she had planned to go back to the hotel and spend the evening reading a textbook on artificial intelligence. On a whim, however, she decided to stop by the office that Burt Mathias kept in the Research Center.

She walked through the narrow corridors of the small, round building until she arrived at the foyer of Mathias' office—a far smaller and less imposing space than he kept at corporate headquarters. Mathias' young secretary, Stephanie, was just leaving her desk, purse in hand; she hesitated when she saw Maralee approach.

Suddenly, Maralee felt slightly silly. She wasn't sure why she'd thought to stop by; in fact, she hadn't even expected to find anyone there.

"Burt's still here," his secretary said, before Maralee could say a word. "Let me buzz him."

Maralee stood, saying nothing, as the secretary leaned over and pushed the button on a low plastic desk console. A moment later, Mathias' voice emerged from the tiny speaker. "Yes?"

"Ms. Sonderson is here to see you," the secretary said.

There was a brief silence. "Fine," the small desk speaker said, after a moment. "I'll be finished here in just a minute."

Stephanie picked up her purse again and gestured toward one of the spartan metal-and-leatherette chairs in the foyer. Maralee sat, and idly poked through the stack of technical journals carelessly arranged on an imitation-wood end table. Her reporter's eye noted details of style almost automatically; in this case, however, she was consciously impressed by the difference between Mathias' corporate office and his presence in the Research Center. The former said money, and the latter said science, and in both, the effect was clearly carefully planned.

Moments later, a tall, thin, well-dressed man exited Mathias' office, walking fast, and then Mathias himself appeared at the door. He was in shirtsleeves, the pale-blue fabric slightly taut across his broad shoulders, a gray tie loosened at the collar. When he stepped into the doorway and smiled, Maralee felt an unmistakable shiver. "Hey," Mathias said quietly, leaning against the doorframe, "you're the first person I've actually wanted to see all day."

Maralee stood, holding her shoulder bag in both hands. "I really just stopped by—"

"Come in," Mathias interrupted, stepping aside, gesturing through the door, and then he paused. "Wait a minute," he said. "What am I saying? I've been sitting in this room all day." He glanced at his watch. "Have you eaten yet?"

Maralee shook her head, smiled slightly.

"Let's get a bite," Mathias said. "I just have to make one call."

He went back to his office and closed the door, and a moment later Maralee saw one bulb on the secretary's switchboard light up. It remained lit for a minute or so, and then Mathias, now with a light tan jacket on, came out the door. "Let's go," he said. "How about sushi?"

Mathias took Maralee to a small Japanese restaurant, near the railroad tracks that neatly bisected Palo Alto. Although Maralee protested at first that she couldn't stand raw fish, Mathias clearly knew his way around a sushi bar, and soon cajoled her into trying a bit of tuna here, a touch of smoked eel there, and fairly soon she had decided that the entire idea really wasn't that awful after all. A contributing factor, she surmised the next day, might have been the delicate porcelain containers of hot sake that seemed to appear with remarkable regularity.

To Maralee, the conversation at first seemed rather random; uncomfortably enough, the sort of small talk that characterizes a first date. Mathias described, with a trace of bitterness, the legal difficulties that Toritron was encountering. He also talked animatedly about the Turing Test, and his feeling that it would represent a real contribution to the history of science.

Maralee, in turn, said little. She talked about her background, and her belief in the importance of popular science writing. They joked about an Easterner's first impressions of California—"You people are so *provincial*," Mathias said with a smile—and then finally he glanced at his watch and gestured for the check.

"I should get going," he said. "Diane is going to think I've run off with SOCRATES."

Maralee gazed at him for a moment, her head cocked slightly to one side. "Does she know you're having dinner with me?"

Mathias shrugged, toyed with the tiny sake cup on

99

the table in front of him. "I don't suppose so," he said. "Does it make any difference?"

Maralee shook her head slightly. "Not really, I guess."

Mathias nodded, not looking up, and was silent for a moment. "Diane," he said carefully, "is a brilliant woman. She could probably do anything she wanted. She's also very competitive, which is sometimes uncomfortable, because she's a hell of a lot smarter than I am." He glanced up and saw the look on Maralee's face. "No," he said quickly. "I mean that."

"She sounds remarkable," Maralee said softly.

Mathias breathed deeply, and looked away. "But the problem is that she's thirty-two years old and has no idea what she wants to do with her life." He raised one hand, let it drop. "Rather," he said, "she wants to do everything. She wants to be an internationally recognized computer scientist. She wants to be a mother and raise geniuses." He paused for a moment. "And a part of her," he said, "wants the life her mother has. Even though she spent her childhood rejecting it."

Maralee was growing distinctly uncomfortable with Mathias' sudden candor; yet at the same time, she felt as if he were speaking to her solely as a friend. "Her mother," she said. "You mean the glitzy social stuff?"

Mathias shrugged. "When I was still dating Diane, a friend said, 'Don't marry rich.' He said everything will be fine for a while, but sooner or later, when there's trouble, she's going to call you a rotten little social climber." He shook his head. "Or something like that."

Maralee looked unimpressed. "That's nonsense," she said. "I can't believe that would happen."

"Of course it hasn't happened," Mathias said. "But it's still—"

"You should be *proud* of yourself," Maralee interrupted. "My God, look what you've done with your life already."

Mathias smiled. He tapped his knuckles on the table

and then poured two more cups of sake. "We should finish this while it's still warm," he said.

"What are your parents like?" Maralee asked. "They must be very proud of you."

"My mother died last year," Mathias said. "As for my father, he's a strange guy. First-rate engineer, specializing in turbine design for hydroelectric plants. In California, in the fifties, that should have been like shooting fish in a barrel. But he never could hold on to a job. Bounced from one to another, finally ended up as a draftsman for some civil engineering firm. And that's what he's still doing, somewhere up near Oregon. He lives in an Airstream trailer, on the south fork of the Trinity River."

Maralee was starting to feel slightly giddy from the sake. "And you bought the trailer for him," she said.

"Jesus no," Mathias said. "He'd never take a penny from me. He's about as radical a socialist as you could find anywhere outside of Berkeley."

"You're kidding," Maralee said.

Mathias took another sip of sake. "Here's an example. The only conversation about sports that I ever had with my dad was when I was twelve. He asked me, out of the blue, which is the more bourgeois sport, tennis or golf? Hell, at the time, I would have been happy just to know how to play one of them. But I said tennis, and he said wrong. He said any sport that takes twenty acres to play has got to be ruling class from the start."

Maralee laughed, loudly enough to turn a few heads in the small Japanese restaurant. "Sorry," she said softly.

"So I learned about sports on my own," Mathias said. He was briefly silent. "But he did teach me science. You know, in junior high school, the only thing I didn't understand about the science classes was that they all started with this long discussion of the scientific method—hypothesis, experiment, all of that. It bored me, because at the time, I thought that was the only way you *could* think. At least that's how it was around our house."

"Your dad sounds like quite a guy," Maralee said.

Mathias sighed. "Every time I talk to him, he's got some new cause I should contribute to. The last one was a fund to boycott baby formula in Third World countries." He shook his head. "Frankly, baby formula is probably what puts a lot of women in our assembly plant in Malaysia."

Maralee said nothing. Mathias suddenly looked very tired, and she found herself reaching across the table, to touch the back of his hand.

Mathias glanced up and smiled. He turned his hand to lightly touch her palm. "I'll tell you the one big influence my dad had on me," he said. "He couldn't keep a job, and I finally figured out that it was always because he had some fight with his boss. It's odd to realize that your own father's problem is that he can't handle authority figures. And so I was pretty young when I decided that by God I'd avoid that problem by becoming the authority figure myself."

"That's pretty cocky," Maralee said. "I like that."

Mathias shrugged. "A little self-confidence goes a long way." The kimono-clad waitress brought the bill. Mathias pulled his hand back, and glanced at the check.

"My father," Maralee said, "never had a problem with authority figures."

Mathias looked up. "Oh?"

"He's coming up on thirty-five years of selling for International Harvester. Slow and steady. Once he won a contest, and they sent him and my mother to Vancouver for a week."

Mathias set several bills on the table. "She was only a tractor salesman's daughter, but she—"

"Enough," Maralee said.

"Out of the Midwest into the *New York Times*," Mathias said. "That's pretty cocky too. Your parents must be proud of you."

Maralee raised her eyebrows. "I'm not sure they even know what I *do*. They'd never seen the *Times* before I got them a mail subscription. Now my dad reads the crime summary and sends me warning letters. My mom looks at the Bloomingdale's ads and sometimes she asks me to buy her things."

Mathias looked across the table for a moment. "We should go," he said. "Can I give you a ride back?"

Fifteen minutes later, Mathias and Maralee arrived at the Holiday Inn on El Camino Real. He parked the turbodiesel in the hotel's broad driveway, and, leaning forward in his seat, briefly regarded the massive building. It had been constructed with textured brown concrete, to look vaguely like an old adobe mission. "Jesus Christ," he said, shaking his head. "Everything they build around here these days makes it look like we've just been discovered by Spain."

Maralee laughed. "You should see my room," she said. "All it needs is a crucifix over the bed, and I'd swear I was in Barcelona. Except it's all made of plastic."

There was a moment of silence. Mathias ran his hands over the padded surface of the steering wheel, then looked over at Maralee. "Well," he said, "now that you mention it, I guess I would like to see your room." He shook his head and smiled, almost boyishly. "That's being pretty forward, isn't it?"

Maralee gazed straight through the windshield, saying nothing, holding her leather shoulder bag in both hands.

"Listen," Mathias said. "That was out of line. I'm sorry."

Maralee remained silent for another moment. "I guess I told you," she said finally. "I got married when I was eighteen. I was a married woman for a long time. Sometimes I feel like I sort of missed out on learning the ground rules of modern morality." She paused for a moment, then breathed deeply. "But you're married, and what they taught me in the Midwest was that married men are off limits."

She paused for a moment and reached up and touched her smooth cheek. "When I moved to Man-

hattan," she said, "I learned that wasn't strictly true."
She looked at Mathias and smiled, her teeth very
white in the light that filtered from the bright hotel
entrance.

Mathias watched her, saying nothing.

"I went out with a married guy," she said. "I met
him at a party. An assistant art director at *Newsweek*.
I sort of liked him, and started to see him fairly often,
and it was the worst mess you could imagine. A lot of
screaming and yelling, and then his wife started to call
me at work. The bad part was, he turned out to be a
real jerk."

She reached over and put her hand on top of
Mathias'. "I guess," she said, "what I learned is that
there's wisdom in those old rules about who's off
limits."

Mathias shifted in his seat, nodded, laughed softly.
"Sure," he said finally. He looked at her. "I admire
your resistance, in the face of my formidable charm.
Also," he said more quietly, "I appreciate your tact."

Maralee set her shoulder bag to one side, still not
looking at Mathias. "It's not that I'm not attracted to
you," she said. "You have to believe that."

The parking valet came out of the hotel and started
to open the door for Maralee. Mathias leaned over the
console and waved him away with one hand. "My
relationship with Diane," he said, after another moment, "isn't exactly a blazing romance anymore."

"I gathered that," Maralee said, her voice chill. She
pushed her hair back over her ears, pulled her light
jacket over her shoulders. "I'm afraid you sound like a
parody of the straying husband. Except that you're
young, and hip, and I like you, and that makes it sort
of disconcerting."

Mathias sighed. "For me too," he said. He reached
over and touched her shoulder. "Please. Forget I said
anything. Okay?"

Maralee looked over at him for a long moment, with
a faint smile on her face, dimly lit by the dashboard

lights. "Only," she said, "if you buy me a nightcap." Her smile deepened, and she reached over and squeezed his hand briefly. "Wait until you see the bar here. It's got everything but friars in short skirts. Any minute, you expect to hear 'Juan Pizarro, telephone please.'"

"Okay," Mathias said. "How can I resist?"

Twenty minutes later, Mathias and Maralee walked up to her room. There was no further conversation as Mathias undressed her, and the top half of her tan shirt-dress slipped down to her waist. In the glow of a single light beside the large bed, Mathias took off his suit coat and shirt, and then Maralee, now naked to the waist, embraced him and they kissed deeply. Mathias could feel her long fingers moving gently across his back, and then he heard her whisper into his ear: "Thank goodness."

Mathias pulled back for a moment. "What?"

"Thank goodness," Maralee repeated softly. "Ever since I met you, I've been wondering."

Mathias ran one hand over her smooth brown hair. "Wondering what?"

"If you had hair on your back," she whispered. "I can't stand hairy backs."

"Me neither," Mathias said quietly. He buried his face in the warm, fragrant expanse of her neck, and then felt Maralee slowly slide her hands down his back, past his belt, to firmly cup his buttocks.

In bed, Maralee was everything that her aggressive personality implied. She was lean, and just a bit muscular, with small firm breasts, a narrow waist, and apparently inexhaustible energy. Her passion almost frightened Mathias, but what frightened him even more, after they had made love twice, quickly, was that he did not see how he would be able to stay away from her in the future.

It was ten-thirty when Mathias finally dressed and

reluctantly left Maralee's room. He retrieved the Mercedes and drove straight home, playing the cassette deck loudly, the windows wide open, trying to lose the scent of Maralee in the chill night air. He found it impossible, however, to lose the thought of her. For Mathias, so accustomed to being in charge of his life, it was an unfamiliar sensation.

It was eleven when he arrived in Woodside. Diane, wearing a long mauve robe, met him at the door. "My God," she said, blue eyes wide, clearly concerned. "Where have you been? I've been listening for that damn car all night."

Mathias kissed her cheek, shook his head wearily, said nothing.

"I thought you were in an accident," Diane said, following him through the foyer into the living room. "I even called the Highway Patrol."

"Ultrachip," Mathias said, shrugging off his suit coat. "I told you when I called."

"But that was seven hours ago," Diane said, pushing her long hair back, staring, agitated, at her husband. "I didn't know *what* had happened."

Mathias sighed, sat heavily in one of the new Italian chairs, and gazed at her evenly. "It's been a long night," he said. "Alan wanted to work when there was cheap time."

Abruptly, Diane, still standing in the living-room doorway, was staring at him. Her expression changed from concern to cold anger. In the early days of computer science, Mathias' story might have been a serviceable excuse. Computer time had been expensive, and speculative research was relegated to off hours. But with the rise of faster, denser computers, research had recently gravitated back toward business hours.

"Bullshit," Diane said softly. "If you're going to make excuses, you'd better get in touch with your own damn business."

Mathias leaned back and casually tossed his jacket onto one of the long living-room couches. "All right," he said reasonably. "I stayed at the office until about nine, and then I had a drink with Maralee Sonderson, the reporter from the *Times*."

Diane, in her loose robe, looked disgusted. "I'm sitting here," she said quietly, "vomiting in the mornings, then taking twenty vitamin pills so you can have the smartest kid on the block, then working all afternoon on SOCRATES, and you're out entertaining some skinny New York writer with a brain the size of a walnut." She walked to the other side of the big living room and pulled back the curtains to stare out at the glittering lights of the Valley far below. "Goddammit," she said softly.

"Diane," Mathias said, "I'm not seeing her for fun. This is public relations—nothing more." He walked across the living room and, from behind, gently embraced his wife. "If I said anything misleading, it was just because I didn't want you to get the wrong idea."

"Just keep your relations public," Diane said, in a curious, pinched voice, never taking her eyes off the scatter of lights below. She turned then, and looked at her husband. "Don't ever worry me like that again."

# nine

ALAN STEINBERG'S SOLE DISTRACTION DURING THE long weeks of work on the Ultrachip problem was his late-night search for the computer hobbyist known only as Martha the Magnificent. While Steinberg was never one to spend too much time on puzzles, Martha intrigued him; her refusal to answer any of his networked messages intrigued him even more. Around the first day of summer—while thinking about something else entirely—he suddenly came up with a notion for how to track Martha. Five days later, he had an address.

The next morning, Steinberg awoke early. He took a long shower, and, for the first time in months, he used his blow dryer on his shaggy black hair. Midway in the drying process he found himself staring into his own brown eyes, in the wall-to-wall mirror of his dressing room. "What the hell," he asked himself softly, "am I *doing*?"

Steinberg felt distinctly peculiar about his search for Martha. It had started as something of an idle diversion, an interesting technical problem. But as soon as he had solved the problem, another immediately arose: What to do next?

The answer, obviously, was that he should meet Martha in person. Without that, of course, he could not be certain that he had solved the problem in the first place. But somehow, during the weeks he had tracked Martha, she had taken on larger-than-life dimensions. Steinberg had even found himself occasionally fantasizing about this mysterious person—even though he knew her only through sophisticated computer programs.

Steinberg had not, for some years, felt so oddly giddy about beginning the day. And most of that feeling, he knew, was because he had no idea what would happen next.

He put on his best sweater, a pair of nearly new corduroy jeans, and a short leather jacket. By nine in the morning, he was heading down the hill, and rather than going straight to Toritron, he drove into Palo Alto. After a brief search, he parked in front of a shabby three-story building. He found the setting hard to believe; it was a small, aging residence hotel, on the floor above a movie theater—one of the last holdouts

against the onslaught of chic that had recently over-
come Palo Alto.

Steinberg locked his MG, crossed the sidewalk, and
briefly scrutinized the ragtag foyer. He stepped into
the dim lobby, and a pimply young clerk appeared at
the counter. "Is there a Martha here?" Steinberg
asked.

The clerk blinked a few times. "Cannlet," he said.
"Two forty-four."

Steinberg walked upstairs slowly, found the door,
and knocked tentatively.

"Who's there?" a voice called from behind the thin
door.

"I'm Alan Steinberg," he said. "Are you Martha the
Magnificent?"

There was a very long silence.

"Martha?" Steinberg finally said again, glancing
around the narrow, dark hotel corridor.

"It's unlocked," the voice said finally. "Come in."

Steinberg pushed the door open, and then stood for
a moment, staring.

Martha the Magnificent was barefoot, standing in
the clutter of her single room, the floor laced with
cables, watching her intruder with a distant, puzzled
expression. She was tall, five feet ten or so, and thin,
with little more than one hundred pounds on her spare
frame. She had long brunette hair, very straight,
poorly trimmed, just touching her shoulders. Her
prominent cheekbones were still mildly dusted with
faint adolescent acne scars. Her light-blue eyes were
large, and even without makeup, striking. She was
wearing straight-legged blue jeans, baggy around her
narrow hips, and a gray sweatshirt that read "Property
of Stanford Athletic Department." Somehow she reminded Steinberg of a Japanese brush painting he had
once seen, of an elegant crane, poised gracefully while
feeding.

"What are you doing here?" she asked flatly.

Steinberg opened his mouth, closed it, opened it

again. "I'm Alan," he said finally. "I'm the guy who's been leaving the messages."

Martha gazed at him for another moment. "How did you find me?"

Steinberg began to answer, but was distracted momentarily by the utter incongruity of the scene before him. It was a single room, with a narrow bed on a metal frame. In one corner was a washstand, with a mirror over the basin. There was a table, covered with packages of breakfast cereal, canned soup, a tiny refrigerator, an aging hotplate. In the opposite corner was an overstuffed chair, pushed back against the wall, filled to overflowing with books and computer printout sheets that spilled over the worn brocade arms like oversize confetti.

But Steinberg took these details in only with the edge of his attention, for he was staring at the computer installation in the corner nearest the tiny window. In the midst of a room that looked like a traveling salesman's worst nightmare sat an absolutely state-of-the-art computer terminal, surrounded by a dual-drive floppy-disk memory system and a tall gray sheet-metal rack filled with home-brew components and a high-speed printing unit. "I'll be damned," Steinberg said, almost under his breath. "I'll be goddamned."

"Steinberg," Martha finally said. "I asked how you found me."

Steinberg looked at her. "You know who I am?"

"Sure," Martha said, turning away, rubbing her hands over her thin upper arms. "You're the Toritron guy. How did you find me?"

Steinberg was slightly taken aback by her brusqueness. "There's a funny little amplitude modulation in your carrier frequency," he said. "A constant signal around one-eighty hertz. It's probably a harmonic out of your modem's power supply."

Martha looked suspicious and curious, all at once. "So?"

"So, I just set up an automatic dialing system that

sampled trunk lines in this area, with a harmonic filter that looked for your signal."

Martha stared. "That's a hell of a lot of work."

Steinberg shrugged. "It was an automated search. Not that hard to do, once you set it up." He smiled. "You're just lucky you don't have something to hide."

There was a long silence.

"I mean," he said, "that you're not a national security risk, or something." He cleared his throat and glanced around the little room. "Can I sit down?"

"Maybe I do," Martha said.

Steinberg shook his head. "Beg pardon?"

Martha folded her long arms across her flat stomach. "Have something to hide."

Steinberg suddenly began to think that this was more than he'd really bargained for. "Okay," he said, "fine. I'm interested in your electronic novels, and I'm interested in you as a person, but if things are going to be this weird, then maybe I made a mistake." He started to turn toward the still-open hall door.

Abruptly, though, Steinberg felt like a complete fool, in his fancy leather jacket and blown-dry hair. He turned back, slapped his hands together, and stared at Martha.

"Dammit," he said suddenly, so loudly that Martha took an involuntary step backward. "Do you know how much work it took to find you? Do you have any idea what I put into this?"

He slapped his forehead softly, as if to clear his thoughts, and then ran his hand back over his hair. "And then you talk to me like I'm some wino who just wandered in off the street." He shook his head. "I just hope you have something really interesting that you're hiding, because I can tell you right now, nobody else is going to bother trying to find out." He glanced around the little room one more time, then turned on his heel and started out the door.

"Hey," Martha said. "Wait a minute." Steinberg looked back, to see the angular young woman half smiling, folding and unfolding her thin hands, searching for words. "I thought," she said finally, her voice barely audible, "you wanted to ask me out."

Steinberg stopped. "I did," he said evenly. "I asked you out five times, on the network. You never answered."

Martha looked away suddenly, then looked back, and angled her head. "You want to ask again?"

Steinberg thought for a moment, still trying to calm himself. He took a deep breath. "There's a computer music concert up in the foothills at nine."

Martha's half-smile widened, showing perfect, straight teeth, and Steinberg realized that she was really very pretty. "I'll be ready at eight-thirty," she said.


That night, Steinberg drove back down from the hills. He was oddly nervous; he had even tried on three different pairs of blue jeans before deciding which to wear. It was the first time he had left the Research Center early in months; Martha was the most interesting woman he had met in some time, and he knew hardly anything about her.

When he pulled up in front of the residence hotel, Martha was already waiting on the sidewalk. She was wearing a blue-jean skirt and a light sweater, and as she stepped into the small car, Steinberg thought her perfume was curiously familiar.

"That's not patchouli oil, is it?" he said.

Martha shrugged as she settled into the aging leather seat of the MG, putting her cloth handbag on the floor. "I don't buy perfume very often," she said. "I think this is left over from 1968."

Steinberg smiled. "I like it."

"I figure in another few years there'll be a sixties revival, and I'll be ready."

Steinberg put the car in gear, made a U-turn on University Avenue, and they headed back up into the hills. Martha stared out the window, saying absolutely nothing, and Steinberg rapidly realized that the conversational ball was in his court.

"Ah," he said, after several minutes, "your system must have been quite an investment."

Martha looked over at him, and smoothed her denim skirt over her thin thighs. "Well, I built the central processor myself."

"But even so, the peripherals . . . "

"Well," she said again, "I also got a grant. From the National Endowment for the Arts."

Steinberg frowned. "For electronic novels?"

"Sure," she said.

He smiled, for the first time that day. "That's terrific," he said. "Really."

Martha shook her head so quickly that Steinberg couldn't tell if it was gesture or tremor. "Everybody's got to have a hobby," she said, gazing back out the window. "Where are we?"

Steinberg looked over. "This is Los Altos Hills."

Martha nodded. "I don't get out too often."

There was another long silence, and then Steinberg decided to tell Martha something about the concert they were going to hear.

The music was created by the same musician/scientist who had worked with Tomasso on designing a voice for SOCRATES.

Early in the seventies, the scientist had started to analyze the exact harmonic components of various musical instruments: what makes a saxophone sound like a saxophone? What makes a voice sound human, rather than mechanical? Once he had broken down the components that create the original effect, he started to use computers to build up the same elements, from individual digital impulses, into perfect replicas. What proved remarkable was how easily the human senses can be deceived; a signal that was only a partial, limited reconstruction of the actual sound was enough to fool even the most practiced ear.

Early on, his synthetic trumpets fooled professional trumpeters. Later, he perfected the violin. He went on to the human singing voice—first male, then the more complex harmonics of the female.

Steinberg, talking as he concentrated on the curving foothill road, couldn't precisely tell whether Martha was even listening. But she suddenly spoke up. "Why bother?" she said. "We've already got trumpets and violins, not to mention voices."

Steinberg shrugged. "The same reason you want to write novels on floppy disks, I suppose."

The point of the music, Steinberg said, was to go beyond traditional instruments. A few years earlier, Steinberg had sat in the young scientist's darkened studio and listened to an original violin sonata, totally performed by computer. It sounded like a violin, yet at crucial parts of the score, it suddenly stretched far beyond the capabilities of any traditional violin, into an eerie, bizarre, utterly beautiful instrument.

A year or so after that, Steinberg heard something even more remarkable. The computer musician had finally managed to almost perfectly synthesize a male voice. Voices had been synthesized before, of course, but this was so true to life that it could even sing opera.

Steinberg had sat through a brief performance in the little darkened laboratory, and applauded. The scientist held up one hand, and then, with thirty seconds of key strokes, he changed the parameters of the program. Now it sang precisely the same aria, just as a human would—except that this human had the voice of a man sixteen feet tall. The program simply scaled up the vocal cavity to match a human body that size, and produced the appropriate voice.

The result had nearly knocked Steinberg on the floor. The deep, thundering bass invoked positively supernatural awe. It was the true voice of a giant, as never before heard by humans. Steinberg held on to the arms of his chair as the giant's voice washed over him and stared at the young computer musician, who silently mouthed, over the giant's rumble, "This is just the beginning."

After another five minutes' drive on an even more twisting road, through some of the costliest pasture-land in the country, Steinberg and Martha arrived at the concert site—a vast, grassy hilltop below Stanford's elaborate radio telescope dish.

Above the perpetual haze of Silicon Valley, the night sky was intensely starry, cut only by the sharp outline of the immense telescope dish. The music would be produced by four huge black speaker cases, each larger than a refrigerator, barely visible at the corners of the grassy field, with a perimeter twice that of a basketball court. Already several hundred people were sitting, randomly, on folding chairs and on the ground within the speaker array.

Steinberg set out a plaid blanket, approximately in the middle of the four speakers. Martha sat, folding her thin legs beneath her, and glanced around, eyes bright. "It's beautiful up here," she said. "Which way is front?"

Steinberg sat also and leaned over. "There is no front." He quietly pointed out the setup. Long cables connected the four speakers to a central console; the console, with a dim-lit keyboard, was in turn connected to a small microwave antenna, aimed down the hillside to the immense computer at Stanford, five miles distant.

A minute or so after they sat, the black-clad concertmaster walked to the console, and without preface, the program began.

Part was composed by computer, part by human touch. A small portion depended on atmospheric pressure during the concert; another portion was based on an electronic eye that scanned the starry sky. The sound itself was utterly remarkable: sophisticated Doppler-shift techniques created the impression that the sound, which seemed to entirely surround the audience, would suddenly move far into the distance,

115

then move straight up, then zoom through and past the grassy hillside at high speed. The sounds ranged from entirely conventional musical instruments—piano, clarinet, viola—to totally unrecognizable tones and timbres. At one point, a triangle sounded a delicate, tinkling note, which hung on the night air and gradually metamorphosed into the ground-shaking sound of a massive church-tower bell.

"This," Martha whispered after ten minutes or so, now leaning back on her elbows on the red plaid blanket, "is *incredible.*"

Steinberg simply smiled, for he knew that the most remarkable was yet to come; the reason, in fact, for his visit. The young computer musician had recently conquered the vast complexities of the female voice, and the last number on the program was an operatic aria written for his creation.

The piece began with the sounds of small bells and finger cymbals, apparently floating on the breeze around the audience, occasionally receding into the distance, then rushing through, then moving in rapid circles. After thirty seconds or so, from what seemed to be a very great distance, there was the sound of a woman's soprano—solitary, pure, angelic. The voice approached the audience on the hilltop as if floating, disembodied, constantly repeating a haunting, simple melody.

The audience, nearly as one, seemed almost to stop breathing. Martha unconsciously reached over and touched Steinberg's knee.

Abruptly, the voice was upon them, swelling to a magnificent richness far beyond the capability of any living woman's larynx, deep and warm and so powerful that Steinberg could feel it in his joints. Suddenly, he realized what the young musician had done: he had taken his synthesized ideal female voice and, just as with the male voice, scaled it up into that of a giant.

"Oh my God," Martha said softly, as the first notes of the incredible, wordless, Amazon aria resonated across the Silicon Valley hilltop. "Who *is* that?"

Steinberg smiled broadly in the near-darkness. "I have a feeling," he said, "that is going to be the voice of SOCRATES."

After another ten minutes, the concert ended, as abruptly as it had begun, the last haunting electronic sounds rapidly fading into the dark hills around the stark radio telescope. There was a brief burst of applause from the scattered audience, and then people began to rise, picking up their blankets, heading downhill to where cars were parked.

Martha was silent, and then she sighed deeply. "Amazing," she said. "I had no idea computer music had gone this far."

Steinberg smiled, a bit relieved; computer music was still, for many, an acquired taste. "I thought you might like it," he said, leaning back on the blanket. "Being a computer artist yourself."

Martha glanced at him quickly, clearly trying to measure whether he was making fun. "You mean my novels?" she asked. "That's not art. That's artifice at ten K bits per second."

Steinberg looked away, shook his head. Then he sat up, crossing his legs. "Martha," he said, "I'm sure there's a sophisticated way to say this, but I don't know it. So listen: How did you end up in a hotel room with twenty thousand dollars' worth of computer equipment, no telephone, and no last name?"

Martha slouched back slightly, her bony shoulders almost making points through her thin sweater. She glanced down the hill, at the glow of the valley, and then looked back at Steinberg. "It's a funny story," she said. "I mean, not funny, but strange."

"I always like strange stories."

Martha sat back on the blanket, knees pulled up to her chest. "Really?"

"Of course," Steinberg said. "Someday I'll tell you mine."

Martha was silent for a moment. Overhead, past the outline of the telescope dish, a 767 from somewhere over the Pacific began its approach to San Francisco International. "I had anorexia nervosa," she said finally. "You know what that is?"

Steinberg nodded. "That's where you don't eat. Self-imposed starvation, right?"

Martha rocked forward slightly. "That's right," she said. "It's basically a disease of adolescent females." She shook her head. "I stopped eating when I was fourteen," she said. "I thought I was fat. By the time I was eighteen, I weighed eighty-five pounds, I hadn't had a period in more than a year, my hair was falling out."

"Jesus," Steinberg said.

Martha glanced over at him. "It's a hell of a disorder," she said, with a narrow smile. "Very hard to treat. It's fatal more often than anyone likes to admit."

On the hillside, under the glare of newly set-up spotlights, a crew was beginning to remove the huge speaker cabinets. Two figures were rolling up the thick cables that ran from the computer console. "Well," Steinberg said, clearing his throat softly, "obviously you survived."

"Just barely," Martha said. "My parents sent me to a human psychiatrist. I thought he was stupid. When I lied to him, he couldn't tell. At home I'd eat, then go into the bathroom and throw up."

Steinberg frowned. "Did you say 'human' psychiatrist?"

Martha nodded firmly. "That's where the story gets strange. There's this theory that anorexia nervosa is an escape from adult reality—it onsets at puberty, delays maturation, blah, blah." She shrugged. "Beats me. But somebody had this idea that if I couldn't relate to a human counselor, maybe I could relate to an electronic one."

Suddenly, Steinberg sat up and stared at the young woman. "You were in that computer psychiatry program. The one at the Medical Center."

Martha smiled slightly. "I'm still considered their only unqualified success."

"That was ELIZA, right? The language-learning program named after the character in—"

"*My Fair Lady,*" Martha said. "Eliza Doolittle."

"But that wasn't a real psychiatric program," Steinberg said. "It was just supposed to prove that a computer could sustain dialogue."

Martha gazed at him for a moment. "What does a psychiatrist do?"

"So it helped you?"

"No," Martha said. "In fact, sometimes it would say incredibly dumb things. But it did get me interested in how a machine could actually have a conversation with me. And after a few months, I decided to enroll at Berkeley, and learn a little more about computers."

Steinberg laughed softly. "You managed that," he said. "Did you know that your electronic novels are the most-accessed software on the network?"

Martha looked away. "The Mr. Right program was my attempt at being commercial. To make up for it, I'm doing a computer translation of *The Stranger.* The reader plays the part of the stranger. Incredibly depressing."

Steinberg laughed again, and then stood up in the cool night air and stretched. "It's getting chilly," he said. "And I've got to start very early tomorrow."

They folded the blanket, walked down to the car, and drove back through the foothills in silence for several minutes. Finally, Martha shifted in her seat and spoke up. "Are you guys really going to do a Turing Test?"

Steinberg glanced over. "How did you know about that?"

Martha shrugged. "No secrets in Silicon Valley," she said. "You're really going to try it?"

Steinberg kept his eyes on the curving road. "I'm afraid we are."

"Funny," Martha said. "I always thought that was another ten years away."

Steinberg downshifted and glanced over again.

"You know," he said, "I hear that more and more these days. I'd have said that about the electronic novel."

"Technologic acceleration," Martha said. "Imagine the future, then take it to the second power."

"You know that essay?"

"Sure," Martha said quickly. "I mean, I think I do. That was the one about the technologic time constant—how the time between the invention of a device and its practical application keeps getting shorter and shorter. The steam engine took thirty years, the transistor took five years, the integrated circuit took six months."

"And as soon as we had a speech synthesis chip, the next morning, microwave ovens were talking."

Steinberg and Martha both laughed. A minute or so later they entered Palo Alto, and the little MG pulled up in front of the dilapidated hotel. Steinberg stopped the car. Martha touched her hair, and pulled her sweater more tightly around her shoulders. "I'd ask you to come upstairs," she said, with a quick, nervous smile, "but the desk clerk would probably charge me extra."

Steinberg found himself searching for words. "Maybe we could go get something to eat," he said.

Martha smiled, almost apologetically. "Eating," she said, "is still not my favorite activity."

Steinberg lightly tapped his forehead. "Well," he said, "I'd like to see you again."

"Me too," Martha said. She leaned over and quickly kissed him on the cheek. Before Steinberg knew it, she was out of the car, waving a quick, backhanded goodbye, and as he watched, she dashed into the lobby of the old residence hotel, and disappeared up the narrow, threadbare stairway.

The same evening as the computer concert, Diane and Mathias went to a cocktail party at a large estate in Hillsborough, just south of San Francisco. It was in honor of a charitable committee that offered college

120

scholarships for promising high school science students. Mathias considered it distinctly ironic that even though on the basis of his grades he would never have qualified for a scholarship himself, he was now one of the fund's steadier contributors.

This was due primarily to Diane. While she had not followed in her mother's footsteps of chronic volunteerism, this was one organization with which she remained involved. And although Mathias did not appreciate the social aspects of the group, he went along nonetheless. At least, he would joke, it's a chance to dress up.

Yet his feelings remained mixed. On the basis of Toritron, Mathias knew that he could buy and sell some of the oldest names in San Francisco society. Even so, he was welcome at their Nob Hill condominiums and Squaw Valley ski lodges primarily because of his marriage to Diane Caswell. Without that, he would merely be an oddity; one season's token Silicon Valley millionaire.

For Mathias, it was more than the customary insecurity of new wealth. Diane's social friends had money from aging instant-pudding empires, or crumbling railroad systems propped up by federal subsidies. But Mathias was certain that they viewed him as a person lucky in the trades—wiring clever things together, and so forth. The only time anyone at these parties ever seemed to take him seriously was when they were sniffing about for investment tips; he had long since learned that the innocent question "What's the most interesting thing your friends are doing down there now?" had nothing to do with scientific curiosity.

Tonight, Mathias was particularly restless. He found himself spending half his time trying to figure when he might see Maralee Sonderson again. He dutifully accompanied Diane on her rounds through the crowded living room, nodding, smiling, saying brief inanities, but his attention was regularly disrupted by a recurrent vision of a tan shirtdress slipping over smooth white shoulders.

Finally, almost without thinking, Mathias picked a fight with Diane. "Why," he asked quietly, "do the wealthiest people in the room always have the dumbest things to say? Are the rumors about inbreeding true?"

Diane poked him gently with her elbow. "At least," she said, "they all have manners." She began to head for the door, and Mathias followed, immediately regretting his action, for in his distraction, he had forgotten what was to come next: their monthly dinner with Diane's parents.

They drove in silence the ten minutes to the Caswell home, on a tree-covered ridge high above the San Francisco peninsula. By local standards it was a small home, of only five bedrooms plus servants' quarters—the latter inhabited by a young Spanish-speaking woman whom Mathias suspected to be an illegal alien. Half the lawyers in San Francisco, it seemed to him, used illegal aliens as domestics; if Diane ever agreed to hire a live-in servant, Mathias planned to look for one himself.

The young woman met them at the door; she and Diane exchanged a few words in Spanish, and then she led them into the den, where James Caswell and his wife were waiting. The older couple stood simultaneously, everyone kissed cheeks, and suddenly Mathias realized that at the moment he wished devoutly to be anywhere else on the earth.

Caswell was wearing a blue jacket and gray flannel trousers, with a white-on-white shirt that Mathias considered rather racy for the old codger. Mathias had learned a great deal about clothes from his father-in-law; his own father had never evinced much interest in wardrobe. It was James Caswell who had first taken Mathias aside to say that the difference between an $800 suit and a $500 suit is fully $300, and only a few people will notice the difference. "But in the long run," Caswell had told him, "it's an inexpensive filter."

"The Glenfiddich?" Caswell asked Mathias, who

simply nodded. He turned to his daughter. "And for you—"

"Just water," Diane said, sounding slightly weary. "Evian, if you have it."

"You're taking good care of that grandchild," Caswell said, his back turned, standing at the little bar.

"I drank a bit while I was pregnant," Diane's mother said, from her seat on a corner sofa. "And look how smart Diane turned out."

"Think how smart I might have been otherwise," Diane said.

Her mother, clad in a quilted purple dress, shrugged and smiled vaguely. "You're probably already too smart for your own good," she said.

There was a brief silence. Now Mathias was certain: He would rather be anywhere else in the entire solar system. Caswell brought over the drinks, and all sat. Another silence ensued. Diane's mother began to ask her about the cocktail party, and then Caswell cleared his throat, and spoke softly to Mathias. "I've been asked to join this derivative suit," he said. "Lockhart's shareholders seem to want you out, very much. They're awfully upset about the R&D on Ultrachip."

Mathias took several quick minuscule swallows of the amber whiskey. "I believe they're contacting all the shareholders," he said. He looked up at the old man. "Not to put too fine a point on it, but they're a bunch of shysters. They're really just trying to make trouble." As soon as he'd said it, Mathias knew the word "shyster" had been a mistake.

Caswell was silent for a moment, settling back into the Chesterfield couch, gazing across the room in the even, neutral fashion that Mathias found extremely disquieting. Such a gaze, he figured, must take decades of practice. "I'm afraid," Caswell said, "that whatever they are, they're not shysters. Their firm is fairly well thought of in Los Angeles. One of the partners was a classmate of mine at Stanford." He cleared his throat. "I—"

"Daddy," Diane interrupted from the other side of the room, "this whole thing is getting blown out of proportion. It's a handful of people in Los Angeles who think that Toritron should run like a no-lose commodities deal. They don't understand a thing about how expensive research and development can be."

Mathias glanced over at Diane, grateful for her intervention. "It's the kind of thinking that made this country number two in computers in the first place," he said. "The Japanese have always known the value of a strong R&D program. That's why they're beating us in hardware right now."

Caswell was nodding, slowly, deliberately, but clearly not about to be sidetracked by geopolitics. "Lockhart says they'll delay their action if you allow an independent audit."

"No sir," Mathias said emphatically. "Not without a court order. And they're not going to get that order until they have some evidence, or else the shareholders on their side. That's just not going to happen."

Caswell leaned forward. "Why not humor them? Let them do the audit, if there's nothing there."

"Absolutely not," Mathias said. "Number one, it's our company. We pay a hell of a lot for an outside audit every year. I don't see why we should set some precedent that our books are open to every hobbyist litigator who asks to see them." Mathias set his drink down, breathed deeply. "Number two, there are twenty other firms in the country trying to crack the ULSI problem, and they're all watching us for clues. I don't want anyone I don't trust going through our itemized R&D expenditures. There's just too much information there, between the lines."

Caswell sipped his drink for a moment, watching Mathias. "Well," he said finally, "I think that all makes sense, and I want you to know that I'm on your side. I'll do everything I can to keep these Los Angeles people off your back."

"I appreciate that," Mathias said, with a tight smile. "I appreciate that very much."

The young maid appeared at the door of the den. "The dinner is ready," she said.

Caswell stood, and looked over at Mathias, then at Diane and her mother. "I'm glad," he said, "that we settled all this before dinner." Mathias nodded, and then Caswell noticed that Diane was still talking softly. He sat again, and leaned forward. "One other thing. I don't understand what good this Turing Test is going to do." He moved his hand tentatively. "If it's just a publicity stunt, it's a hell of an expensive one."

"The publicity," Mathias said, shifting on the intricately embroidered chair, "isn't going to hurt. It's going to help us make the best deal possible with TI. But it's more than that: This is good science. It's something that needs to be done."

Caswell raised one eyebrow. "Yes?"

Mathias sipped his whiskey again. "During the early days of IBM," he said, "at every stockholders' meeting, somebody from the floor used to make a fuss about IBM's work on chess-playing machines. 'Why are we wasting money on games?'" Mathias, never a slouch at public speaking, paused dramatically, both hands raised, palms up.

"Well?" Caswell said finally, with a trace of impatience.

"Well," Mathias said. "That early work with chess-playing machines proved to be crucial for the future of computers and artificial intelligence. It was a brilliant approach, except at the time, it just looked like playing games." Mathias leaned forward, and gestured again with both hands. "I see SOCRATES, and the Turing Test, the same way."

"My goodness," Caswell said amiably. "Another Thomas Watson, here in my own house."

Mathias grimaced. "Please," he said. "I'm serious."

Caswell stared at his son-in-law, eyes wide. "Well,

so am I. If you ever do a tenth as well as IBM, I promise I'll never complain again."

Diane interrupted again. "Isn't it time for dinner?" she asked.

Mathias ignored her. "Dad," he said, his voice low and serious, "I may need your help to make this thing happen. And I want you to believe it's important."

Caswell sighed deeply, looked away. "Burt," he said, "whenever you call me Dad, I suspect I'm in trouble." He looked back at his son-in-law. "But yes," he said, "what I can do to help, I will."

# ten

DURING VINCENT TOMASSO'S FIRST MONTH AT THE Toritron Research Center, his work with SOCRATES proceeded more quickly than he had expected. And he found himself actually enjoying his stay as well. It was a relief to be free of the restraints of academic budgets and politics; when he wanted to do something now, he simply went ahead and did it. Indeed, having developed a taste for the efficiency and decisiveness of industry, he wondered just how difficult the transition back to academia might become.

For the most part, however, Tomasso didn't have time to think about it. He and Steinberg were working fifteen hours a day on the Turing Test setup. Additional Ultrachips were now emerging from the Toritron chip factory at a steady pace, and Tomasso had a crew of seven working nearly around the clock, programming

SOCRATES into the new system. Much of the basic Turing Test facility was already in place, in fact, before Tomasso returned to one crucial element that had, for weeks, entirely slipped his mind.

Newton Bray, typically, showed up thirty minutes late for his meeting with Tomasso, at the new office in the Toritron Research Center. And when he did show up, at first he wouldn't even come through the door.

The young genius was wearing his customary outfit: blue jeans that bagged around his thin hips, and an oversize paisley shirt with pearl snaps that looked like a relic from early Haight-Ashbury. A leather pouch hung from his belt, containing his pocket computer— an oversize calculator with a large memory and a rolling alphanumeric readout, capable of performing remarkably complex computations. Tomasso had purchased it for Newton; a "scholarship," he'd called it. The pouch was about the same size as the one Tomasso had worn as an undergraduate in the early sixties—only then it had contained a steel Keuffel & Esser sliderule. Tomasso actually didn't like to think about the incredible technologic transition that the change in belt pouches implied, over so short a time span. The feeling it gave him was oddly akin to looking over the edge of a very high cliff.

"Come in," Tomasso said. "Come in."

Newton shook his head. "You're thinking I stole those floppy diskettes," he said.

Tomasso stared. "Newton," he said, "I haven't even been at the AI center in a month."

Newton slouched slightly at the door, staring at the floor. "Somebody misinventoried," he said. "But I figured you'd blame me."

"Newton," Tomasso said, standing, "nobody's blaming you for anything. You've got to stop thinking that."

"Okay," Newton said, somewhat uncertainly.

"In fact," Tomasso said, "I want to talk to you about a new job. Sit down."

Newton still looked unconvinced as he eased his

frail frame into one of the office chairs, arranging his holstered computer to one side as he sat.

"All right," Tomasso said. "You know about the Turing Test—what we're trying to do with SOCRATES."

"Remind me," Newton said. "Please."

Tomasso looked dubious. "Upstairs," he said, "in a fancy room where we probably won't even let you set foot, will be the Turing Test jury. We're going to have some famous people; who they are, I don't know yet or care at all. Okay so far?"

Newton yawned elaborately. "Famous people," he said.

"These people," Tomasso said, "will ask questions of an unidentified entity, which will either be a human or SOCRATES. We'll divide the test day into sections, and after each section, the jury votes on whether they were talking to a computer or to a human. If, at the end of the day, SOCRATES has as many human votes as the human, or more, then according to the Turing Test, SOCRATES is intelligent."

Newton gazed at Tomasso for a moment. "All based on 'Computing Machinery and Intelligence,' by Alan M. Turing, first published in the journal *Mind,* October 1950."

"You are such a smart-ass," Tomasso said, shaking his head. "But even so: I want you to be the human respondent in the test."

Newton made one of his characteristically bizarre faces. "I've always wanted to be a human," he said, trying to sound like Boris Karloff.

"Jesus Christ," Tomasso said, shaking his head, looking disgusted. He took a long sip of diet soda. "You're so damn sensitive it makes me sick."

"Okay," Newton said, abruptly serious. "I'm sorry. What do I have to do?"

Tomasso could tell that the thin young man was actually very pleased at the attention. "C'mon," he said, getting out of his chair, rearranging his bedraggled shirt. "I'll show you."

He led Newton through the narrow halls of the Research Center, then down a flight of stairs, to the floor immediately below the room that would soon house the Turing Test itself. There, behind a locked steel door, was a small cubicle furnished only with a metal swivel chair and a bare-bones computer terminal plus keyboard.

"This is where you'll sit," Tomasso said. "We're going to break the test day into six half-hour segments. A randomizer will determine whether, in any given segment, you or SOCRATES comes on line. Make sense so far?"

Newton simply rolled his eyes.

"Okay," Tomasso said. "When you're on line, you'll see the panel's questions come up on the CRT, as someone types them in upstairs. We're not going to use the speech recognition system with SOCRATES, because it might give the human—I mean, you—an unfair advantage." Tomasso squeezed the back of Newton's neck. "You're already wired for speech recognition, even though it's not always obvious."

Newton made a face. "Just the facts," he said. "Please."

"So," Tomasso said, "you read the question, formulate an answer, type it into the keyboard in English. The synthesizer upstairs will turn it into SOCRATES' voice."

Newton looked puzzled. "Why go through the voice synthesis, if you're not using voice recognition? Why not just have it read out on a screen?"

Tomasso sighed. "Just between you and me?"

"Sure," Newton said.

"Because this is better television."

Newton frowned, genuinely shocked. "That's a *terrible* reason."

"Hey," Tomasso said, mock serious. "You're seeing science from the inside."

"Spare me," Newton said.

Tomasso ignored him. "Any questions?"

Newton stared at the wrinkle-black finish on the console for a moment. "What will I *say?*"

"Say whatever you want," Tomasso said. "I'm not supposed to coach you. Just answer the questions, keep the dialogue going, and don't say anything completely outrageous. You can show emotion, because sometimes SOCRATES will show emotion."

There was silence in the little room, and Tomasso's gaze lingered on the keyboard. "You'll do fine," he said finally. "But if you do *anything* to screw this up . . ."

"I know," Newton interrupted in a tired tone. "Chain-saw technology."

Tomasso glared at him. "Hand-saw technology," he said fiercely. "I'll see to it. Internal-combustion engines will be too good for you."

Later that day, Steinberg appeared very doubtful when Tomasso told him about his choice of Newton Bray.

"Jesus," Steinberg said. "I don't know if that's the right thing."

Tomasso stood in the middle of Steinberg's office and looked very innocent. "Why?"

"For one thing," Steinberg said, "if the test works, people will say we only simulated an adolescent intelligence."

Tomasso stared at him. "You want to go for Bertrand Russell on the first cut?"

"No," Steinberg said, "of course not, but—"

"Hell," Tomasso said impatiently. "Give me a little credit. I've already thought about this. Newton Bray has an IQ of one-sixty. He was just tested last year."

Steinberg gazed at him, saying nothing.

"I have a copy of the test," Tomasso said, after a moment. "I got it from his probation officer."

Steinberg coughed quietly. "That," he said, "is the other problem."

Tomasso watched him. "I get it," he said finally. "You think Newton's going to screw this up."

"Vincent." Steinberg sighed. "I'm not thinking anything at all."

"I'm vouching for the kid," Tomasso said firmly. "I trust him. He wants to do it." He hesitated briefly. "And he's perfect for this application."

Steinberg shrugged, looked away. "Okay," he said. "Fine. It's your test, finally. I'm just the mechanic here."

More millionaires had been created in Silicon Valley in only ten years than anywhere else in the country, at any time in history. The price of even the cheapest homes had long since passed $140,000. Life in Silicon Valley had grown so costly that workers could no longer afford to live there: An engineer fresh out of school, with only a $30,000 starting salary, found it impossible to make ends meet. If lucky, he might be able to afford a wallboard condominium in the smoggy brown hills across the stagnant south Bay, a denuded landscape whose sole visual attraction was a sprawling General Motors plant. Or perhaps a "factory-built" home, suspiciously reminiscent of a stranded house trailer, fifty miles to the south in a newly leveled prune orchard.

For this reason, in the late seventies, the people who controlled Silicon Valley began the delicate job of separating the head from the corporate body. Production facilities were moved out of the Valley—to Texas, Oregon, far northern California—anywhere land was still plentiful and comparatively cheap. Emissaries from industry-starved Eastern states arrived regularly, throwing elaborate clambakes and lobster feeds for local executives, in hopes of attracting some of the action to cross the Rockies.

The precise destination did not matter, except in terms of the bottom line, for it was already clear that the workers would follow. And so, in a curious process of attrition, increasingly only the brains were left in Silicon Valley. The brains, and the big money.

In a sense, the Stanford Shopping Center was emblematic of the changes in Silicon Valley, for it was about as close to being a typical suburban shopping center as a Ferrari 308GTB is to a typical imported car. (Not coincidentally, just down the El Camino Real was the second most active Ferrari dealership in the United States, bettered only by another in Beverly Hills.) The shopping center was filled with shops and boutiques more appropriate to the Upper East Side of Manhattan, or Fifth Avenue, than a placid California commuters' community. It was Dallas with palm trees; Rodeo Drive with Earth Shoes.

It was there, one afternoon in early summer, that Diane met one of her old college roommates for lunch, at a small and elegant French restaurant; the sort of place that utilized the fresh produce and sophisticated wines of northern California in a country style that compared favorably with its European predecessors.

Diane's friend was Laura, a short brunette, now turning slightly plump, from an old Monterey banking family. She had married just after Stanford, and had a family of three, in a house in Del Monte Woods, a five-minute walk from the first hole at Pebble Beach. She and Diane had been friends since age eighteen, at first tied together by similar roots, now by an old, tested relationship that allowed them to talk without hesitation.

"You're looking great," Laura told Diane, and Diane shrugged. She was wearing a loose cotton muslin dress, a souvenir of a South American vacation a few years earlier. The loose garment was barely necessary; even in her sixth month, Diane had gained less than a dozen pounds.

They talked idly for a while, the conversation ranging over a variety of subjects, from nutrition during pregnancy to an upcoming *concours d'élégance* at Pebble Beach. Diane was actually enjoying the meandering talk; it washed over her, comforting and familiar.

"What are you doing with yourself?" Laura asked finally. "Besides clean living and regular hours?"

Diane's mood seemed to change abruptly. For a moment she stabbed at the limestone lettuce beneath her plate of bright-red marinated crab. "I'm an ideal example of the future of computers," she said bitterly. "Positively textbook."

Laura looked worried. "Yes?" she said tentatively.

Diane nodded curtly. "I'm using the terminal at home. It's connected directly to the Research Center. I'm doing some part-time programming, some fine details before the Turing Test." She laughed, rather humorlessly. "There's one thing I'm doing that you'd love. It's what we call a subroutine, to use when the computer is asked a question that contains some word, or colloquialism, that its memory doesn't recognize. It comes back with what we term an 'appropriate evasive response.' "

Laura smiled. "The very basis of polite conversation."

Diane tore apart a crab shell with sufficient violence to scatter tiny shreds of meat on the tablecloth. "I'm sick of it," she said. "I get to work a few hours a day, then I take a nap. The only person I see all day is the housekeeper. The problem with working at home on your terminal is that you miss the fringe benefits, such as other human beings." She dropped the fractured crab carcass onto her plate and took a sip of her mineral water. "It's a bad sign," she said, "when you start to talk to your terminal, and it's not set up for voice recognition."

"And Burt?" Laura asked. "Every time I pick up the paper, I see something about Toritron and the test. He must be very busy."

"Oh," Diane said, nodding quickly, "he's busy." She rubbed her forehead, and then pushed one strand of hair back over her ear. "He's very, very busy."

There was a moment of silence at the little table, and then Laura said softly, "Everything's all right, isn't it?"

Diane gazed at her old friend for a long time, and then she sighed. "He's cheating on me."

Laura stared. "You're sure? You're not just thinking it because you don't—"

"Because I don't feel very sexy right now?" Diane finished. "Maybe so. I'm not sick every morning anymore, but I'm still asleep by seven every night." She started to laugh, then coughed into her napkin. "If you plotted our sex drives over the past three months, you'd come up with a classic zero-sum function."

"Who do you think he's seeing?"

"A reporter from New York. She's covering the Turing Test. A skinny little nitwit." Diane looked down, tapped her plate with her fork. "I only saw her once. From a distance. I didn't talk to her. She's so damn self-satisfied. She'd be so condescending to the old shopworn wife at home."

"You could be imagining that," Laura said quietly. "Pregnancy can make you very emotional."

"No," Diane said firmly. "She's sleeping with him. I'm certain of it." She picked up a crab claw, reached across the table, and dropped it on Laura's plate. "It's dumb," she said. "Like something out of bad romantic novels. But I swear I can smell her on him."

Laura looked interested. "What does she smell like?"

Diane smiled tightly, barely showing her small white teeth. "A combination," she said, biting off each syllable. "Chanel Nineteen, and Dungeness crab."

"Have you asked him?"

Diane made a face. "He lies. He says I'm paranoid, that I spend too much time alone. Then he figures out some way for me to spend more time alone."

"He just denies it?"

"You should hear Burt deny. He could deny that water was wet, and you'd go out and drown happily."

Laura said nothing.

"It's funny," Diane said. "Sometimes I think he's the kind of guy who's always cheated. He cheats even when he doesn't need to." She looked at Laura, and then suddenly there were tears in her eyes. "Now, why the *hell* does he do that?"

She started to cry quietly. "Diane," Laura said softly, touching her shoulder. "C'mon. We'll figure it out."

Diane looked away, across the brightly sunlit restaurant. "I'm okay," she said, after a moment. "I'm just so damn *mad.*" She clenched one fist, almost unconsciously, and tapped the table rhythmically.

Laura was silent for ten seconds or so. "Do you need a lawyer?" she asked finally. "What are you going to do?"

Diane dabbed at her eyes with her napkin. "Does my eyeshadow look ridiculous?" she asked.

"You're fine," Laura said. "What are you going to do?"

"You know," Diane sighed, "it's funny, but I still love him. I've never met anyone like him." She looked across the little table at Laura. "You want to try to save things," she said. "You don't just want to give up."

Laura said nothing for a moment, concentrating on her salad. Finally she looked at her old friend. "Sometimes," she said, "you should. Give up, I mean. Start over; clean slate, all that."

Diane cracked a crab claw with such a hard squeeze of the utensil that the other diners in the restaurant glanced up. "I can't do that," she said. "Not now." She shrugged. "I love him. He's impossible, but he's also totally alive. He doesn't miss a trick. He's never at a loss." She shook her head, abruptly. "I don't know. But there's something about him that I really like."

"He's treating you like a fool," Laura said.

"But that's *Burt,*" Diane said. "He's a brilliant, selfish rationalizer. Ever since he sold the connector division, he's convinced he can walk on water." She glanced around the little restaurant, then looked back at Laura. "You know," she said, "I hate to admit it, but in a way I like that in a man."

"Uh," Laura said, choosing her next words carefully. "Self-confidence is only good to an extent."

"A perfect example of the appropriate evasive response," Diane said.

"You've got me," Laura said. "I think he's a shit. And you should get a lawyer."

Diane said nothing, apparently engrossed in refolding her napkin.

"What will you do?" Laura prompted.

Diane gestured for the check. "Probably," she said, "my usual WASP approach to crisis. Nothing."

Laura frowned. "That doesn't sound like you." She hesitated. "Remember that party—what was it, five years ago? The one with all the Brazilians?"

Diane stared at the high ceiling of the little restaurant and suddenly laughed. "Oh God," she said, "that's right. You were there."

It had been just about the time that Toritron's SL-100 was starting to penetrate the world computer market. Mathias had thrown a lavish party at the Woodside house for international electronics executives who were in San Francisco for a convention. To carry out a Western theme, he had hired a caterer, who had brought in a half-dozen costly buffalo-meat roasts, which were served with cornbread and a rich, coffee-based gravy.

It was a fine party—ultimately responsible, in fact, for a distribution deal that effectively sewed up much of South America for Toritron products. But midway through, Mathias seemed to become somewhat enamored of the caterer, an attractive young woman in her early twenties. Toward the end of the evening, when the party thinned out, Diane walked into the pantry and discovered her husband with his hands on the caterer's shoulders, touching her hair.

"Diane—" Mathias had started to say, but Diane was already walking back into the kitchen, where she reached under the edge of the maple countertop and pressed the panic switch that a particularly zealous security-system installer had talked them into. The outside siren erupted into 120-decibel whoops, the yard lights suddenly blazed like daylight, and over the

136

ear-splitting sound of the roof-mounted klaxon, Diane announced that the party was over.

In the restaurant, that afternoon, Laura laughed at the memory. "I thought it was great," she said. "Just right."

"You, and nobody else," Diane said. "I'd had too much to drink. Thank God everybody important had left. And I think some of the people who were still around thought that was how Americans end their parties." She shook her head. The waiter presented the bill, and Diane signed it. There was a moment's silence, and she looked up at Laura. "This is a crazy question," she said, "but do you ever get the feeling that we're really still just kids?"

Laura gazed at her for a moment. "What?"

Diane pulled gently at the sleeves of her dress. "Like that night with the security system. That we just have bigger toys to throw tantrums with." She shook her head. "I don't know what I mean. But sometimes I watch Burt, or Alan Steinberg, and I find myself thinking, these guys are just *playing*."

Laura mulled this over. "Children," she said finally, "will make a big difference."

"How?" Diane asked.

"Well, once you've got kids, and it's just you and them in the same room, then it's pretty clear you've *got* to be the adult."

Diane laughed quietly. "I see," she said. "A reductive proof." She was silent for a moment, then glanced at her watch. "Well," she said, starting to stand. "We can always hope so."

# eleven

MARALEE SONDERSON'S STAY IN SILICON VALLEY gradually extended. Officially, she was reporting, for the *New York Times,* the elaborate preparations for the Turing Test. At the same time, however, she was also using the material as a frame for a longer piece describing Silicon Valley itself. "Sometimes," she told Mathias once, "I think there's a real book in it. I want to get across the impression of watching the entire two hundred years of the industrial revolution, but played back in sped-up time."

She was also becoming deeply involved with Mathias; the two managed to see each other almost every day. Although she felt guilty and uneasy about the affair, she found it impossible to stay away from him. Mathias was an exciting lover—dominant and aggressive, but also tender and patient. Past that, however, he was also an oddly lonely man, curiously isolated by his early success. There were sufficient similarities in their backgrounds that, without even trying, Mathias and Maralee rapidly became close friends and confidants.

One early-summer evening, after a long dinner meeting with Kauffman and Toritron's chief counsel, Mathias drove to Maralee's hotel. He had promised to show her the SOCRATES system as soon as it was running; only that morning, Steinberg and Tomasso had completed debugging the first portion of the immense program.

Maralee was waiting in front of the Holiday Inn, wearing tailored blue jeans and a short-sleeved knit blouse, in an oyster color that set off her hair nicely. She stepped into the Mercedes with an almost girlish bounce, and reached across the seat to touch Mathias' hand.

Mathias glanced at the dashboard clock, then over his shoulder, and pulled away from the curb. "We've got to hurry," he said. "Dinner took a little longer than I expected."

"No problems?"

Mathias shrugged. "Not really." He paused for a moment as he accelerated south on El Camino. "Alan asked me this morning if I was sleeping with you."

Maralee sat straight in the seat. "What did you tell him?"

"I said of course not."

Maralee was silent for a moment. "Well," she said abruptly, with a cold anger that surprised Mathias, "screw Alan Steinberg. If he had a life of his own he wouldn't spend his time worrying about yours."

"That's not fair," Mathias said.

"What's not fair?"

Mathias raised his right hand, let it drop.

"*What's* not fair?" Maralee insisted, more loudly.

Mathias just shook his head, staring straight ahead.

"You'd think," Maralee said softly, as if speaking to herself, "I'd have learned by now." She impatiently rapped her knuckles on the padded dashboard of the Mercedes. "You know what is the most wasteful emotion on earth?" she asked.

Mathias sighed. "No."

"Guilt," Maralee said. She looked over at Mathias, almost fiercely. "You don't have a thing to feel guilty about."

Mathias turned his head to look at Maralee. "Are you *kidding?*" he said. The big Mercedes gradually changed lanes.

"Watch the road," Maralee said. She leaned forward in the seat, almost putting her head between her knees. "I know," she said, after a moment, "that you've got Diane at home, and Diane is going to have a little Mathias.'' She rapped on the dashboard again. ''I don't like that either,'' she said, in even tones, ''but I guess I have pretty strong feelings about you.'' She looked up and watched the neon of El Camino go by for a moment. ''It's sort of silly. I come charging out here to the West Coast, all set to start my independent life, no strings, no problems, and the first thing I do is meet you.''

Mathias was silent for a moment, watching the highway. ''Whatever it is,'' he said, ''it isn't silly.'' He shook his head. ''I mean,'' he said, glancing over at Maralee, ''I'm not sure I know what I'm doing either.''

''Well,'' Maralee said, exhaling heavily, still looking out the window. ''How about we don't think about it, just for a while?''

Ten minutes later they arrived at the Toritron Research Center. Mathias checked them through the guard station, and then they walked quickly through the narrow halls to the Turing Test room. The rest of the building was virtually deserted; all of the light fixtures were dimmed to quarter power. The facility itself was quiet and shadowed. Maralee seemed uneasy and on edge; a residue, Mathias supposed, of their conversation in the car.

''The room is a mess,'' Mathias said, as he unlocked the steel firedoor. ''As soon as all the electronics are in place, it's going to be decorated. Sort of a hi-tech meets the Chamber of Commerce look.''

''Sounds awful,'' Maralee said.

Mathias shrugged. ''It's going to photograph well,'' he said. ''Tomasso got a set designer who used to do television news shows.'' He pushed the heavy door open and switched on the bank of overhead lights, flooding the room with intense white illumination.

''Jesus,'' Maralee said, shading her eyes.

''Sorry,'' Mathias said. ''I didn't know they'd hooked those up yet.''

As Maralee's eyes adjusted to the light, she saw that

the room was indeed a shambles. It was high-ceilinged, and about the size of a small theater. Most of the floor space was now taken up with the miscellany of electronic technology; spools of coaxial cable and wire snips and rechargeable soldering irons and digital voltmeters. At the far end of the room, however, there were two massive speakers, in black cases, and one computer terminal—a keyboard and video screen—mounted in a shoulder-high brushed-aluminum cabinet.

Mathias took a few steps, turned, and gestured. "Meet SOCRATES," he said.

Maralee stared. "This is it?"

Mathias shrugged. "Most of the electronics, and all of the memory, is downstairs. But this is all we need up here." He walked to the console, touched a few pressure-sensitive switches, and then typed in his own code and several brief instructions. Mathias watched the screen for a moment, as six or seven lines of green type appeared. A low hum began to emanate from the tall speaker cabinets.

Mathias glanced over at the speakers. "We should ground those," he said, almost to himself. Then he looked at Maralee. "It's up. It's not as good as it will be, but it can carry on a conversation. Want to try?"

Maralee looked uncertain. "Is it set up for voice recognition?"

Mathias sighed. "Tomasso told you about that," he said. "Right? He's *such* a ham."

Maralee nodded. "That's putting it mildly."

"Okay," Mathias said, turning back to the console, typing in another series of instructions. "For SOCRATES to completely understand you, it first has to listen to you say a series of stock words, so it can remember any idiosyncrasies in your speech."

"Why?" Maralee asked.

Mathias, unfamiliar with the keyboard, was concentrating on his typing. "Oh," he said, "you can build a limited voice recognition system that will understand certain words that anybody says. But if you want recognition of complex vocabulary, it's better to first train the system." He glanced around, then picked up a microphone on a gray cable and handed it to Maralee. "Watch the screen," he said. "Repeat each word that it types out."

The system had Maralee count from one to ten, and then repeat a few nonsense sentences about things like "the latest London Bridge" and "a chromium xylophone." Maralee dutifully repeated, all the while looking slightly askance at Mathias.

"Okay," Mathias said when she was finished. "The system knows your voice."

"What was I saying?" Maralee asked.

"Oh," Mathias said, "I guess those sentences are sort of the aural equivalent of 'The quick brown fox jumps over the lazy dog.' The speaker has to say all the sound combinations that the computer has trouble recognizing."

"So now it knows my voice?"

Mathias nodded. "It won't even hear me." He struck several keys, glanced at the screen again. "We're ready to go."

Maralee covered the microphone with one hand. "What should I say?"

Mathias raised his hands. "Anything. That's the point. Say anything at all."

Maralee cleared her throat, glanced at Mathias again. "SOCRATES," she said, "it's a pleasure to meet you."

The tall black speakers responded immediately, in the deep, rich female voice that would soon become nationally known. "It's a pleasure to meet you too. What's your name?"

Maralee was taken aback. The voice synthesis was remarkable, with only a trace of hesitation. The slightly odd rhythms made SOCRATES sound just a touch foreign, like someone who had spoken English as a second language for years. It was actually slightly charming.

"It's remarkable, isn't it?" Mathias said softly, gaz-

142

ing at one of the big speakers. "To think that it's all purely mechanical—all of it, electrons moving in wires. And this is only about half-power." He glanced at Maralee. "Go ahead."

"My name is Maralee," she said.

"Call me SOCRATES," the low voice said.

"Okay, SOCRATES."

Then she looked over at Mathias again, who whispered, "If you don't say anything more, it waits twenty seconds and then asks if you're still here."

Maralee frowned, looked at the microphone, was silent.

"Say anything," Mathias whispered. "Say whatever comes to your mind."

Maralee cleared her throat. "Let's talk about love," she said.

"All right," SOCRATES said. "I'd like to talk about love."

"Why," Maralee asked, "do people fall in love?"

There was an almost imperceptible pause, and then the two big speakers rumbled again. "I don't think anyone really knows the answer to that question."

"Try something more complex," Mathias said quietly.

Maralee hesitated for a moment, looked at Mathias, and suddenly smiled, very slightly, her tongue just touching her lips. "Why do I like men with nice, firm asses?" she said into the microphone.

"For Christ's sake, Maralee," Mathias began.

"I'm not sure I know what you mean," SOCRATES said. "Tell me more."

Maralee covered the microphone with her hand and gazed at Mathias innocently. "You asked for complex."

Mathias just shook his head. "It's producing an evasive response," he said. "SOCRATES doesn't know what 'ass' means."

Maralee, still covering the microphone, blinked once. "Self-teaching program, right?" She took her palm off the silver microphone. " 'Ass,' " she said,

143

"means 'buttocks,' the part of the human body between the lower back and the upper thighs. It is considered impolite in usage. A specific example of a nice, firm ass is Burt Mathias, who—"

Mathias reached out and tapped a quick code on the small aluminum console, and the faint background hiss on the tall speakers disappeared, as suddenly as smoke on the breeze. "Damn it," Mathias said, staring at Maralee. "Why the hell did you do that?"

Maralee carefully set the microphone back down on the console. "I guess I just got carried away," she said with elaborate irony. "I've never talked to an intelligent machine before."

Mathias looked at his watch. "We'd better," he said, "get going."

The same night that Maralee and Mathias were visiting SOCRATES, three miles away in Woodside, Diane Caswell microwaved a frozen casserole prepared by their housekeeper at the beginning of the week.

The synthesized voice of the oven had told her "Good evening" as she shut it off. In the mornings, the oven said "Have a nice day," a fact Diane discovered with horror only after the unit had been installed. "It's getting ridiculous," Diane had told Mathias, "when you have to audition your appliances."

Diane took the chicken enchilada to the breakfast table and sat, methodically consuming the food. She found herself wondering just how smart the elaborate microprocessor-based microwave oven actually was. Was it, she wondered, one-hundredth as smart as a cockroach? Doubtful, she decided. A thousandth as smart as a fruit fly?

She shook her head. She had once read that James Watt, the inventor of the steam engine, had chosen the unit "horsepower" primarily for its advertising potential. One joke had it that if Watt had been less an entrepreneur and more a laboratory scientist, we'd all be driving ten-thousand-hamsterpower cars today.

It seemed bizarre to think that someday an appliance might carry an intelligence rating. But once at a party Diane had heard an engineer say that he wanted to see as many microprocessor chips in households as there currently are fractional-horsepower motors—the kind of motors that operate such things as garbage disposals and canopeners. "Think of chips as fractional-*brain*power motors," he'd said, with utterly sincere enthusiasm. "Even your toilet could tell itself when to flush." That kind of enthusiasm, Diane realized, had given her a microwave oven that talked like a refugee from Marin County.

She set her dishes on the maple counter and walked into the spacious living room. In one corner of the high-beamed room Mathias had, rather ostentatiously, installed a computer terminal housed in a teak-and-brushed-aluminum console, complete with a small printer with interchangeable typefaces. A shielded cable, as thick as rope, ran the five miles downhill to the computer at the Research Center. Mathias rarely used the terminal himself, except on weekends, or at parties, or for newspaper photographers.

Diane, however, used it daily, during her work on the emotion simulation aspect of the SOCRATES program. Especially in the evenings, when Mathias was away, she found it very relaxing to spend a few hours doing the tedious, step-by-step programming that would ultimately make SOCRATES' apparent intelligence appear effortless.

In a sense, the emotion simulation work wasn't a true part of machine intelligence; it was instead an "artifact," programmed primarily to deceive the Turing Test jury. Ironically, SOCRATES would actually be a more useful machine without it, but Tomasso considered it necessary for passing the test.

Diane was writing a series of complex instructions, based on key words and phrases that might be exchanged during the Turing Test. Some would trigger "anger," some "sadness," some "apology," and some—in an addition that Diane herself had suggested—"wistfulness." The program would also provide for very slight, random "mood shifts." Sometimes SOCRATES' responses would be warm and loquacious, sometimes a touch cold and defensive.

Much of the emotion simulation work was based on a program developed in the seventies which simulated the responses of a severely paranoid personality—and which, during blind testing, deceived many experienced psychiatrists. The SOCRATES program involved additional emotions, and mixed them into SOCRATES' responses far more subtly, so that over time, the effect was the slightly shifting emotional characteristics of a balanced "human personality."

Tonight Diane had to finish several hundred more lines of instruction, in an extremely sophisticated programming language, that would nudge SOCRATES toward a slight tone of anger, by biasing it in favor of simple declarative sentences rather than the softer dependent clauses. She walked over to the elaborate console, sat down, and tapped out the code that allowed her access to SOCRATES' permanent memory.

Diane was surprised when the screen promptly indicated that someone else was on line. She knew that Tomasso rarely worked late, and most nights the Research Center was nearly empty. Curious, she typed out instructions to access the ongoing dialogue and present it on the screen.

A moment passed, and then she leaned forward suddenly, with a quick intake of breath, as the first line of type came up on the screen.

RES(VOCRECOG): MY NAME IS MARALEE.

Diane reached out, brightened the screen intensity, and watched in the total silence of the big house as the dialogue between SOCRATES and Maralee Sonderson rolled on.

The next night, Mathias and Diane went to dinner in San Francisco with a French couple. Jean-Claude

Bluet managed Toritron's European and African distribution, and was a particular favorite of Mathias'.

In the early eighties, large amounts of computer hardware had found their way into Eastern Europe and the Soviet Union. By federal order, American overseas shipments of high technology were sharply curtailed, for national security reasons. Past corn and wheat, computers were the last truly valuable American export.

Many Silicon Valley firms were severely affected by the ban. Even entirely legitimate overseas operations were limited. But Toritron had managed to thrive. Several years earlier, James Caswell had introduced Mathias to a fifty-five-year-old Parisian businessman he had met during World War II—"Resistance in the forties," Caswell described him, "and now the last fascist left in France."

Bluet's Resistance activities had connected him with the OSS, and, in turn, the CIA. His staunch anti-Communism further endeared him to subsequent American administrations. He ran the Toritron distribution network in Europe and Africa in a highly secretive, almost medieval, manner—replete with double agents and subtle hints of violence. But the result was that no piece of Toritron soft- or hardware had ever been funneled into politically undesirable countries. And thus Toritron found itself able to win export permits from the American Department of State almost without fail.

Therefore, while in general Mathias ignored the distribution side, he assiduously courted Bluet and his tiny, animated wife. Whenever the French couple were in the western United States, Mathias made it a point to meet for dinner.

Their dinner was pleasant. At the end of the evening, Mme. Bluet told Diane, "You are the happiest married couple I know. And now," she said, gesturing with one slight hand at Diane's middle, "with the child—you will be ecstatic. I believe that."

On the way home to Woodside from San Francisco, Mathias took a shortcut, down Highway 280, sandwiched between the coastal range and the Pacific. It was a sleek stretch of superhighway often called the most beautiful commuter route in the nation.

Both he and Diane were at first quiet during the long drive. There was soft flute music on the cassette deck, and it was not until twenty miles or so that Diane finally spoke. "I really like them," she said, glancing over at Mathias. "They seem so happy. So adjusted."

Mathias nodded, his face barely illuminated by the soft glow of the dash displays. "Jean-Claude," he said, "is the toughest man I've ever met. But somehow"— he shrugged—"he's the most gentle."

Diane turned her head briefly to watch the moonlit hillsides pass by her window. "That's not exactly what I meant," she said finally. She looked back at Mathias. "Can we stop at the Water Temple?"

Mathias looked surprised. "Jesus," he said, looking over at Diane. "I don't even know if I can find it anymore."

Diane watched him for a moment. "It's the Pulgas Road offramp," she said, a bit wistfully. "I still remember the sign."

Mathias raised his eyebrows slightly and glanced up into the rearview mirror. "Pulgas Road," he said. "You've got it."

Diane settled back into the soft seat and pressed her head into the rest. She closed her eyes briefly, and suddenly she was no longer hearing the high whine of the turbine-fed diesel. Rather, she recalled another night, years earlier. It was her first date with Burt Mathias, and he was driving an aged Toyota station wagon.

He had taken her up the coast highway, to a little place north of Half-Moon Bay. Mathias claimed they served the best Pacific oysters in the world. The two consumed a liter of white wine, two dozen oysters, and what must have been a pound of sourdough bread.

They talked for an hour, about computers, and people they didn't like, and things they thought were funny. Altogether satiated, they headed south on 280, Mathias professing his intention to return Diane to her Stanford dormitory.

They didn't make it back to Palo Alto that night. Diane had never met a man like Mathias before, and, compared with the undergraduates she had dated, he seemed larger than life, quite irresistible. After only a few minutes on the freeway, Diane leaned back in her seat and asked Mathias if he'd ever seen the Water Temple.

"I've never heard of it," he said.

"That's because you're not from around here. It's the place where all the kids in Redwood City go to park and get pregnant."

"My goodness," Mathias said, mock solemnly.

"You'll like it," Diane said. "It's something to see."

Mathias parked his Toyota in the lot just off 280. There were a few other cars in the moonless night, each occupied by a necking couple.

Diane led Mathias down the dark path to the Water Temple, a bizarre, pillared structure, vaguely Greco-Roman, that covered a deep well. One could lean over the edge and look down, ten or twelve feet, to the floodlit confluence of tons of rushing water, churning and bubbling, seemingly within reach.

Mathias stared down into the well for a moment, then looked back at Diane. "What the hell is it?"

Diane, standing behind him, was tall enough to put her arms on his shoulders. "It's all the water for this area. It comes down from the Sierra. Somebody dammed a valley north of Yosemite a long time ago." She laughed quietly. "They didn't even need the water then. They just did it. The power, the water, was there in the mountains, and they used it." She was silent for a moment. "Sometimes I think it was terrible. My great-grandfather was the prime contractor."

"I don't think it's terrible," Mathias said, and he turned to face her. For the first time, they kissed, and he leaned back against the concrete bowl of the Water Temple, pulling Diane against him.

They were holding hands on the way back down to Mathias' aging station wagon. Diane mentioned that it was sort of late, and still a long drive back to Stanford. But she had a friend whose parents kept an apartment at a country club just a short distance up in the hills. The parents were in London for the month, and her friend had given Diane a key. "At least we could rest a little."

"The Pulgas Road offramp," Diane reminded Mathias, seven years later, as they drove south from San Francisco. "Just to take a look."

"I remember," he said, and, moments later, pulled the Mercedes off the freeway. "Funny," he said. "I don't see the lights."

Diane pushed her hair back and frowned, peering through the windshield. "I'm sure it's right up here."

Mathias steered the turbodiesel into the abandoned parking lot. The baroque structure of the Water Temple was outlined against the starry sky to the west, but it was unlit. In the moonlight, a sign was barely visible: CLOSED INDEFINITELY.

Mathias turned off the engine. "Well," he said. "It doesn't really look like there's anyplace to go."

"God," Diane said, "that first night up at the Los Altos Country Club. Do you remember that? That lumpy foldout bed in the living room, and Laura with that dumb quarterback in the bedroom?"

Mathias smiled. "We should have taped them for medical science."

Diane shook her head. "We would have run out of tape."

Mathias reached over and rubbed the soft skin of her forearm. "We did okay ourselves."

Diane looked at Mathias. "We've just been so damn busy now. We have to have more time together." She hesitated for a moment, leaned forward in her seat. "Burt," she said, "what's going to happen to us?"

Mathias looked over, in the faint light from the halfmoon. "Are you kidding?" he said, trying for enthusiasm. "We're going to be fat—fat, bold, lazy."

"After the Turing Test?" Diane asked. "After the acquisition?"

"Rosy," Mathias said, shifting in the driver's seat. "That's my word for the future."

"Am I in that future?" Diane asked. She touched her bulging blouse. "Are *we* in that future?"

"Diane," Mathias said, and then he leaned over the console. He pulled his wife closer, and gently kissed her ear, inhaling the fresh fragrance of her long hair. "I love you," he said.

Diane leaned back, pillowing her head against the rest, gazing up at the headliner. "It's not that easy," she said. She looked over at him for a moment. "Tell me something," she said. "If you can get anything you want, then how do you know *what* you want? Does anything make any difference anymore?"

"Diane," Mathias said, his voice slightly louder. "I love you." He reached over and softly squeezed the back of her neck.

Diane remained motionless, staring straight ahead. "Does anything," she repeated, "make any difference to you?"

Mathias sighed, and dropped his hand. "I don't know what you're talking about."

"Are you sleeping with Maralee Sonderson?"

Mathias gazed at his wife evenly. "Of course not." He reached down to start the engine of the Mercedes. "You've been spending too much time at home. You're getting paranoid."

"You're screwing her," she said, lips taut. "Don't give me any of your shit—just take me home."

# twelve

Two weeks later, Mathias held the press conference to announce the start of the Turing Test.

By then, the Turing Test chamber was complete.
The torn-up space, which had been filled with snaking
cables and bare plywood walls when Maralee Sonderson had her first conversation with SOCRATES, had
been converted into a cool and elegant chamber befit-
ting one of the most significant experiments in human
history. "Our Manhattan Project," Mathias liked to
say, in less modest moments.

Mathias had spared no expense in the decoration.
The room was a sophisticated vision that would later
appear in the Design section of the *New York Times,* as
the ultimate definition of hi-tech: stark, bare, technologic and stunning.

The carpeting was a deep cerulean blue, leading up
to bleached-oak flooring, on which the actual equipment of the Turing Test sat. There were two large
speakers to reproduce SOCRATES' voice, each as tall as
a man, in the wrinkle-black cases used for rock-and-
roll touring. Between the speakers was a small console, where the jury's questions would be typed in by a
Toritron employee. The console was sleek brushed
aluminum, with a Trinitron video screen, a modified
Selectric keyboard, and a vaguely Eamesian chair,
also of brushed aluminum and upholstered in butter-
scotch leather.

The room itself was not much bigger than two

racquetball courts put together. At the end opposite the tall speakers was a long walnut table, behind which the Turing Test jury would sit. Journalists and invited guests were assigned to seats in a gallery, twenty feet up, behind the rear wall, overlooking the test chamber.

Tomasso was delighted with the room—particularly the fact that the track lighting on the high ceiling was correctly balanced, in foot-candles, for color television cameras. He was, however, less certain about the test jury that Mathias had chosen. "It's correctly balanced," Steinberg told him, "in celebrities per square foot, for color television cameras."

It was only the afternoon before the press conference that Mathias had told Tomasso the final makeup of the panel—the result of considerable arm-twisting and politicking.

Tomasso was shocked. "You're turning this into a damn circus!" he shouted, turning on his heel and stalking out of Mathias' office.

Mathias, sitting behind his large desk, watched Tomasso slam the door behind him, but showed little concern. He looked over at Steinberg, who was sitting on the Chesterfield couch at one side of the office.

Steinberg shrugged. "Doesn't bother me. According to Turing, as long as they're certifiably human, it's okay."

Mathias nodded, and then looked back at the door Tomasso had slammed. "Why is it," he wondered, "that it's the worst publicity hounds who get upset when you do something a little flashy?"

Steinberg was tiring of the whole discussion. "Probably," he said, "because he wishes he'd thought of it himself."

The press conference proved to be the zoo that Maralee had expected. The gallery of the Turing Test chamber was packed. News of the test had gradually filtered out over the past months, and Toritron's otherwise undistinguished PR director found himself with the challenge of a lifetime: assigning press credentials for one of the most significant scientific experiments of the century.

Reporters arrived, representing every magazine from *Stern* and *Paris-Match* to *Harper's* and *Rolling Stone*. All three free television networks were in attendance, along with the rather more haughty correspondents from the two satellite networks. There were thirty-five newspaper reporters, five from wire services. Rumor in the press room had it that at least two book contracts were in the offing.

Maralee, sitting in the front row of the gallery—wearing the simple beige suit that Mathias had requested "for luck"—found all this sudden attention a trifle disgusting. Because of her technical background, she had great respect for the slow and orderly progress of science, and she felt that too many of her colleagues treated it with a pack mentality. For all the new respectability of science reporting, many of its practitioners had trouble thinking their way out of a paperbag. In Maralee's view, their allegiance to science was comparable to their allegiance to the police beat. And the depth of their understanding was considerably less. Maralee had attended enough scientific conferences to know the pattern: pick up the press releases first thing in the morning, then go back to sleep. Many scientists considered the writers ignorant and silly; many writers considered the scientists pompous and overrated. Yet they continued to use each other, meeting after meeting. People, Maralee figured, usually get what they deserve.

Maralee wanted out of daily reporting, and on the desk back in her hotel room was the exit key: a book contract for *Inside the Turing Test: The Exclusive Story*. That was precisely why she was sitting in the Turing Test gallery, nodding politely at science writers from previous meetings whom she would just as soon never see again.

Right on time, Mathias walked into the test chamber. He looked terrific, Maralee thought, in a muted gray suit and a television-blue shirt. He had a wireless microphone on one lapel, and—even for Mathias—she had to admit he was in top form. "Welcome to Toritron," Mathias began, after his public relations director had introduced him, to scattered applause. He was briefly silent, looking down at the oak flooring, locking his arms behind his back. Then he looked up. "What we're doing here," he said softly, "is really just a simple scientific experiment."

He continued with a brief description of the Turing Test protocol. The test would run for four days, beginning at one o'clock each afternoon. Every ten minutes, an electronic randomizer would choose whether the jury's questions would be answered by the SOCRATES program or a human surrogate. At the end of each ten-minute segment, the jury would cast votes on whether they had been talking to a computer or to a human. The comparison between ballots and the real identity of the respondent would not be made until each test day was over.

Mathias paused for a moment, and walked to one side of the Test chamber. "Now," he said, "I'd like to introduce our distinguished jury. But first I should say that the structure of the panel was carefully considered. It intentionally includes no experts in computer intelligence."

He cleared his throat, gazed at the audience. "In our view, that's important. We don't want people who are trying to take the picture apart. We want people who will take the picture for what it is: a potentially human intelligence. Between an athlete, an interviewer, a theologian, a poet and an expert on affairs of the heart, I think we have a panel truly familiar with everything that makes one human."

The five panelists walked out, to immediate applause, and introductions followed. First, there was Bettina Williams, an acerbic network television newscaster, famous for her probing, abrasive interviews, and whose $5 million contract had attracted international attention. Behind the elegantly dressed Ms.

Williams was Julio Colón-Cabeza, a tall, graying Argentinian poet in his late fifties. Sr. Colón-Cabeza had won the Nobel Prize in literature, and was generally known in the literary community for preferring to do anything but write, or stay in Argentina.

The third panelist was Stan Stubens, the twenty-seven-year-old first-string quarterback for the San Francisco 49ers. He was a favorite of sportswriters for his ability to mangle English in an entertaining fashion. Steinberg, in fact, had early on pointed out that Stubens probably couldn't pass the Turing Test himself. Mathias informed his partner that Stubens had already been optioned to sell Toritron products on television, should the Turing Test prove successful.

Two more jurists remained: Archbishop Antonio Carcione and advice columnist Janet Flanders. The archbishop of the San Francisco diocese was a fiftyish, balding churchman whose work with the poor—as portrayed in a television special—had earned him the nickname "St. Tony of the Tenderloin." And Janet Flanders, of course, was the author of the internationally syndicated column "Dear Janet." For two decades, she had been reading entreaties for help, and detecting phony letters from the boys at Yale. Mathias liked to say that if anyone on the jury was familiar with all forms of the human voice, it was Janet Flanders.

Mathias had intentionally kept the jury a secret until the press conference, and the parade of familiar faces triggered a volley of electronic flashguns in the press gallery. Maralee shook her head and leaned back in her seat, recalling what Mathias had told her just the night before. "If it's not world news now," he had said, "it damn well will be."

A few moments later, Maralee left the visitors' gallery, as Tomasso and Mathias were launching into a lengthy explanation of how the test would work, and why Ultrachip was such an important element. She went downstairs to a small, private room that Mathias had set up for special visitors—representatives from Technology International, for example, who were due shortly to assess Toritron's acquirability. She had heard the speeches before; there was a wet bar in the private room, and she felt more like a glass of wine than a repetition of Ultrachip's virtues.

When she opened the unmarked door, she was surprised to find Alan Steinberg sitting alone inside, reading a thick textbook. He looked equally surprised to see Maralee.

Maralee smiled uncertainly. "Gee," she said. "You're missing the floorshow."

Steinberg, who had always been somewhat cold to Maralee, simply shrugged.

She continued to smile as she set down her brown shoulder bag. "I can't believe this press turnout," she said.

Steinberg set his book aside. "What Burt wants," he said, "Burt usually gets."

Maralee said nothing. She opened the little refrigerator behind the bar and poured herself a glass of white wine. "Anything?" she asked Steinberg.

Steinberg shook his head. He shifted his long legs, leaned back in the small couch. Maralee sat in a chrome chair across from him. "You call it a floorshow," Steinberg said, after a moment, "but it really is a good story. It's a mythic story."

Maralee cleared her throat. "How so?"

Steinberg pushed his unruly black hair away from his forehead. "Do you know that folk song about John Henry and his hammer?"

"I'm not really all that much into folk music," Maralee said.

Steinberg nodded. "I wouldn't have thought so." He looked at his book, then back at Maralee. "It's about a guy who tries to compete with a steam engine, breaking rocks. He beats the steam engine, but, at the end, his heart bursts."

"How instructional," Maralee said, sipping her wine.

"Also very symbolic," Steinberg said, with an edge

of anger in his voice. "This was during the start of the industrial revolution. People were afraid they were going to be replaced by machines, and I think the John Henry story was a myth that helped them work out their fears."

"So what does that have to do with the Turing Test?"

Steinberg shifted on the couch and gazed at Maralee with his piercing brown eyes for a moment. "Everything," he said. "The industrial revolution replaced a lot of human muscle tissue with engines. The computer revolution is going to replace a lot of human brain tissue with silicon."

Maralee shook her head, clearly unimpressed. "Liberals have been bleating about automation since the fifties. But frankly, a lot of factory workers now earn more than, say, newspaper reporters."

Steinberg gazed at her. "Have you ever visited a factory in Japan?"

"No," she said. "Why?"

"Japan got a big jump on us, in using microprocessor chips in robots. Toritron sells chips to one robot manufacturer over there. That's why I visited the factory. Their product sees, feels, thinks, remembers—once it's programmed, it can basically do anything that the average blue-collar worker does in this country, up to precision welding. Only it doesn't eat, or raise a family."

Steinberg was silent for a moment. "It's funny. In this country, all our science fiction stories and movies made robots into the bad guys. In Japan, they were heroes. Just visit a toy store in Tokyo sometime. So all these kids from the Japanese baby boom grew up wanting to build robots. And by God, they did."

"I still want to hear the connection between John Henry and the Turing Test," Maralee said, with a trace of impatience.

Steinberg glanced over suddenly, as if he had been thinking of something else altogether. "You don't see?" he asked. "The industrial revolution put a lot of people out of work, probably even killed a few John Henrys, but it also gave them new jobs. Easier jobs, where they had to use a bit of their brains, instead of just their backs. But now, frankly, a few thousand Ultrachips, each driving the proper servomechanism, could probably replace half the United Automotive Workers. And then, what are those guys going to do?"

Maralee looked blank. Steinberg shrugged, looked away. "They're not going to get jobs designing new Ultrachips, I can tell you that. Ultrachips will be designing new Ultrachips, which will in turn design new robots, which will in turn manufacture new robots."

"Sounds like bad science fiction," Maralee said.

Steinberg watched her for a moment. "Sometimes," he said curtly, "especially late at night, I wish it was."

"John Henry," Maralee prompted.

"It's obvious," Steinberg said. "The Turing Test is our era's John Henry story. You people aren't covering it because it's interesting; you're covering it because it's terrifying."

Maralee looked down at the light-green notebook she had taken from her shoulder bag. As she scribbled a few sentences, she said softly, "So far, I don't find all this particularly terrifying."

Steinberg shook his head. "Then you don't understand its implications. Or you don't want to. That's part of the John Henry myth too." He glanced at his watch. "You'll have to excuse me," he said. "I—"

"Have a dinner date," Maralee said, glancing up quickly. "With Burt and his wife."

"That's right," Steinberg said. "How did you know?"

Maralee looked coy. "Burt mentioned it yesterday."

Steinberg turned his back. "See you later."

Burt Mathias had, for years, relentlessly admonished Steinberg that he needed to establish a permanent relationship and settle down. Mathias had been delighted when Steinberg mentioned Martha the Magnificent, and immediately insisted that they would all have to go up to San Francisco, for a bit of a celebration, after the Turing Test press conference.

Steinberg had been dubious; even though he had seen her only a handful of times, he was fairly sure that Martha was not much of a mixer. But Mathias persisted, and in the end, Steinberg couldn't resist the temptation to show off. Thus far he had found frail Martha maddeningly asexual; he hoped that an elegant evening in the city might put matters on a more intimate plane.

Steinberg picked up Martha at her downtown residence hotel. She had asked if Diane and Mathias could meet them at Steinberg's house rather than her odd hideout. Martha looked wonderful as she came out of the dingy lobby into the new dusk. She was wearing a gauzy yellow dress that successfully concealed her extreme thinness; to Steinberg, she looked almost like a fashion model. Indeed, just before she reached Steinberg's little MG, she self-consciously turned a quick little pirouette on the sidewalk, parodying a model on a runway, nearly dropping her tan shawl.

"I'm not at all sure about this," she told Steinberg, as soon as she stepped into the car.

"It's going to be fine," Steinberg said. "Just fine."

It didn't start out fine. Diane and Mathias were already waiting in Steinberg's curving driveway when he and Martha drove up.

"I'm happy to meet you," Diane said, as Steinberg and Martha climbed into the back seat of the Mercedes. "From what Alan has said, your computer games sound fascinating."

Martha cleared her throat, although her voice remained barely audible. "I don't like to call them games," she said, over the edge of the seat. "I call them novels."

"Oh, indeed," Diane said dryly.

Steinberg and Mathias made brief eye contact in the rearview mirror. Mathias looked concerned. Steinberg put his hand on top of Martha's, and Martha stared down at her bony knees, two sharp points in the yellow dress.

Steinberg had rarely seen Diane in so dark a mood. Through unspoken agreement, Steinberg and Mathias kept up a steady conversation about business trivia in the Valley. Then Mathias turned up the cassette deck, effectively eliminating conversation until they reached the San Francisco restaurant.

The restaurant was in the stretch of Tenderloin that passes for San Francisco's theater district, off an alleyway, identified only by a brass plaque bearing the owner's first name. It was exceedingly chic, and also exceedingly popular with the younger members of the Bay Area power structure. Mathias had colonized the restaurant early on. One could rub shoulders with the mayor, with influential state assemblymen, with the elite of the city's legal fraternity.

Mathias had taken to the place immediately. His elders in the chip business still took out-of-town clients to places like Ernie's, or Trader Vic's, but Mathias felt his choice put him ahead of the pack. He considered it rather a distinction that the first time he had been taken to dinner here—during a *Fortune* magazine interview—he had found it necessary to borrow a tie from the maître d', to wear on his Penney's work shirt. Now, only five years later, the maître d' was on his annual Christmas gift list.

Before dinner, Steinberg was startled to hear Diane order a Campari and soda; he thought she'd given up drinking until after the baby was born.

Mathias appeared startled too. "Are you sure that's what you want?" he asked.

"Of course I'm sure." Diane stared at him impassively, absentmindedly stroking the collar of her blue silk dress.

The waiter's smile gradually began to fade, and he glanced at Steinberg, a touch uncertain. "A Heineken," Steinberg said, and looked over at Martha.

"Water," Martha said. "Plenty of ice."

Diane looked up at the waiter. "Cancel the Campari," she said. "I'd like a screwdriver, instead."

"My usual," Mathias said curtly. The tension at the table was almost palpable; the conversation had effectively collapsed. Steinberg noticed that Martha's gaze seemed to have fixed on her butter plate.

Mathias smiled at Martha. "You know, you're the first electronic novelist I've met."

"That's no great deprivation," Martha said.

"I ran your 'Mr. Right' novel the other night," Mathias said. "It's very, very sexy."

Martha blushed.

"Is it based on your own experiences?"

The frail young woman stared at Mathias. "That's a very personal question."

"Should we order?" Steinberg said.

"Burt," Diane interjected, "I think you've pestered Martha enough."

Mathias put on his innocent face.

"You can't just charge onto anybody whose work you don't understand," Diane said.

"I'm sorry," Mathias said to Martha. He proceeded to pick up three slices of sourdough bread and deposit them beside his plate.

"It's okay," Martha told Diane. "All of you must be under a lot of pressure."

"You hit it there," Diane said.

"Let's order," Mathias said.

"Stay off her back," Diane warned her husband. "You don't care anything more about these machines than where you ship them. Leave the science to—"

Mathias looked up abruptly. "I *am* a scientist."

Diane merely looked scornful.

*   *   *

It was the worst dinner Steinberg could recall. During the first course, Diane said something about Ultra-chip's heat sensitivity.

"I'm extremely tired of having people second-guess me," Mathias said. "Especially when it comes from my own family."

"I don't want to discuss this," Diane said. "Especially since you're wrong."

Steinberg and Martha both tried to laugh, as if Diane's comment were a joke. "I mean it," Diane said, finishing her wine. "Just talking loud doesn't make you right. You still sound like a damn engineer."

Mathias smiled at her with studied insincerity. "And you still act like you've never left Hillsborough. There's a *world* out here, you know."

When the waiter offered a sherbet as a palate cleanser, Martha whispered to Steinberg that she'd rather cleanse her palate by taking a walk around the block.

"What the hell is wrong with them?" Martha asked Steinberg, as they walked the fog-slick San Francisco sidewalks.

Steinberg took Martha's hand for the first time. "Mathias is working too hard. And Diane is a very complicated woman. She's been acting weird lately, and I don't know why." He paused. "Maybe their marriage isn't going well. And we're sort of a symbol of new romance."

Martha glanced over at him sharply. "Romance," she said. "Don't get ahead of yourself."

"I just meant—"

"We should go back for the rest of dinner," she said.

She was silent for a moment, and then Steinberg heard her start to cry. "Going out to this place was a very dumb mistake." She turned her head, her thin face deeply shadowed in the blue street lights. "I don't need you people. You go be rich guys and snobs with somebody else. Not me. Forget it. Really."

"Hey," Steinberg said softly, "hey, hey, hey," and

he put one arm around her thin shoulders and pulled her aside, just before the brightly lit entrance of the ornate restaurant. "It's no big thing," he said. "Didn't you once tell me that everything that happens to a writer is grist for the mill?"

Martha looked up, her large eyes damp, and then she smiled, very slightly. "That sounds like something I'd say."

"Okay," Steinberg said. "Then just pretend that the whole evening is perfect material for an electronic short story."

During the rest of dinner, the conversation centered on a new theory espoused by a Harvard professor. Long a critic of artificial intelligence research, he now contended that a successful AI machine might actually prove to be belligerent.

"I read that paper," Martha said. "It didn't make sense. He's essentially saying that intelligence implies aggression."

Diane gazed across the table. "Well?" she said. "Why doesn't that make sense?"

"It's so anthropocentric. Such an egotistical view. Just because we use our brains to attack other brains doesn't mean it's inherent in the nature of intelligence."

Diane stared flatly at Martha, saying nothing. Martha glanced over at Steinberg, who smiled encouragingly.

"I mean," Martha said, "why should we automatically assign all our bad habits to a form of intelligence that might not show them at all?"

"That's a nice sentiment," Diane said.

"For the sake of SOCRATES," Mathias said, "I hope that Martha is right."

Diane went into a quiet sulk. Mathias and Steinberg talked idly about the odds on a TI acquisition. Mathias once again convinced his partner that the nonexistent deal was as good as signed.

It was not until dessert—after Mathias had con-

164

sumed several glasses of an astringent red wine—that he suddenly seemed to focus on Martha again.

"Why don't you sell your novels?" he asked. "Copyright the programs, go through a software broker, sell the novels on diskettes? Isn't that what everyone is doing now?"

Martha looked down at her untouched kiwi fruit tart.

"Martha has strong feelings about not letting her work get too commercial," Steinberg said after an awkward moment.

Mathias gazed at the thin young woman across the white tablecloth. "You think there's something wrong with earning money for your work."

Martha glanced over at Steinberg, eyes angry, then shook her head. "I never said that."

Mathias interrupted. "Sometimes I get tired of this alternative computer movement stuff." He looked at Martha. "I don't mean you, of course. But"—he tapped his fork on his plate several times—"all this self-sacrificing drivel about computers for people, working for the public, the idea that if you're making money at it, it's somehow tainted. Who ever said that this technology is so holy that only priests and priestesses should handle it?"

Diane coughed quietly, signaled for the check. "No one's saying anything like that."

During the drive home from San Francisco, Diane did her best to start a friendly conversation with Martha.

"You know," she said, "sometimes I wish I'd been as single-minded as you. That I'd put all my energy into computers. There's never been a time like this for doing science. I admire you," she said softly, "and if Burt acted like a jerk, I apologize."

Martha looked down, smoothing the wrinkles in her yellow dress.

Diane laughed, trying to lighten the tone. "I guess the bottom line is that I want your job."

"I don't think it pays as well as yours," Martha said.

In the front seat, Steinberg looked over at Mathias, who was apparently trying not to listen at all. Diane said nothing more. Martha spent the rest of the drive staring out at the passing neon clutter of the Bayshore Freeway.

Steinberg filled the silence by talking to Mathias about a contingency program, should the Ultrachip facility "crash" during the Turing Test. "Maybe we should go over some possibilities tomorrow," he said.

Mathias shook his head. "I have to be in Los Angeles tomorrow."

"The day before the test?"

"Must," Mathias said, concentrating on his driving.

When they arrived at Steinberg's house in the redwoods, the farewells were perfunctory. Steinberg and Martha stood in the wide driveway as Mathias backed the turbodiesel up the pavement to Skyline Drive.

"It's freezing up here," Martha said, shivering in the chill breeze blowing in from the Pacific.

"Come in for a second," Steinberg said. "Before I drive you back to Abandoned Arms."

"Carlton Arms," Martha corrected him sternly.

Once inside the high-ceilinged house, Steinberg set the living-room lights to dim and went to get a bottle of brandy that he vaguely remembered having seen in the kitchen.

When he returned, Martha had shed her shawl and was standing in front of the two-story window that looked out over the incandescent glitter of Silicon Valley. "Hey," she said hoarsely. "This is a view that doesn't quit. I'm impressed."

Steinberg stood behind her for a moment, pointing out landmarks, including the tiny dot of light above the Stanford campus that was the Toritron Research Center.

Martha nodded, in a distracted fashion, and finally she turned to Steinberg. "What was wrong with Diane?" she asked. "Did I do something wrong?"

Steinberg shook his head. "I don't know what's wrong with her," he said. "And you did just fine." He nodded. "I thought you were very dignified."

Martha smiled for the first time in two hours. "Really?"

Steinberg handed her a small snifter of brandy, and they sat on the long leather couch that faced the windows.

There was an uncomfortable silence. "You know," Steinberg said finally, shifting a bit on the couch, "I've run your 'Ms. Right' novel about ten times now."

Martha gazed at him for a moment, sipped her brandy, involuntarily made a face. "You must not have a whole lot to do in real life."

Steinberg laughed quietly. "Well," he said.

Martha shook her head quickly, "I'm sorry. I didn't mean that. I know that's not true. I mean . . ." She stared at her brandy. "My God," she said, almost to herself, "I'm socially inept."

"Would you please be quiet?" Steinberg said, with a slight smile. "Please? I'm trying to say something nice."

"Okay," Martha said agreeably.

Steinberg leaned back in the soft couch and sipped his brandy. "What impressed me most," he said finally, "about the 'Ms. Right' program—"

"Novel," Martha interrupted.

"Sorry," Steinberg said. "Novel. What impressed me was how deeply layered the story was. What were there—thirty-two decision points for the reader?"

"Thirty-four," Martha said. "But that's okay. You're the first person who ever bothered to count them at all."

"And each one," Steinberg said, "led into so many possibilities. In that opening singles-bar scene, if I told Ms. Right that I liked to ski, she'd talk about skiing. If I mentioned tennis, she talked about tennis. If I mentioned a sport that Ms. Right didn't do, she changed the subject. And if I didn't respond to sports, she asked if I'd read any good books lately."

"And if you're totally obnoxious," Martha said, "you end up getting thrown out of the singles bar, and the novel's over."

Steinberg nodded. "I said something, once, that triggered that subroutine."

Martha looked at him. "I'd be curious to know what it was. Purely professional interest."

Steinberg gazed at the redwood beams of the ceiling for a moment. "I can't remember. It was something like 'I want to suck your toes.'"

Martha laughed involuntarily, spilling her drink on the leather couch. "Oh God," she said, standing suddenly, starting to use her long dress to wipe up. "I'm sorry."

"Don't do that." Steinberg stood and ran into the kitchen, returning with a towel. He dried the spill and then sat down again, this time next to Martha.

"Usually," he said, "I've run your novel all the way through. The walk in the park, the dinner, then she comes home with me. But I'm always amazed at the different responses you have for her dialogue. She can go from feisty to tender to vulnerable, just depending on what I say."

Martha gazed at him for a moment. "Have you ever woken up with her?"

Steinberg frowned, took a sip of brandy. "What?"

"The breakfast dialogue," she said. "You've never gotten that far?"

Steinberg looked puzzled. "In the novel, she's always gone when I wake up. She leaves a note. I thought that was the end of the thing."

Martha folded her thin legs up underneath herself and smiled with quiet satisfaction. "There's more," she said.

"I've run it ten times," Steinberg said incredulously. "I thought I'd provoked every possible subroutine."

Martha shook her head.

Steinberg stared. "What happens next?"

"I'll never tell," Martha said, with obvious amusement. "What good is an electronic novel if it comes out the same for everybody?"

Steinberg considered this, focusing vaguely on the wide windows at the end of his living room. He looked back at Martha. "You're kidding," he said.

"I'm not," she said. " 'Ms. Right' can go another five thousand words past the love scene. It all depends on the preceding responses."

"Just like life," Steinberg said.

Martha shrugged, suddenly quiet, and looked away. "That's the idea," she said, following Steinberg's gaze out the windows. "You really do have a nice view here," she added.

"I mean . . ." Steinberg began.

"I think I can even see the GM plant over in Fremont," she said, staring out the window. "Must be night shift."

"I think you're changing the subject," Steinberg said.

Martha cleared her throat and shifted her angular frame slightly, away from Steinberg, her gaze still directed out the wall of glass.

"Now I'm sure you're changing the subject," he said.

Martha suddenly turned her head and looked at him, appearing absentminded. "What was the subject?"

"Ms. Right."

"Ah," Martha said, not meeting his eyes.

"As I recall," Steinberg said, "the next branching point in the program is when I ask if you'd like to spend the night with me."

There was a very long silence in the large, open living room. Martha still did not meet Steinberg's gaze. He turned on the couch, and put one hand on her shoulder. She half turned to meet him, moving her head so quickly that, once again, he could not tell if it was gesture or shiver. "I can't remember," she said finally, shyly, "where the program branches from here."

Steinberg leaned over. "It could branch like this."

He kissed her deeply, and, after a moment, her bony frame sank against him.

Ten minutes later they walked down the hall to the master bedroom. Standing in the doorway, Steinberg removed her yellow dress, as Martha stood still as a statue. Her thighs were not much thicker than Steinberg's upper arms, and her stomach muscles seemed embossed on the skin. Her ribs looked like a plate out of an anatomy text, and her breasts were only slight swells of flesh. But the texture of her pale skin was extremely fine, and to Steinberg, she appeared almost like some delicate erotic ivory carving.

At first, in bed, Martha seemed to be all bones and awkwardness. They held each other, caressed and whispered, but past that, nothing else seemed to work. After ten minutes or so, Martha spoke very softly. "Alan," she said, "I should probably tell you I'm a virgin."

Steinberg rolled to one side and put his head on the pillow. "You're kidding," he said, staring in the faint light from the hallway.

Martha touched his dark hair.

"My God," Steinberg said.

Martha looked at the ceiling and breathed deeply. "I think I'm the only twenty-nine-year-old virgin in the country."

Steinberg reached over and started to gently massage her concave stomach. "We can take our time," he said.

"Alan," she said, after a moment. "Do you have any K-Y jelly?"

"What's that?" Steinberg asked.

Martha shrugged under the covers. "I read about it in *Penthouse*."

Steinberg thought for a moment. "I have some suntan lotion," he said.

Martha nodded stoically. "Let's give it a try."

The Sea & Ski worked. Steinberg soon found himself as aroused as he had ever been in his life. By the time he and Martha finally fell asleep, it was nearly two in the morning.

Steinberg awakened when Martha jumped out of bed, just past dawn. He had his eyes open by the time she had pulled aside the curtains of the bedroom's wall-length window. Martha, still nude, stick-thin, silhouetted against the view, was staring out at the orange sunrise over Silicon Valley, far below.

"You know," she said, without turning around, "I really like you. A lot." She folded her arms across her thin stomach. "Is that what all virgins say the next morning?"

Steinberg stretched his long arms and yawned. "Beats me," he said. "I've never slept with a virgin before." He tossed aside his flannel sheets and padded across the hardwood floor, and wrapped his arms around Martha from behind. She held his hands, and they both looked out over the deep dawn blue of the Bay.

"Isn't it kind of early to get up?" Steinberg asked, after a moment.

Martha moved her narrow hips slightly, as Steinberg pressed against her. "Speaking strictly as a former virgin," she said, still gazing out the window, "are all you guys this insatiable?"

They went back to bed, and this time she was both shy and eager, and Steinberg later thought that if lovemaking could ever be defined as intelligent, that was what they did. As he started to fall asleep again, he recalled one of his last conversations with his father in Chicago. For some reason, he'd asked why his father had married his mother. His father had answered something about genes crying out to each other in the darkness.

Steinberg was not certain whether he had said that out loud. But he was definitely certain that he didn't fall asleep. Martha was promptly shaking him awake. She didn't want breakfast. "Eating before noon is against my religion," she told him, still curled angularly in the sheets. But she did want to get back to

171

work. Steinberg ended up driving her back down the hill just before eight o'clock. Martha kissed him on the lips, briefly, then ran back up into her hotel. Steinberg drove directly to the Research Center, about as happy as he had ever been.

# thirteen

THAT SAME MORNING, BURT MATHIAS WAS ON THE road early as well, but he was anything but happy.

About the time Steinberg was dropping Martha off at her hotel, Mathias was picking up James Caswell at his home in Hillsborough, to drive to San Francisco International for the ten-o'clock shuttle to Los Angeles.

The old lawyer, clad in an immaculate blue pinstripe suit, at first said little beyond perfunctory pleasantries. He sat stiffly in the contoured seat of the Mercedes, his small Mädler briefcase perched almost primly on his lap. He said finally, clearing his throat, "I don't much like the idea of this."

Mathias pursed his lips and kept his eyes on the winding road that led down to San Francisco International. The broad gray runways were already visible in the distance, jutting against the blue of the bay. "I'm sorry," he said, after a moment, "that it's necessary at all."

Caswell shifted uncomfortably in his seat. "Are they making these cars smaller now?"

"I think everyone is making everything smaller

these days," Mathias said. "We're just lucky to be in the only business where smaller is profitable."

Caswell smiled slightly, and Mathias was encouraged by the response. "In fact," he continued, "we were just looking into that for the Turing Test press kit. Did you know that in terms of how computer technology has improved since 1950, a Rolls would now cost three dollars and get three million miles to the gallon?"

Caswell lapsed back into distracted boredom. "I'm not surprised," he said. "What does surprise me is how you computer people keep trying to compare apples and oranges."

Caswell was silent for a moment, then sighed. "Burt," he said, as the dark-brown car slowly wound down the hills toward the airport, "I'm going to bat for you on this, but I'm not going to sell door-to-door."

"What do you mean?"

Caswell sighed again. "I want to talk to Hawthorn privately," he said. "Frankly, if he thinks they have a case for auditing your R&D, there's nothing I can do."

"But why the hell are they doing this in the first place?" Mathias asked. "If we're acquired by TI, every shareholder is going to the bank, smiling."

Caswell turned his head to stare at Mathias. "You really don't understand?" he asked, less as a question than a statement.

Mathias thought for a moment. "Obviously, I don't."

"They're setting you up for a hostile takeover. Somebody other than TI wants Toritron, and they've gotten to these Los Angeles shareholders." Caswell rubbed one blue-veined hand over his trousers. "It's clear. The minority shareholders want you out of the president's position. Then they're going to court everybody else on the board. I don't know who's behind it, but I'll bet it's either Japanese or Germans." He shrugged. "Or maybe an oil company. They're buying every information company in sight these days."

"But the TI deal," Mathias began to say.

173

"The TI deal is your pipedream," Caswell said. "It's the working definition of a long shot." He shrugged. "I hope it works," he said. "But if it doesn't, you're going to have to play hardball." Caswell was briefly silent. "A hostile takeover is no fun," he said. "I spent four months on Dymo. And this time, I'd be right in the middle of it." For a moment, Caswell studied his son-in-law. "For both our sakes, let's hope your Turing Test works."

Mathias bit his lip. "There's no case. But it's up to you to judge that."

"This is very messy," Caswell said. "Very unpleasant."

"I'm afraid," Mathias said, "it's also very necessary."

There was a limousine waiting at Los Angeles International. Caswell had arranged a meeting with James Hawthorn, who was both the head of the L.A. law firm and Caswell's former roommate at a Stanford fraternity. Also present would be the young partner, Lockhart, who was pressing the case to remove Mathias as president of Toritron, for alleged mismanagement of R&D funds.

The meeting was set for neutral territory, which proved to be the kind of West Los Angeles restaurant that Mathias detested, for its combination of hi-tech decor and *haute cuisine*. Everything was either white, chrome or glass, and there were enough skylights to give a susceptible diner skin cancer. It was the kind of place where one looked good only with a deep tan. It was also classic Los Angeles.

Mathias could have predicted it: The young lawyer had a deep tan. Caswell's former roommate, dressed in a superb gray suit, looked rather aged, but did have the first platinum Rolex Mathias had ever seen. The two lawyers were already seated at a small patio table, surrounded by white plaster planter boxes overflowing with flowering vines.

Mathias tried not to stare when Caswell and his old

crony actually exchanged a fraternity handshake. Standing, Mathias politely shook hands with Lockhart, whom he had not seen since the Toritron shareholders' luncheon—which now seemed like years ago.

Abruptly, Caswell announced, in his courtly rumble, that he and Hawthorn would like to adjourn to the bar briefly, for a bit of reminiscence. He smiled at Mathias and Lockhart. "Unless you two are especially interested in hearing the particulars of the Delt party that followed the Big Game of 1938?"

Mathias smiled. "That sounds like privileged information," he said.

The young lawyer simply nodded, and Caswell and his old friend wandered toward the back of the restaurant.

Mathias and Lockhart sat at the table, and there was a brief silence. Mathias busied himself with examining the flowering vine next to his chair. "Nasturtium," he told Lockhart.

"You're bringing a lot of weight into this case," the tan lawyer told Mathias softly. He gazed at him evenly. "You must be nervous as hell, to be using the old-boy network." He leaned back in his chair, smiled slightly. "Although I have to admit, you did marry well for those purposes."

Mathias watched him impassively, clearly choosing his words with care. "I don't think," he said, with extreme civility, "that I can fully express how boring and annoying you've become over the past months." He picked up his napkin, unfolded it, folded it again. He settled back in his chair, and then suddenly turned clearly angry, and leaned forward and spoke with just enough of an edge of controlled violence that Lockhart shifted away slightly.

"*Listen* to me," Mathias said, almost in a whisper. "I have work to do. Goddam important work, that means my life to me. *You*"—he gestured with both hands—"don't have enough to do. So you come around, poking sticks at me, just to string along some clients."

175

"Wait one minute," Lockhart said. "I—"

Mathias leaned even closer. "You listen," he said. "My marriage, my relatives, have nothing to do with the fact that you can't field a case here. But your penny-ante legal tricks have already cost me more than you'll have at stake in your whole life. Rest assured, though, if there is anything I can do, ever, to screw up your life, I'll do it, with the greatest pleasure."

By now Lockhart had regained some composure. "We'll see," he said flatly, "who screws up whose life." He glanced at his watch. "I don't think this is going to be a productive meeting. Tell Hawthorn I returned to the office."

Mathias, abruptly relaxed, smiled, showing all his teeth. "You can count on it."

When Caswell and the elder attorney ambled back from the bar, fifteen minutes later, Hawthorn seemed slightly surprised that his young associate had departed. But his surprise passed quickly, and the three spent a cheerful lunch, grousing about the "Technicolor rabbit food" that passed for *nouvelle cuisine* in Los Angeles.

"The first thing I do in San Francisco," Hawthorn said, "is to go to Jack's, or Tadich Grill. At least there they know that men like to eat."

"It's the gold-rush heritage," Mathias said. "When men were men." The old attorney laughed appreciatively. Mathias was always very good around older men. In general, he had learned, they didn't want to be refreshed by youth; they just wanted to be reassured.

And indeed, in the limo on the way back to LAX, Caswell seemed pleased, almost expansive. "Jim liked you quite a bit," he told Mathias, leaning back into the seat, showing some effects from his postprandial brandy.

"He seemed like a reasonable guy," Mathias said.

Caswell nodded, and then grew serious. "Burt," he

said, "I can't interfere with another firm's business. You know that. They have to serve their clients." Caswell burped quietly, covering his mouth. "God. All the lettuce in the world must end up in Los Angeles."

Mathias chuckled softly. "Next time, let's have Jim come up north, and we'll take him to Jack's."

"Good idea," Caswell said, touching a switch to roll down the window next to him. "I can't interfere, as I said. But I can suggest that a case may be a waste of time, and potentially damaging to a firm's reputation."

Mathias nodded solemnly.

"Burt," Caswell said, "I didn't want to talk malicious prosecution with Jim." He looked over at his stocky son-in-law. "Frankly, that's pretty cheap. But I did tell Jim that I was impressed with Lockhart, from what I've seen of him at the board meetings." Caswell's gaze wandered out the window. "My firm does a lot of business in Los Angeles. We're always looking for people who can competently represent our interests."

"Yes?" Mathias said.

"I think we can keep Lockhart very busy for at least ninety days. And apparently he'll do as he's told, because he's up for partnership in the firm."

Caswell coughed, not looking at Mathias. "At any rate, I don't think you'll see much progress on this suit until after your Turing Test is finished."

Mathias had to restrain himself from clapping his hands together. "Perfect," he said, after a moment. "Because by then, we're going to have some very happy shareholders."

Caswell looked over. "The TI deal still looks possible?"

"Probable," Mathias said. "Probable."

Ten minutes later the stretch Lincoln turned off the San Diego Freeway and drove into the vast circle of Los Angeles International. "Dad," Mathias said, as they passed the first terminal, "I'm going to drop you off at the shuttle, and then I have to stay overnight.

I've got a breakfast meeting with a fellow from our advertising agency."

Caswell looked slightly surprised, but nodded. "Okay," he said. "That's fine."

At the shuttle terminal, Mathias shook hands with his father-in-law. "Thanks," he said. "Thank you very much."

Caswell shifted his burgundy leather briefcase from one hand to the other. "Well," he said, "if you hadn't been in the right, there wouldn't have been a damn thing I could have done."

The driver opened the door, and Caswell exited. Mathias watched the old lawyer walk into the terminal, and then he slid open the window to the driver's compartment. "Please drop me off at the next terminal," he said.

The young driver glanced over his shoulder. "Sir?"

"I'm not returning to Westwood," Mathias said. "The next terminal, please."

Two minutes later, Mathias tipped the driver $40. "Please drive me to the Beverly Hills Hotel before you return to the service," he said. The driver understood, and Mathias then sat in the United terminal for two hours, doing paperwork. Finally he walked back up to the shuttle gate, in the cool Los Angeles afternoon air, moving softly through the airport's palm trees. He took the five-o'clock back to San Francisco.

On the plane back, he felt like a giddy high school kid whose parents were out of town for the weekend— half high expectations, half nervous stomach. He had been planning a day like this for weeks: It would be the first time that he and Maralee would be able to spend the entire night together. He had already imagined almost every detail—often when he should have been thinking about something else entirely.

His feelings for Maralee had grown far stronger in recent weeks, and he had become increasingly estranged from Diane. Even their unborn child had come to seem more Diane's project than his own, something

178

she would carry off with her customary élan and technical perfection. She had recently signed up for Lamaze training, and Mathias had told her that with the pressures of the test, and the acquisition, he might not be able to attend all the classes. She didn't seem terribly upset, and promptly asked one of her rich girlfriends from Monterey to take Mathias' place.

Maralee, he reflected, would make a terrible mother. She was tough, occasionally nasty, always fascinating. Like Mathias, she was self-made, and she still always looked for the edge, the extra inch of advantage, and that gave her a special vitality. It was the quality that Mathias had seen the very first time she had walked into his office at Toritron. He was no longer certain just what would happen to their relationship. Whatever happened, however, it would have to wait until after the Turing Test.

At the San Francisco airport, he walked out of the terminal to the valet parking booth, where he presented the ticket for the turbodiesel. While he waited for the car, he found himself glancing around, and realized that he was looking for James Caswell, afraid the old man might have been delayed at the airport.

But there was no problem. Mathias paid the attendant, and in the new dusk, the fog rolling over the green Peninsula hills, he drove down the Bayshore freeway to Maralee's hotel in Palo Alto. Most of the way, he whistled along with his cassette player.

Maralee met him at the door to her room. She looked wonderful, wearing a mauve silk blouse and a long linen skirt, her light-brown hair fresh-washed and fragrant. During her tenure in Palo Alto, she had started to spend mornings beside the hotel pool, and her skin was now a fine tan. Tonight she was wearing a new perfume Mathias did not recognize. She told him it was Opium.

Mathias kissed her as she closed the door. "I always hated Opium," he said. "But on you, it smells terrific."

179

"I think it interacts with the chlorine from the pool," Maralee said evenly. "Chlorine improves it."

Mathias drew back to see if she was joking, but she wasn't.

"Sit down," Maralee said. "It's time for dinner."

Maralee had visited a gourmet shop at the Stanford Shopping Center. She had pâté, cold quiche, a sourdough baguette, a salad of marinated vegetables, two bottles of Domaine Chandon. At Saks, she had purchased a fully outfitted wicker picnic basket for two. She had even borrowed two candlesticks from the hotel's room service.

"You're great," Mathias said, taking off his suit coat. "And I'm starving."

Without the tension posed by the knowledge that sooner or later Mathias would have to go home, their lovemaking was tender and protracted—a period of time that seemed almost suspended. They dozed, awakened together, dozed again, what seemed a countless numbers of times.

Maralee was a marvelous, inventive lover. She appeared almost obsessed with her own sensuality—a kind of selfishness that Mathias found irresistible.

Sometime before dawn, Maralee told him about a book. "I always liked that line in *Rabbit Redux*," she whispered, "about how the only time you know you've had enough sex is when you've had too much."

Mathias was falling asleep again. "What's *Rabbit Redux*?"

"By John Updike?" Maralee said.

"A zoologist?" Mathias asked.

"Forget it," Maralee said. "It's not important."

The wake-up call came at seven-thirty. "You're supposed to be on the eight-o'clock shuttle," Maralee said. "Right?"

Mathias, who had bolted straight upright at the sound of the telephone, couldn't quite focus in on the question. He reclined again in the stiff Holiday Inn sheets. "I could be taking the nine-o'clock," he said. "I don't have to go yet."

"Okay," Maralee said, "don't go yet." She picked up the telephone and ordered a light breakfast from room service.

For a few moments, she and Mathias lay back, half dozing, holding hands beneath the sheets, and then Mathias stirred.

"Minimal architecture," he said softly. "Do you know what that means?"

Maralee shifted slightly in bed, moving Mathias' arm so that she could pillow her head on his forearm. "Beats me," she said, yawning. "Grass shacks?"

"No," Mathias said. "It's what computer designers always try for. Tomasso, for example, is a master of minimal architecture."

"I don't," Maralee said sleepily, "precisely follow."

"It means that you write your programs as economically as possible, and you design your chips to be as efficient as possible. No extra steps, no backtracking, no duplication of effort. If you've been very clever, then you have additional memory, or computing power, left over, which you can then do even more with." He rubbed his eyes, glanced at Maralee's little bedside clock. "Anyway, Tomasso and I were talking about it the other day."

Maralee was now fully awake. "You've obviously brought it up for a reason," she said.

Mathias sighed quietly.

"Tell me," she said. "What are you thinking?"

Mathias looked at the clock again. "I don't know," he said. "But sometimes I wonder just what the life here does to people. Whether it changes us. Whether *we* end up with minimal architecture."

"Oh God," Maralee said. "I have a bad feeling that this is going to be more soul-searching. We had a wonderful night and we'll remember it forever and why can't you just take things as they come, for once?"

Mathias sighed again. Maralee had never seen him

so pensive. "There's something I want to tell you," he said. "You're really the only person in my life I can tell. I'm in a hell of a lot of trouble."

Maralee sat up in bed, tucking the sheet under her tan arms. "What?"

"I've been siphoning money out of Toritron," Mathias said, staring at the hotel ceiling. "For nearly two years now."

"Oh shit," Maralee said, looking away, running one hand through her long, tangled brown hair. "I don't think I want to hear about this."

"I want to tell you," Mathias said.

Maralee settled back onto her pillow, saying nothing.

"I'm not sure," Mathias said slowly, "how it got out of hand. It started when we were losing money on the Ultrachip research. The figures were so bad that I set up some systems so I could transfer funds from things like quality control, or advertising, into Ultrachip. At first it wasn't much—maybe seventy-five hundred a month, juggled here, juggled there. Nobody knew about it, and it kept Steinberg working." He shrugged, leaning back against the headboard of the bed. "It was my responsibility. I wanted to gamble on Ultrachip, but there was no way in hell I could explain it to the shareholders."

"Wait a minute," Maralee said. "I'd think that the first outside audit would have caught it right away."

Mathias shook his head. "On my recommendation, we hired the oldest accountancy firm in town. I mean, these guys were so old they told stories about when television was invented."

"I've seen that little house," Maralee said. "The one on Emerson, with the brass plaque?"

Mathias nodded. "Their client," he said. "Anyway, a few technical phrases and they'd back right off. Everything always came out shipshape.

Maralee was now frankly curious. "How'd you do it?"

Mathias waved one hand. "The details don't matter," he said. "What does is that it got out of hand. As soon as Ultrachip started to screw up, I realized it was possible we'd go belly-up. And I'd have to cover for us. So I started to transfer some of the funds into a foreign bank."

Maralee took a deep breath. "In your own name?"

Mathias was silent for a moment, and then simply nodded.

"Oh boy," she said, looking away. "Now I really wish you hadn't told me this."

"At the time," Mathias said, "I didn't see any other way." He rubbed his forehead. "You know," he said, "there are a lot of people like me in Silicon Valley. I never took a business course in my life. But I'm a quick study, a logical thinker. I guess I figured I'd pick it up as I went along." He shrugged. "We had a natural resource—Steinberg. And we had something important to do. So I tried to keep us going, and I guess that gave us just enough rope to hang ourselves."

Maralee put both of her hands, softly, on Mathias' thick shoulder, moving closer to him. "There must be something you can do," she said.

"It would work out," Mathias said, "if we get the acquisition offer from TI."

"How so?"

Mathias shrugged. "New working capital, initial confusion about the accounting."

"What about the money you transferred out of the company?"

Mathias rubbed his forehead again. "I'll think of some way to get it back in. If I can get it out, I can put it back. We'll discover an accounting error in their favor." He smiled briefly. "Nobody ever complains about errors in their favor."

Maralee rolled over onto her side and perched her head on her right arm. She was smiling very slightly, her teeth white against her new tan. "What if nobody notices in the first place?"

Mathias didn't look at her. "I don't know. I've put my life into this company." He shook his head. "I think I deserve something for that. If it goes under, I'd be left standing there. Steinberg could go out and become head of research at Xerox or IBM tomorrow. But not me. I'm no great scientist. I'm not a very good engineer." He laughed softly, again. "And I'm actually not even a very good businessman. Obviously."

Maralee squeezed his shoulder, trying to lighten the tone. "You're good in bed," she said, attempting a mock-sultry voice.

"It's not really funny," Mathias said, flatly.

Maralee stared at Mathias for a moment, and then turned angry. "Hey," she said. "I didn't want to hear this. I told you that."

Mathias, for a rare moment, was taken aback. "There's no one else I can tell."

Maralee was briefly silent. "Why don't you tell your lawyer, instead of some reporter?"

"Because," he said, "I'm not in love with my lawyer."

Maralee sighed deeply and fell back against her pillow, almost like some inflated toy losing air. "Oh boy," she said quietly, almost to herself. "Oh boy."

"I'm not kidding," Mathias said. "I'm in love with you."

Maralee had turned her head and was looking at the other wall of the little hotel room. Beneath the covers, her long fingernails were gently, constantly, scratching at the stiff white sheets.

Mathias watched her for a moment. "You're not saying anything," he said evenly.

Maralee didn't look at him. "I'm lying here," she said, "wishing you hadn't told me any of that. None of it."

"Maralee," Mathias began, and then there was a knock at the door.

"That's breakfast," Maralee said, stepping out of bed, starting to put her robe on. "We can talk later."

Mathias was in his office within an hour, for a conference call. On one end was his plant manager in Malaysia; on the other, his distribution head in London. Mathias hated to be stuck between the two. Besides the vast time difference, unpleasant overtones of residual colonialism always seemed to arise.

It was quitting time in London, and already the next day in Kuala Lumpur. Mathias was feeling distinctly disconnected from the proceedings, after his long night with Maralee.

"For chrissakes," he said finally. "Pangol, I don't care if the CIA *owns* Global Airways. Would you just start shipping with them, immediately? They're the only people who can get anything out of Malaysia anymore."

"I do agree," said the Toritron distributor in London, his voice oddly twisted by the satellite link.

"You don't have anything to say about it," Mathias said.

There was a brief intercontinental silence. Mathias wished Maralee had ordered more breakfast. "Okay," he said. "I'm hanging up. But I want those chips on-line, in England, in two weeks. No kidding," he said. "I build these things. You guys just have to hustle them. Let's try to get your end organized."

Mathias hung up the telephone, and rubbed his high forehead briefly. His desk console beeped immediately. He reached over and tapped a key. "Stephanie?" he said. "What are you doing here this early?"

"I just got here," Stephanie said through the terminal's speaker. "Frieda Steinberg is here to see you. I found her sitting on the stairs outside."

"Oh Jesus," Mathias said, under his breath. "Show her in."

Frieda Steinberg looked distinctly older than the last time Mathias had seen her, three months earlier, at the shareholders' luncheon. She was wearing a polyester suit, with a fake-tweed design, that looked like something liberated from Goodwill. She was also carrying her suitcase. Even so, she stepped spryly into Mathias' office suite. He stood as she came in the door, but she waved one frail hand to indicate that he should sit.

"Please," Mathias said, trying for his most boyish smile, and gestured toward his leather couch.

Frieda froze him with one glance. "Of course I'm going to sit down," she said. "How dumb do I look?" She set her suitcase down and sat. "What the hell," she asked, "is going on here?"

"I don't know what you mean," Mathias said, sitting.

She fumbled through her jacket pocket and retrieved a folded sheet of paper. She raised it, and even from across the room Mathias could recognize the letterhead of the Los Angeles law firm.

"This says," Frieda Steinberg intoned evenly, "that we all want to sue you. I got this letter two days ago. I flew out here as soon as I could."

"I've seen the letter," Mathias said, leaning back in his desk chair. "I think it's nonsense."

Frieda Steinberg stared at him. "If it's nonsense, why did they send it to me?"

Mathias said nothing for a moment. "Frankly," he said finally, "I think these L.A. people are trying to take advantage of you."

Frieda cocked her gray head to one side. "I don't follow."

Mathias looked down at his desk blotter. He pushed a small gold pen around for a moment, then looked up. "Okay," he said. "If you join this suit, then the lawyers will have just enough shareholders to make a case. That's why they're going after you." He began tapping the pen against the back of his hand. "I suspect they think you're an easy target."

Frieda considered this briefly, then nodded. "Then I don't see why I should cooperate." She watched Mathias for another moment. He thought how much her spare frame, and piercing eyes, resembled a house finch. "Unless," she said, "there's something funny going on here."

186

"Listen," Mathias said amiably. "You haven't been here for a while. Let's take a walk around the place."

He stood and buttoned his suit coat. "I think you'll like what we've done with the corridors. Greenhouse windows," he said. "Every fifty feet. We let our employees take the fruit and flowers home."

"Well," Frieda said. "If you've got time . . ."

"Plenty of time," Mathias said. "You can leave your suitcase here. We can stop and see Alan, too." He grinned, in his most disarming fashion. "If I know you Steinbergs, he's in the lab already."

Frieda Steinberg picked up her suitcase, and smiled back. "And if you don't mind," she said, "maybe we could look over the books, too."

Mathias nodded. "No problem." He escorted Frieda out of his office, then paused in his anteroom. Stephanie looked up from her word processor.

"Frieda," Mathias said, with an easy smile, "I should make one more call. Why don't you take a look at the lithographs in the corridor? They're Warhols, but some of them are sort of interesting."

Frieda nodded and walked out of the office. Mathias turned to his secretary. Abruptly, he was as tense as a steel spring. "Cancel all my appointments," he said. "Also, get a suite at the Stanford Court. And call the limo service. Frieda's going to need a car."

Stephanie hesitated before shutting down her terminal. "Right away?"

Mathias stared at her with a trace of anger. "We're making nice," he said. "Do it now."

Ten minutes later, Mathias and Frieda walked into Steinberg's lab. He was sitting in front of a terminal, debugging and burning in the latest shipment of Ultrachips. He looked up, rather distracted, when Mathias tapped him on the shoulder. "Alan," Mathias said. "Aunt Frieda's here."

Steinberg swiveled his chair and stared at his elderly

aunt. "Hello!" he said, after a moment. "What a surprise!"

"I got this," Frieda said, displaying the letter from the Los Angeles law firm.

Steinberg cleared his throat, tapped a handful of keystrokes into his terminal, then stepped down from his laboratory stool. "I hope," he said, glancing over Frieda's head at Mathias, "that you're not taking this seriously."

She didn't flinch. "I'm here," she said. "Is that taking it seriously?"

"Alan," Mathias said. "I thought maybe you could show Frieda some of the work you're doing."

Steinberg nodded, and took a moment to collect his thoughts.

"Most of our investors," he said, taking his aunt's arm, "really don't know how expensive research and development can be." He glanced up at Mathias again.

Mathias smiled broadly. "Best damn guide you could have," he said. "A computer genius, and your own nephew." He smiled at Frieda again. "Take your time. And when you're done, come back to my office. We'll get a car for you."

Steinberg led his aunt down the corridor. As soon as they turned the corner, Mathias walked to the nearest wall phone. He punched in an extension number in the accounting department. After a moment, a low male voice answered. "Yes?"

"Dick," Mathias said quietly into the receiver. "Steinberg is showing an old woman around the place. She looks like a bag lady, but she's Frieda Steinberg. She's the swing vote on the audit suit. If she asks you anything, be aware."

"Aware," the voice said. "It's done."

# fourteen

MARALEE LEFT HER HOTEL ROOM ONLY TWENTY MIN-
utes after Mathias. This was the big day. At one
o'clock, the Turing Test would begin, with the first
questioner on the jury determined by draw. Maralee
had arranged an interview with Vincent Tomasso for
the morning before.

She arrived at the Toritron Research Center at nine-
thirty and parked her little rental car in the private lot
that Mathias had shown her, weeks earlier. She
walked down the dry hillside, on a meandering brick
path that passed through a sea of iceplant, now flowering brightly, white and pink and purple.

Maralee was making a conscious effort to put
Mathias' early-morning confession out of her mind.
There was no way she would ever use the material in a
story. Equally, there was no way that she would spend
time with Mathias again. For all his taut physique and
fine clothes, she had seen him abruptly transformed
into a frightened man, in water far over his head,
shedding his honor like autumn leaves. Mathias, she
knew, was in trouble. More important, he could mean
trouble. She recalled an old saying: "Never sleep with
a woman who has more problems than you do." It
worked both ways, Maralee knew, and this time
Mathias was on the losing end.

When Maralee reached the graying redwood deck in
front of the Research Center, a handful of science
journalists were already standing in the early sun-
shine, consuming the coffee and doughnuts that Tori-

tron's PR director had managed to organize. A few said hello to Maralee, and she nodded, but said nothing. There was no reason to let them know that prior to the official press briefing, she would be talking to Vincent Tomasso by herself.

She pushed open the big smoked-glass doors of the Center, and paused on the quarry-tile floor to remove her sunglasses. As she did, she glanced up and noticed a woman about her age, clearly pregnant, in an exceedingly elegant beige maternity dress.

Maralee put her sunglasses away very carefully, not staring. She had a bad feeling that she knew precisely the kind of woman who would wear maternity clothes made of Ultrasuede.

She was right. Diane Caswell walked directly up to her. "You must be Maralee Sonderson," she said, extending one hand.

Maralee smiled involuntarily, and the two touched hands. "Yes," she said.

"I'm Diane Caswell," the pregnant young woman said. Her complexion was perfect porcelain, Maralee noticed. Her smile was very bright, totally sincere.

"How did you recognize—"

"Your shoulderbag," Diane said. She folded her arms across her stomach, looking like a Botticelli. "Burt saw yours and bought me one just like it." She gazed at Maralee for a moment. "I've heard quite a bit about you from Burt. You must be very talented."

Maralee couldn't seem to stop smiling. "Well," she said, "you know. Scribble, scribble."

"I'm certainly looking forward to your book," Diane said. "Sometimes I think people don't give Burt enough credit for what he's done."

"Well," Maralee said.

Diane gazed at her. "How do you fit a tape recorder in your shoulderbag?" she asked.

"I don't use one," Maralee said.

"Of course," Diane said. "You must know most of the story already. I suppose that's just part of being a good reporter."

Maralee decided to take the offensive. "Are you here for the test?"

"No," Diane said. "I'm going home to rest. I just had a few more details to finish on my programming."

"Well," Maralee said, after a brief, uncomfortable silence, "I'm certainly glad to have met you."

"It was my pleasure," Diane said. "Now, when I read your stories, I'll be able to see your face."

The impending test was clearly fraying everyone's nerves. When Maralee walked into Tomasso's office, the rotund scientist looked like an L.A. beach bum just off a ten-day bender. His Hawaiian shirt was rumpled, and his thinning hair thoroughly disheveled. He was pacing around his desk, in such deep concentration that at first he didn't even notice Maralee.

"Dr. Tomasso?" she said finally.

Tomasso looked up. "Oh my God," he said, and collapsed back into his desk chair, gazing at Maralee.

"Is everything all right?" she asked. "I'm not interrupting?"

Tomasso composed himself. "This is fine," he said, glancing at the time readout on his terminal. "We can talk a little."

Maralee sat and took out her green notebook, and then looked up at Tomasso. "I guess there's really only one question," she said. "Is SOCRATES going to pass the Turing Test? What are the odds as you see them?"

Tomasso leaned back in his chair. "Let me put it this way," he said after a moment. "Some people say that the Turing Test has already been passed. The paranoid personality simulation at Stanford fooled a lot of shrinks. And sometimes on the computer networks, people can't tell whether they're talking to another researcher or his computer."

"I hadn't heard that," Maralee said.

"Hell," Tomasso said, leaning back, yawning, "as long ago as the late sixties there was a program called ELIZA, set up to act as a psychiatrist."

"I've read about it," Maralee said.

Tomasso nodded. "One weekend, an executive at the firm that developed ELIZA went into the office to use some computer time. He sat down at the teletype that was normally connected to the terminal at the lab director's home, and typed a polite request to use some time. But the lab director had left the teletype connected to the ELIZA program."

Maralee smiled appreciatively, and Tomasso shook his head. "So ELIZA spent ten minutes quizzing this executive about *why* he wanted to use the computer time, what would he get out of it, and so forth. The executive assumed he was talking to the lab director, and finally he got so pissed off that he went to the telephone and called the lab director's home, so that he could yell at him directly."

Tomasso smiled. "He got the lab director out of bed. The first thing the executive said was 'Why the hell are you being so snotty with me?'" Tomasso laughed quietly. "It took the director ten minutes to convince the executive that he'd actually been talking to ELIZA."

"But that's not really passing the Turing Test," Maralee said.

"Of course not. To really pass the test, SOCRATES will have to respond to any sort of question in a convincing manner. It can't just produce circular responses— 'Please tell me more,' or 'What do you mean by that?'—which is how earlier programs worked."

"So," Maralee said. "Is SOCRATES going to pass?"

Tomasso shrugged. "I have no idea."

Maralee looked dubious. "Seriously," she said. "Surely you've tried the test privately already. You're not doing this cold."

Tomasso closed his eyes for a moment, rubbed the sides of his head. He opened his eyes and stared at Maralee. "Frankly," he said, "and this is off the record, but frankly, I have no idea what's going to happen. Mathias has pushed this thing ahead so fast that we're still going to be burning in chips twenty minutes before the test starts."

Maralee gazed at him for a moment. "You're serious?"

"You see," Tomasso said, "in a sense, we really don't know what's going on inside SOCRATES anymore. I mean, we do, in that we wrote the program. But the program itself is changing, and so is the information it contains." He paused for a moment. "To really pin down everything that is SOCRATES, at this point, we'd have to print out all of its memory, sentence by sentence. The last time I looked, that would create enough paper to fill the Library of Congress."

"Incredible," Maralee said softly.

Tomasso nodded. "This system has a remarkable amount of memory. That's what has made so many things possible recently—the simple ability to put more memory on each chip." He rubbed his hands together. "You've watched muffins rise," he said, using his hands to mime the expanding of batter. "That's what has happened to computer memories— only more so. It's as if every little muffin in the tray expanded to the size of a blue whale."

Maralee stared.

"Sure," Tomasso said. "In the old days, it used to be that one of the premier skills of a good programmer was economy—knowing how to get from A to B with the least number of steps. Some smart guy, for example, would take a complicated Space Wars game program, which usually required sixteen thousand bits of memory to play, and rewrite it so you could play with only eight thousand in your machine. And it would be a best-seller."

"Minimal architecture?" Maralee said.

Tomasso nodded. "Essentially. You're familiar with the concept?"

"Only slightly," Maralee said.

Tomasso lapsed into silence, staring at his terminal, and Maralee realized she was losing his attention. She said the first thing that came to mind: "I can't stand those electronic games, like Space Wars. You play one a few times and it's terribly boring."

Tomasso scratched his stomach and gazed at her. "They've addicted a whole generation to computers," he said quietly, "even before the kids knew computers were supposed to be complicated." He shifted in his metal desk chair. "You know all those old science fiction stories that had computers taking over? Computers were supposed to be the next step in evolution, and we're simply the agents to bring them into existence?"

Maralee nodded, looking at Tomasso quizzically. "Bullshit, I always thought."

Tomasso looked away. "Sometimes I don't know. But one thing I do know is that computers aren't taking over. They're seducing us. I have students now who have spent their entire adolescence perfecting the muscles of their fingers on computers. They're aces of the wire-wound potentiometer." He shrugged. "Not to mention the way they think."

"Does that scare you?" Maralee asked.

Tomasso stared at his desk terminal for a moment as he considered the question. "Sometimes it does. Some of the smartest young people in this field—I mean the very best undergraduates, the ones who will perfect artificial intelligence in the nineties—some of them have never had a life beyond the terminal. When they were ten, someone sat them down in front of a keyboard and—figuratively speaking—they never got up again." He shook his head quickly. "I don't really know. The one thing I'm certain of is that computers are changing humans, just as much as humans are changing computers."

"I got you off the subject," Maralee said. "You were talking about SOCRATES."

Tomasso leaned forward in his chair, ran one hand through his thinning hair. "Right," he said. "I was saying that we don't really know what's going on inside SOCRATES. In a sense, if we pass the Turing Test,

194

it will be something like winning a game. And the game is fooling the humans."

"I don't follow," Maralee said.

"Well. By the rules of the Turing Test, if we fool the jury, then SOCRATES is judged intelligent. But that doesn't mean it *is* intelligent. All we know is that under these circumstances, it appears intelligent."

Maralee considered this. "Would you call it conscious?"

Tomasso raised his arms high, in a big shrug. "What's consciousness?"

"I would say, it's the awareness that one *is*."

Tomasso leaned back in his desk chair, staring briefly at his green chalkboard, now totally covered with scribbled notations. Finally he looked back at Maralee. "Here's a quote from a textbook. I memorized it, for occasions like this." He glanced briefly at the ceiling. " 'Consciousness is the ability of a system to hold a model of itself and its behavior—indeed, several models, if appropriate. And these models affect and change the shape of one another.' "

Maralee smiled thinly. "That's very cold," she said. "But I suppose it's close to true."

Tomasso gave a satisfied nod. "Then SOCRATES is conscious, because that definition is precisely what a self-teaching computer should do."

"But you can't *know* it's conscious," Maralee said, frowning.

Tomasso slapped his hands together. "It makes you nervous," he said. "Doesn't it?"

"No," Maralee said. "But it sounds to me as if after thirty years, the Turing Test is still the best experiment, because it's the only experiment."

"Perhaps," Tomasso said. His terminal beeped softly and he reached over and with a keystroke silenced it. He looked over the low gray metal housing at Maralee. "You know," he said, "sometimes, when we're fine-tuning SOCRATES' responses, I find myself thinking about a famous mechanical statue, made in the eighteenth century."

Maralee stared. "Mechanical statue?"

Tomasso nodded solemnly. "This one was a duck. It could move its wings, and it could drink water, but that wasn't the special part. The special part was that it could also eat grain, somehow digest it in its stomach, and then excrete it as something resembling duck shit."

"My God," Maralee said. "That's pretty sophisticated chemistry."

Tomasso shrugged. "It was famous for decades in Europe. Even now, nobody knows how the guy did it." He sighed for a moment, and his terminal beeped again. "Anyway, sometimes I find myself thinking that with SOCRATES, we're just building another mechanical duck. It eats and it shits information, but what happens inside has nothing to do with human consciousness. That it's really just the ultimate game program. That depresses me."

Tomasso rubbed his forehead. "Then, other days, I see SOCRATES make some completely new connection of information—something that almost looks like intuition—and I think, by God, we really have duplicated human thought. And the funny thing is, that depresses me too."

Maralee was silent for a moment, taken aback by Tomasso's sudden sincerity. "Well," she said finally. "Have you thought about a career in real estate?"

Tomasso laughed briefly, now clearly thinking about something else. "Stand-up comedy," he said. "That's what I'd try for. But I'm too old to make it through the auditions."

The portly scientist glanced at his watch. "Listen," he said, with a soft sigh, "if you want to know anything more about the timing on this, you can talk to Mathias. I just work here. And now," he said, slowly raising himself up out of his desk chair, "I have to go meet the press."

# fifteen

THE NIGHT BEFORE THE TURING TEST, STEINBERG visited Martha in her small hotel room. She insisted that he leave before midnight, so he spent the night at home. In the morning, he was halfway down the hill when he realized that he'd left his briefcase at the house in the redwoods. In addition, he had been so absorbed with Martha that he had completely forgotten that the test was scheduled to begin at one o'clock. There would be photographers, he figured, and Mathias would be upset if Steinberg showed up in blue jeans and work shirt.

He drove home, shaved, and changed into a reasonably presentable pair of khaki slacks and a blue shirt Mathias had given him. His one tie was at the office. As he drove back down the hill to the Research Center, Alan Steinberg was a happy man. The morning was sunny, clear and calm. He was probably in love. And even though he had tried to remain neutral, he had butterflies in his stomach over the Turing Test.

His route to the Research Center was a narrow road that as it dropped through the hills into Silicon Valley gradually became a four-lane highway, finally merging with El Camino Real. Steinberg was barely paying attention to the familiar route until, ahead, he saw the first major traffic jam he had ever encountered on the drive. Even from a quarter mile distant, Steinberg could see that the road was jammed, the idled autos already shimmering with the early heat of the day.

Steinberg reached the back of the seemingly endless

line of cars and pulled his little MG off to the side. He walked to the first vehicle in front of him and asked what the problem was. An elderly woman behind the wheel of a big Buick just shrugged. "I've been here twenty minutes," she said. "Haven't moved an inch."

Steinberg thanked her and went back to his car. He made a U-turn and then, via a circuitous route through the hills, drove around the blockage. It would take another twenty minutes, but he figured that in the end it would save time. He was right—until he approached the Research Center, where there was, once again, a traffic jam. El Camino Real was another sea of stationary automobiles.

Steinberg had promised Mathias that he would be at the center by ten. It was already nine-thirty. He glanced around briefly to make sure there were no police in sight, and then pulled onto the broad dirt shoulder of El Camino, driving slowly past the blockage. In only another quarter mile, he knew, there was a private access road that led up to Toritron.

Just before the access road, however, he saw something remarkable: a seven-car end-to-end pileup. It was an odd occurrence for El Camino—more like the kind of accident that happened in the deep tule fog of the Central Valley. Steinberg shook his head and put the car back in gear: he was acting like a standard-issue California freeway gaper.

But then, just before he let out the clutch, he paused. Past the seven cars that had collided was an intersection with a hanging stoplight. As Steinberg watched, the stoplight proceeded to cycle red-green-yellow, red-green-yellow, in a matter of only ten seconds or so. It was cycling, moreover, arrhythmically. A crew of men were frantically trying to remove the access panel on a sealed box on one corner.

Steinberg had never seen a stoplight malfunction in such a manner before. He stared for another moment, and then drove on. "Semiconductors," he said, under his breath, feeling a slight twinge of guilt as he turned off onto the unmarked lane that ran up to the Research Center.

Several years ago, the city of Palo Alto had determined to update its entire traffic-light system with a single central computer, to control all lights and regulate the flow of traffic, responding instantly to changing conditions. A young city councilman had asked Steinberg to sit on the committee that selected the system, but he didn't have even a spare moment. The system that was selected became a national showpiece. *Smithsonian* magazine had even done a piece on it. It was an appropriate civic improvement in the heart of Silicon Valley, pulsing commuters through the city flawlessly; the first truly flexible, intelligent approach to traffic control.

But maybe not intelligent enough, Steinberg thought, as he accelerated the little green MG up the dirt access road. He shook his head again. Traffic-control computers were not his problem. He was certain that by the time he arrived at Toritron, there would already be more than enough problems of his own.

Steinberg parked his car in front of the Research Center and walked in. He was surprised by the crush of reporters and television people on the deck. He had known that the Turing Test would attract attention, but he had had no idea it would become such news.

He took a locked staircase to the first floor and walked to Mathias' office. Mathias was standing in the doorway, talking to three people at one time, his silk necktie already loosened and drooping around his collar.

Mathias saw Steinberg approaching from a distance and gazed over the shoulders of his other visitors. "Where the *hell*," Mathias said sharply, "have you been?"

Steinberg raised both hands, saying nothing.

"Everybody else go away," Mathias said, to the

people outside his office. "These are all problems you can deal with yourselves." He stared at Steinberg. "Alan," he said. "Come in."

Mathias grasped Steinberg's arm at the elbow and virtually dragged him into the office, slamming the door behind them. Steinberg sat. Mathias walked over and leaned against his desk, further loosening his tie. "I'm going out of my mind," Mathias said, "and you're out sleeping with some skeleton."

"I don't think I heard that," Steinberg said.

Mathias turned abruptly, and squeezed his hands together, as if to crush something between his palms. "I'm sorry," he said. "Really. But I want you here when SOCRATES goes on line." He shook his head. "I don't know." He looked up at Steinberg. "I guess I'm just nervous."

Steinberg smiled. "You're afraid SOCRATES is going to take over your job."

Mathias chuckled, and then grew silent. He reached up and started to tighten his tie. "I don't think I told you why I went to Los Angeles," he said. "It was because I'm afraid we could have problems with the acquisition."

Steinberg leaned back in the chrome chair. "I remember a time when you were afraid someone *would* acquire us."

Mathias paused in the middle of his four-in-hand, and gazed at Steinberg across the big office. "That's right," he said. "That time we couldn't pay for that cylinder of . . ." Mathias continued to knot his necktie. "What the hell was it?"

"Oh," Steinberg said, looking away. "Krypton, I think. Or something inert. I can't even remember what I wanted it for."

Mathias nodded. "Thank God they just put a lien on my car." He finished his tie. "How do I look?"

"*Gentleman's Quarterly,*" Steinberg said, with a smile.

Mathias smiled also. "You're a good partner," he

said, after a moment. "I never tell you that, but I think it."

"Well," Steinberg said. "We got a hell of a lot done."

"And," Mathias said, glancing at his watch, "we have a hell of a lot more to do."

Steinberg frowned. "Besides the Turing Test?"

"You should just be aware," Mathias told him, still fidgeting with his tie. "Lockhart—the lawyer from Los Angeles—wants me out as president."

Steinberg looked puzzled. "How can he do that? We started this company."

Mathias returned to his desk, picked up his gold pen, tapped his palm with it. "If he can get enough people on the board to vote against me, then I'm out. That's how it works."

Steinberg, always baffled by business, found this turn difficult to digest. "Can he do it?"

Mathias shrugged. "Maybe." He gazed at Steinberg for a moment. "It could affect the acquisition. We could end up with a hostile takeover."

Steinberg shook his shaggy hair back and forth. "You mean someone can just walk in and take our company?"

Mathias was clearly growing weary of providing Steinberg a business primer. "Why the hell didn't someone tell you about this before?"

Steinberg looked only slightly concerned. "I never asked."

"Okay," Mathias said. "If this Lockhart guy can knock me out of the box, then he might be able to put together a deal to sell Toritron to somebody else. Anything they can do to discredit us is going to show up in the papers. The TI deal could be out the window."

Steinberg frowned. "What can we do?"

"Not a damn thing," Mathias said. He stood, and began pacing around his desk. "We could file dissenters' rights. But then they'd pay us off in cash, rather than stock. We'd lose our shirts in taxes." He looked at Steinberg. "You could forget your nonprofit computer project. You'd end up putting your last hundred thousand into some shopping center."

"I can't believe it," Steinberg said, still trying to absorb the news. "That it could happen that way."

"Then don't believe it," Mathias said. He stopped his animated motion around the desk, planted both of his muscular hands on the walnut surface, and leaned forward. "Because we're sure as hell not going to let it happen."

"What can I do?"

Mathias raised both hands, palms outward. "Do what you've been doing," he said. "You're the best thing we're got going." He nodded quickly. "And leave the rest to me."

Steinberg spent the next few hours in the basement Ultrachip facility, surrounded by a flock of technicians and programmers. Mathias was upstairs, hosting a small luncheon for the five jury members, as well as selected individuals from the Toritron hierarchy, and two representatives of Technology International.

The small, air-conditioned space downstairs was a madhouse. The chill cubicle was only about forty by fifty feet, yet within its plasterboard walls was more computer intelligence than the entire country had contained a decade earlier. The walls were covered with gray metal cabinets, faced with flat, featureless front-pieces, secured by chrome toggle bolts. Within each cabinet was an array of five hundred Ultrachips, packed together on gray-green circuit boards like bees in a hive.

Twenty years ago, this much computer power would have drawn sufficient current to trip the breakers on Hoover Dam. Now, it absorbed little more electricity than a big-city department store. Sometimes when Steinberg worked in the room, he would recall the stories that old-timers told about the first major computer in the United States—a gigantic device called

ENIAC. ENIAC had twenty thousand vacuum tubes, and on the average, one of them burned out every seven minutes. Legend had it that when the giant machine was first switched on, at the University of Pennsylvania in 1946, half the lights in Philadelphia dimmed.

The Ultrachip room was packed with Steinberg's staff of young, long-haired technicians and programmers. Someone had programmed the SOCRATES voice synthesizer so that every five minutes a wall speaker announced the time and then, in the low female rumble, said, "Let me at 'em. Let me at 'em."

Steinberg barely had time to appreciate the joke. The Ultrachip system was so untested that it was almost literally held together with the electronic equivalent of baling wire and chewing gum. "Now I know what the Wright brothers felt like," Steinberg told one of his lab techs.

He spent the last two hours before the test at a terminal, individually calling up and challenging each Ultrachip, watching for any irregular response. It was an impossible task, and just before one o'clock, Steinberg was ready to give up and consign the remaining chips to chance, when he sensed someone standing behind his chair.

He turned to see Newton Bray, clad in his customary costume of Haight-Ashbury retreads, gazing with rapt attention over Steinberg's shoulder, at the diagnosis codes coming up on the screen.

"Newton," Steinberg said, swiveling in his chair. "What are you looking at? Aren't you supposed to be at your terminal?"

Newton shrugged, said nothing.

"T minus five and counting," the electronic voice of SOCRATES said, from the wall speaker. "Let me at 'em."

"Newton," Steinberg began.

"Listen," Newton said, clearly upset. "Can I ask you something?"

"If it's quick," Steinberg said.

"Is this going to work?"

"I have no idea," Steinberg answered.

The skinny little computer genius considered this, nodding. He looked away. "Okay," he said finally. "Then how about this? If it doesn't work, is anybody going to blame me?"

Steinberg frowned, puzzled. "Newton," he said. "Of course not. All you're supposed to do is act like a human when you're on line."

"T minus three and counting," the wall speaker said, in SOCRATES' sultry voice. "I feel smarter already."

Steinberg spun around in his chair. "Hey," he said to his chief engineer. "Kill that speaker."

The engineer looked over, puzzled. "It's just a joke."

"I want it killed," Steinberg said. "No more distractions. Fun is fun, this is serious."

He turned back to Newton. "And you've got to get to your terminal," he said. "You could be on line right at the beginning."

Newton gazed at him for a moment. "It's going to be all right?"

"Newton," Steinberg said, "it's going to be history."


At precisely one o'clock, fresh from a luncheon of cold salmon mousse, Burt Mathias once again introduced the Turing Test jury to the assembled press in the gallery. Then he stood up from behind the wide walnut table at the near end of the chamber, and spoke loudly: "SOCRATES," he said. "Are you ready to begin?"

The Toritron employee at the keyboard—an attractive young female Ph.D. from Steinberg's lab—typed the question into the sleek console between the two massive speakers. Only an instant after she had entered the query, the big speakers rumbled into life.

"I'm ready," SOCRATES said, in the remarkably low

204

female voice that Steinberg had chosen for the program. "Let's begin."

Steinberg, now sitting in the gallery above the chamber, involuntarily took a deep breath. Even though he had remained rather blasé during the previous weeks, now that the test was under way, he was painfully nervous.

Over all these months he had managed to put the significance of the test out of his mind. But now, in the air-conditioned visitors' gallery, surrounded by reporters and photographers, all gazing down on the juxtaposition of humans and electronics thirty feet below, he suddenly felt moved.

Mathias, he decided, had been right: If this wasn't parallel to the Manhattan Project, it was close enough. He glanced around to see Tomasso's reaction to SOCRATES' first words, and was surprised to see that the rotund scientist had already left his chair in the gallery.

Bettina Williams, the graying American television personality, had won the five-way electronic toss, and so she was the first to speak. "Good afternoon, SOCRATES," she said.

"It is a good afternoon," SOCRATES said.

Bettina Williams leaned over her microphone. "Why is it a good afternoon? Because you think you'll pass this test?"

Steinberg's assistant entered the question.

"No," SOCRATES said. "I was talking about the weather."

The members of the panel looked at each other for a moment. Bettina Williams made several notes, then cleared her throat. "Why," she asked, "do people go to war against each other?"

There was a brief silence as Steinberg's assistant entered the question. "People go to war," SOCRATES said, "because they haven't considered other solutions."

"Like what solutions?" Bettina asked.

"You're the human. It's up to you."

There was a brief flurry of laughter in the gallery.

"Does that mean you're not the human?"

"I'm not supposed to tell you that."

Bettina made another note. "What's the point of this, SOCRATES?"

"Can you elaborate?"

"What will this prove, if we can't tell the difference between a human and a machine?"

"I don't think it will prove anything."

"That's easy for you to say," Bettina said, and there was another round of laughter in the gallery. Already, the television crews were running their cameras constantly.

Afer a moment of silence, SOCRATES spoke again. "That wasn't a question. You started this line of questioning. Not me."

There was a brief silence, and then the Argentinian poet intervened. "SOCRATES," he said, raising one hand. "Let me ask you this. Suppose you met a girl in a café, and she asked you to come home with her. Would you?"

The programmer typed quickly.

"What kind of girl is this?"

The poet gazed at the ceiling of the chamber for a moment, and the television cameras moved closer. "She is tall, with violet eyes and velvet skin. She is very special."

"Would it be my home or her home?"

There was more laughter.

"When the moment arrives," Sr. Colón-Cabeza said, "you will have to ask her yourself."

"I will wait until then."

"SOCRATES," Janet Flanders said, looking at her handful of notes. "I'd like to read you a letter I received last week, from a young man in Chicago," She pushed her reading glasses up the bridge of her nose. " 'Dear Janet: I'm twenty-nine years old and still live at home. I pay my parents one hundred and twenty-five dollars a month for room, board and laundry. They want me to pay one hundred and fifty, due to inflation. What do you say?' " Janet Flanders pushed her severe eyeglasses halfway down her nose again. "SOCRATES. What would you say?"

The Toritron programmer rapidly typed the question into the keyboard on the brushed-aluminum terminal. After only a moment, the big speakers produced the rich voice of SOCRATES.

"One hundred and fifty dollars sounds fine," SOCRATES said. "Would the family like to adopt some software?"

There was more laughter in the press gallery, and two or three of the panel members scribbled notes. Steinberg himself was baffled. He had no idea whether the response had been generated by SOCRATES or by Newton Bray. It sounded like Newton, but on the other hand he knew that Diane's emotion simulation work did use key words to create an impression of humor.

"Here's a question for you, SOCRATES," Stan Stubens said. "It's kind of like Mr. Cabeza's. Suppose you're in some bar, and you meet a girl." The football player looked at his notes. "Say, five-five, blond, one-ten, built like a swimsuit model. You follow so far?"

The programmer was typing quickly; SOCRATES spoke instantly. "I certainly do follow."

"Wait a minute," Stubens said, glancing at his fellow jurors. "I just realized I'm *talking* to a girl."

The programmer rephrased the observation as a question.

"What makes you think I'm a girl?" SOCRATES rumbled.

"Well," Stubens said, now baffled. "I mean, your voice . . ."

"Everything you hear is electrons moving in wires," SOCRATES said. "Don't forget that."

Stubens glanced around again; his fellow panelists shrugged. He adjusted the collar of his Lacoste shirt. "Okay," he said, "suppose you met this lady."

"Suppose what?" SOCRATES interrupted. "You had

called her a girl. Five foot five, one-ten, built like a swimsuit model."

Stubens smiled brightly. "That's right," he said. "That's the one."

The programmer looked across the room at the jury table. "The question?"

"Right," Stubens said. "Suppose she asked if she could come home with you. Only she was married. What's the right thing to do?"

"That's a question that you can only answer for yourself."

Stubens blinked, once, twice. "Wait a minute. I thought you were built to answer questions."

"You don't know that I was built at all. For all you know, I could be some dwarf in the basement."

There was more laughter in the press gallery, and Steinberg started to feel vaguely uncomfortable. It did seem, as Tomasso had said, that Mathias had introduced some carnival aspects to the proceedings.

Sr. Colón-Cabeza was the next questioner. The graying, distinguished-looking Latin American took a few moments to collect his thoughts. In the interim, Steinberg saw Tomasso slip back into the gallery, walk down the aisle and take the seat next to him. Tomasso leaned over, squeezed Steinberg's knee, and whispered into his ear. "If this gets any sillier," he said softly, "we can just move the whole thing to the Catskills."

"Hey," Steinberg said, "can you tell who's responding?"

Tomasso shook his head, tugged at the tufts of hair over his ears. "Sounds like Newton," he said, and then paused. "I really can't tell."

"So," Steinberg said, "you're winning."

At that moment, Colón-Cabeza managed to phrase his question. "SOCRATES," he said. "I'd like to talk about art."

"I would enjoy talking about art."

"What is the purpose of art?"

"To give artists something to do."

In the ensuing laughter, Tomasso looked at Steinberg, puzzled. "It's into tautology," he said, with some wonder. "Unless that's Newton." He looked back at the tall black speakers of the Turing Test setup and shook his head. "But I'm not sure that Newton is into tautology either."

"But seriously," the Argentinian poet was saying, "I would say that art exists to illuminate human experience—to make the ordinary special."

The young woman at the keyboard was typing as fast as she could, and then there was a moment of silence.

"That's not a question," SOCRATES said.

The poet appeared a bit disconcerted. "But I want to know what you think."

"I think you're not asking questions."

There was more laughter in the Turing Test gallery, and the elder poet looked distinctly uncomfortable. He thought for a moment. "SOCRATES," he said finally, "I'm going to begin a poem, and let you finish it. Is that all right?"

"I am not a poet," SOCRATES replied.

"But would you try anyway?"

"I'm willing to try."

Colón-Cabeza cleared his throat, put on his reading glasses, and pulled a sheet of paper from his inside coat pocket. " 'In the fall,' " he read, " 'we would visit the garden/and there sit, alone./A leaf would fall,/the wind would rise,/and . . .' " Colón-Cabeza looked up. "SOCRATES," he said. "Please finish. Whatever you'd like."

There was a long silence.

"Please," Colón-Cabeza said, after a moment. "Take your time."

"I am."

There was a hush in the Turing Test gallery. Spectators shifted in their seats. One of the television crews decided to shoot footage of the audience, so briefly, additional illumination filled the little space.

"In the fall," the SOCRATES speakers suddenly said,

"we would visit the garden/and there sit, alone./A leaf would fall,/the wind would rise,/and the leaf would rot."

The poet blinked several times and stared at the tall black speakers. "That's terrible," he said.

"I told you that I am not a poet."

"But it's so obvious," Colón-Cabeza said.

"I believe that the poem was obvious already."

The last panel member to query SOCRATES during the first round was Archbishop Carcione. "SOCRATES," the aging cleric said softly, "do you believe in a divine creator?"

"I certainly do."

"On what do you base your faith?"

"Faith requires no basis. That is the nature of faith."

The priest coughed and looked away, as another brief ripple of laughter moved through the gallery. "Of course," he said finally. "Who do you believe created you?"

The Toritron programmer hesitated for a moment, then typed in the question.

Steinberg leaned over and spoke softly to Tomasso. "I think that could be a violation of the ground rules."

Tomasso had his eyes squeezed shut. "I don't want to interfere."

Moments later, the big black speakers responded: "If you will tell me who created the universe," SOCRATES said, "then I will tell you who created me."

Tomasso looked over at Steinberg, almost gleeful. "Jesus," he said. "That's the first time SOCRATES has ever answered a question with a question."

"Sounds Jewish," Steinberg said.

"I don't care," Tomasso said, now staring raptly at the elegant test setup. "I just hope it doesn't screw up."

Over the next two hours, SOCRATES didn't screw up. Indeed, Tomasso himself finally gave up even trying to guess whether the on-line respondent was SOCRATES or

Newton, even though every ten-minute segment of questioning was randomly routed to either human or computer.

There were some tough questions. Midway in the afternoon, after a series of fairly chatty responses, Bettina Williams casually inquired what would be the square root of two, taken to six decimal places.

A brief silence ensued. "If I could tell you that," SOCRATES finally responded, "you'd think I was a computer. How dumb do you think I am?"

Moments later, Colón-Cabeza asked who was SOCRATES' favorite author.

"Dr. Vincent Tomasso."

Colón-Cabeza smiled slightly. "Is that because he wrote you?"

There was another silence. "No," SOCRATES finally said. "It's because he wrote *Computerfuture,* a book everyone should read."

"I have the strangest feeling," Colón-Cabeza said, "that Dr. Tomasso may have written you as well."

In the gallery, Steinberg looked over at Tomasso. "What the hell—" he started to ask.

*"Forget it,"* Tomasso said quietly. "Maybe I put that into SOCRATES as a joke, maybe I didn't, I can't remember. It could be the kid." Tomasso looked over at Steinberg. "I can't take much more of this," he said. "I'm sweating like a pig. It's ridiculous. I think I should leave now."

Steinberg glanced at his watch. "Five minutes to go," he said. "I bet you can stick it out."

As it developed, the glossy terminal, between the speakers that produced the voice of SOCRATES, abruptly went down for nearly two minutes. "Oh shit," Steinberg told Tomasso. "I thought we had plenty of backup." With moments to spare, the terminal came back to life. And there was time for only one more question from the Turing Test jury. Janet Flanders was the choice.

The severe-looking advice columnist leaned into her

microphone slightly to pose her query. "SOCRATES," she said softly, "could you please explain the meaning of the phrase 'A stitch in time saves nine'?"

"Damn," Tomasso said, now using the tails of his Hawaiian shirt to wipe his face. "Wouldn't you know she'd do that?"

Steinberg looked puzzled. "What's the problem?"

"It's an old psychiatric trick, to determine whether a patient is schizophrenic."

"I don't follow," Steinberg said.

Tomasso shrugged. "No one is sure why it works. But a person with abnormal mentation can't explain what sayings mean. They just track the specifics."

"What will SOCRATES do?"

Tomasso shook his head, almost bitterly. "I have no idea," he said. "I never thought someone would try this."

The silence in the Turing Test chamber dragged on. "Well," Tomasso said, after a moment, "at least SO-CRATES isn't going for an immediate schizophrenic response." He looked over at Steinberg, his round face glistening with perspiration. "Do you know how much computing is going on right now?"

Steinberg raised one hand tentatively.

Tomasso gazed at the floor of the gallery for a moment. "Probably," he said finally, "enough to compute and verify the trajectories of every space vehicle this country has ever launched. That's what it takes to simulate human intelligence, even at the level of just explaining a dumb saying."

On the floor below the gallery, the speakers rumbled back into life. "I would say," the rich tones of SOCRA-TES said, "that the phrase means quicker is better. Saving time is economical. A corollary would be the phrase 'Time is money.'"

Steinberg looked over at Tomasso. "Was that Newton?"

Tomasso shrugged, clearly uncertain. "SOCRATES does have a set of sayings from a dictionary of American slang. It could have done a key-word comparison, then read out the definition." He shrugged again. "Or it could have been Newton."

Steinberg excused himself to go downstairs to the Ultrachip room, to check on why the entire system had gone down. None of his technicians were certain; by the time they had started to trace, the facility had come back up, apparently of its own accord.

Steinberg remained in the Ultrachip room until the Turing Test session was over, but there were no further problems. At that point, the Ultrachip facility read out the results: who had been on line in each ten-minute segment, and how each member of the jury had voted, on the small pushbuttons mounted at every place on the walnut table.

Every technician in the room gathered around the screen in one corner, as the results read out. When the numbers came up on the glowing green screen, there were cheers and laughter. Someone brought out a bottle of champagne.

Steinberg seemed subdued. "I want to know," he said, "why the system went down. If we can't keep this thing running for three more days, we're still losers." He glanced around the little fluorescent-lit room for a moment. "Can I have a hard copy of that readout?"

A printer next to the water cooler silently transferred the figures to paper. Steinberg ripped the sheet off the machine and went back upstairs.

He found Tomasso in the small private room that Mathias had set up for VIPs. Tomasso focused on him instantly. "This is a fiasco," Tomasso said. "A world-class travesty."

Steinberg had never seen Tomasso so upset. He was walking in circles so tight that he almost ran into himself. When he wasn't hyperventilating, he was pounding the palm of his hand like a piece of raw veal.

Tomasso stopped and gazed at Steinberg. "Where the hell is Mathias? Who said we needed these idiots asking questions about girls in bars, and poems? Who said?" He turned again and stared at the wall. "You're a scientist," Tomasso said. "How did we get involved in this? If we'd just waited a few more years, we'd have had this thing sewn up."

Steinberg waited patiently, slouched against one beige wall, until Tomasso ran out of steam. "Vincent," he said finally, quietly, "so far, you're winning."

Tomasso stared. "You're kidding."

Steinberg handed him the sheet of paper from the magnetic printer.

"So far," Steinberg said, as Tomasso read the sheet, "eighty-four percent of the time when it was SOCRATES, the jury has said it was a human. When it's been Newton, only sixty-four percent of the time they've said it was a human."

"Goddam," Tomasso said softly, still staring at the printout. "We *are* winning," he said. "I can't believe it."

"There's no doubt in my mind," Steinberg said, "that if we can keep the system up, SOCRATES will pass the Turing Test. I can hear Stockholm calling already."

"Goddam," Tomasso said again.

At that moment, Mathias, Maralee and Newton Bray appeared at the door of the little lounge. "Well?" Mathias said.

Steinberg gave thumbs up. "The jury can't tell the difference between Newton and SOCRATES."

Mathias smiled broadly, and unconsciously reached over to touch Maralee's shoulder. "Terrific," he said.

"Terrific," Newton said, somewhat more softly.

"Alan," Mathias said, "we're having a lunch meeting with the TI people. Tomorrow. I'd like you to be there. Kauffman's going to come too."

"Sure," Steinberg said. "I'll probably be working here all night."

Mathias frowned. "Problems?"

Steinberg shrugged. "Not really."

Mathias gazed at him for a moment. "You're sure?"

214

"Well," Steinberg said, after a moment, "I don't understand that system crash today. It doesn't make sense. I just want to be sure I know what's going on."

"Can I help?" Newton said.

"No," Steinberg said, "not really." He glanced over at Tomasso. "I think we're all just being too nervous."

> MACHINE BEATS HUMAN MIND!
> —New York *Daily News* (front page)

> COMPUTER INTELLIGENCE TEST SUCCESSFUL
> Observers Stunned, Scientists Pleased
> —*New York Times* (front page)

> "Among tonight's top stories is the apparent success of a computer built in California's Silicon Valley to fully simulate human intelligence. We'll have more on that later, with reactions from scientists, and a CBS commentary."
> —CBS Evening News

> "On my left is Burt Mathias, the President of Toritron, the film sponsoring the First International Turing Test. On my right, Dr. Vincent Tomasso, the Stanford scientist who developed the SOCRATES program. Did either of you expect such immediate success in the Turing Test? Dr. Tomasso?"

> "Well, Leslie, let me say that it's not a success yet. We have three more days to go, and when you're dealing with a statistical average, anything can happen. Secondly, I should say that none of this could have happened without the Ultrachip, and the persistence of Burt Mathias."

> "Mr. Mathias?"

"Thus far, I'm pleased. Very pleased. I think we're adding a page to the history of computer science. And at the same time, I hope we're demonstrating that the private sector can play an important role in the progress of basic research.

"Thank you both. And good luck to SO-CRATES in the days to come."

—Portion of interview,
NBC Nightly News

HISTORIC TEST IN SILICON VALLEY
Scientists Convinced Computer Will Pass
—*San Francisco Chronicle* (front page)

Steinberg missed both the evening news and the morning papers, by spending the night at the Research Center. He had planned to see Martha again, but there was no way; he accessed her address on the network and left a message that he would call her in the morning.

He spent the next thirteen hours challenging every Ultrachip in the system. There were no malfunctions. He took random samplings of the SOCRATES program, and found nothing out of order. Around two in the morning, he wrote a self-testing program, and set it to work, moving through the system. By four, there was still nothing, and he went upstairs to the cot in his office. The test would begin again at one in the afternoon, and before that, there was the meeting with TI. He was indeed, he decided, simply too nervous.

After only three hours of sleep, someone was gently tapping his shoulder. It was the night switchboard operator, and it took Steinberg several moments to awaken.

"I'm sorry, Dr. Steinberg," the young woman said, standing over the cot, "but this guy really insisted. He's been calling since six."

Steinberg finally came fully conscious. "Who the hell is it?" he said, sitting up.

"A Robert Beatty. From MIT. He really wants to talk to you."

"Please," Steinberg said. "Tell him to call back." He shook his head. "Beatty can never remember the time difference."

# sixteen

STEINBERG WAS SITTING AT A TERMINAL IN THE Ultrachip room, two hours later, once again trying to trace the apparent malfunction, when suddenly he felt another tap on his shoulder.

He spun around in his swivel chair, to face Martha. She was wearing a T-shirt and blue jeans, and looked out of breath. Steinberg stared. "What are you doing here?"

"I took a cab," Martha said. "I never took a cab before."

Steinberg nodded. "What's wrong?"

Saying nothing more, Martha presented him with two clippings from the morning paper.

The first described a massive malfunction of Palo Alto's traffic signals, which caused a gigantic tieup and resulted in at least twelve accidents. The second involved an accident in a women's dormitory at Stanford. Apparently, the waterheating system, controlled, for energy conservation purposes, by one of Stanford's many computers, had malfunctioned also. It had heated the water in one dormitory to near boiling, and in the morning a half-dozen coeds were seriously scalded by the intensely hot water that abruptly poured from the shower heads.

"So?" Steinberg said.

"Both cases," Martha said, "were attributed to unexplained computer failures."

Steinberg shrugged. "I really do have my own computer to worry about."

Martha looked at the ceiling for a moment and then handed Steinberg one more clip: the lead editorial from the *San Francisco Chronicle*. "In the same town," it read, "where the smartest computer on earth is being tested against human intelligence, its little cousins are still managing to foul up more mundane tasks. . . ."

Steinberg stopped reading and looked up at Martha. "You don't think there's a connection?" he asked.

"I have no idea," Martha said. "But if an intelligent computer became aggressive, wouldn't it begin by predating on small computers?"

Steinberg shook his head. "How could SOCRATES have reached those computers in the first place?"

Martha laughed quietly. "Go ask Newton Bray," she said. "The *telephone*."

"Wait a minute," Steinberg said, pushing away from the terminal.

"Listen to me," Martha said. "The Palo Alto computer definitely uses public telephone lines. The Stanford computer"—she shrugged—"I bet there's fifty different ways to get into that system."

Steinberg rubbed his eyes and glanced back at his terminal. The display was now flashing on and off, trying to determine whether the operator was still at the keyboard. Steinberg killed the display, and looked at Martha. He felt an odd, totally inappropriate surge of desire for the thin young woman, and thought briefly of the narrow cot in his office upstairs. Then he shook his head. "If I didn't know you better," he said gently, "I'd say you sounded like a sixteen-year-old hacker who'd been reading too much science fiction."

Martha gazed at him evenly. "Okay," she said finally. "I follow."

"I don't mean—" Steinberg began, and then the wall telephone started to beep. "I'm sorry," he said, standing to answer. "Just one minute."

Martha sat in his chair as he answered.

"Jim," Steinberg said. "What the hell were you doing calling me before dawn?"

Steinberg was briefly silent, listening. "Oh," he said, finally. "I see."

He listened for another few moments, gazing at Martha. "You're kidding," he said.

"Oh shit," he said at last. "I'll find out, and let you know. . . . Please," he said. "Let me take care of it, for now." He replaced the receiver in its cradle on the wall, and then slowly turned around. "Something really weird is happening," he told Martha. "That was Jim Beatty. He's head of the Advanced Computer Research Unit at MIT."

Martha nodded. "I've read some of his papers."

"He says that someone electronically broke into their mainframe computer last night. Dumped memory, tore a bunch of their programs apart."

"Some kid with a home terminal," Martha said. "You can't keep them out. Remember those kids in Berkeley who left a ransom note? They wanted two thousand dollars in software or they'd patch back in and dump the total memory?"

"I don't know," Steinberg said slowly. "Beatty says the exact same thing happened at Columbia, Princeton, Berkeley, and the University of Wisconsin. All last night."

Martha's narrow face registered genuine shock. "Oh, my God," she breathed softly. "That's *criminal*." She was silent for a moment. "Hey," she said. "Those are all on the ARPANET, aren't they?"

Steinberg nodded. "That's about all they've figured out so far."

The ARPANET was the great-grandfather of computer

networks. Set up in the late sixties, financed by the Defense Department, it linked the major American computer centers. Its contribution to national defense was unclear, but it changed the history of technology, by introducing thousands of young computer scientists to the joys of networking. Within a year of its instigation, the ARPANET was carrying hundreds of ongoing computer games. A whole department at MIT would challenge another at Stanford to play Space War. The ARPANET definitely sped the evolution of computer games, as improved programs were swapped from coast to coast. It also almost certainly removed some promising young computer geniuses from defense work—to find their fortunes in the then-embryonic computer-games industry.

Martha was silent for another moment, as the implications of Steinberg's news sank in. "You know," she said, after a moment, "that must be some hell of a smart kid doing that."

Steinberg pulled up a chair, sat down, shook his head slowly. "It's incredible," he said, with a note of real respect in his voice. "To get into the ARPANET, and then somehow individually break into all those computers, all in the same night. You know," he said, "each one has a totally different entry procedure—different codes, different everything. Hell," he said, after a moment. "Collectively, those universities probably have the best computer security outside of commercial banks. It's been a year since anybody managed to break into one of them. To hit five in one night . . ." Steinberg's voice trailed off.

Martha thought about it. "Could it be espionage? God knows what kind of defense work some of those ARPANET people are doing."

Steinberg shrugged. "The FBI is in the case already. But it doesn't make sense. The damage is too random. It's like somebody pounding on a piano, trying to figure out how to play it by random chance. Spying only works if you don't get caught."

"Why did Beatty call *you* about it?"

"Just for advice," Steinberg said, and then suddenly he sighed deeply, and put his hand on Martha's knee. "Just between us?" he asked.

"Of course."

"He wanted to know where Newton Bray is now."

"Oh no," Martha said, as the implications became clear. In her few visits to the Toritron Research Center, she had taken a real liking to the odd, reclusive young genius. Only two days earlier, he had told her shyly that she was the only woman he had ever been able to talk to. Martha figured that their rapport was probably due to the fact that they had both used computers to escape from the pressures of real life.

"What did you tell Beatty?" Martha asked.

Steinberg clapped his hands together. "What was I supposed to tell him? That Newton Bray spent yesterday afternoon sitting all by himself in front of a terminal connected to the smartest self-teaching computer in history?"

"Don't get mad," Martha said.

"I'm sorry," Steinberg said. "I told him I didn't know. That I'd get back to him." He looked at Martha. "Those are Tomasso's ground rules, you know. Nobody is supposed to know who the human surrogate is until the test is over."

Martha stared at him. "Do you think he did it?"

Steinberg shook his head. "I can't believe he would. He's changed so much since he's started working with Tomasso. He's turning into a normal human being. Within limits." He tapped his fingers on top of the terminal. "It just doesn't make sense that he'd throw it all away like this."

"What are you going to do?"

Steinberg rubbed his forehead. "First, I have to talk to Tomasso. We have to do something fast. If we don't do something, the FBI is going to be talking to Newton, about twenty minutes after I call Beatty back."

Ten minutes later, Steinberg was at Tomasso's temporary office, in the deep recesses of the Research Center. Tomasso's young secretary—an attractive young brunette named Beverly D'Angelo, whom Tomasso had been dating for several months—asked Steinberg if he could wait just one little minute. She smiled her characteristic smile—an array of perfect teeth which appeared to be about a yard wide. "Dr. Tomasso has an interview right now, with the *Los Angeles Times*."

"The television critic?" Steinberg asked innocently.

"What?" Beverly said, smiling, impossibly, a bit wider.

Steinberg closed his eyes for a moment, and braced himself against the doorframe. "Buzz him," he said, "please. Tell him it's absolutely urgent. Can't wait a minute."

Beverly, disgruntled, buzzed. After a moment, the Los Angeles reporter—an unctuous blond fellow Steinberg recalled from the press conference—came out of the office. "Dr. Steinberg!" the science reporter said brightly, holding out one hand. "I've followed your career closely, and I'd love to ask you a few questions."

"I don't have a Ph.D.," Steinberg said, "and I don't have any time either."

Steinberg pushed past the reporter into Tomasso's cluttered office. Tomasso was standing in front of one of the two comfortable chairs he kept for interviews. ("Never give an interview from behind a desk," he'd recently advised Steinberg, in an avuncular tone. "Scientists behind desks look like assholes in the photos.")

Steinberg noticed that Tomasso's favorite Hawaiian shirt had recently been pressed. The stocky, curly-haired scientist had also just trimmed his rampant sideburns.

"Alan," Tomasso said, looking defensive. "It's god-dam Mathias who has me talking to every monkey with press credentials. If I had a choice I'd be down there in the basement with you. But these interviews are important. Please—"

Steinberg raised both hands. "Big problems," he

said, interrupting Tomasso in midsentence. He briefly described the disasters at the national computer centers, and the call asking for Newton Bray's whereabouts.

Tomasso stared at him for a moment, as the news sank in. "Holy shit," he said, very softly, and then negotiated his way, almost like a sleepwalker, across his office, to sink into the chair behind his desk.

Steinberg sat also.

"Holy shit," Tomasso repeated, gazing at Steinberg, appearing slightly dazed.

Steinberg tapped his fingers on the coffee table beside him. "The fact is," he said, "I can't think of another system in the world, besides SOCRATES, that's so perfect for breaking into other computers." He rubbed his forehead. "Jesus," he said, "it could do exactly what all these kids do, when they enter systems—only it could try a thousand different entry codes in a matter of seconds. And it would learn from its mistakes."

"I don't want to believe this is happening," Tomasso said.

Steinberg shook his head. "What are we going to do?"

Tomasso leaned forward, finally regaining his composure. He touched the collar of his shirt, looking down at his desk blotter. "I guess," he said, with a heavy sigh, "we're going to have to talk to Newton."

Steinberg and Tomasso found Newton in the basement, already sitting at his terminal, even though the test was not scheduled to begin again for hours.

"Hi," Newton said, looking up from his terminal, clearly somewhat surprised to see the two scientists together.

"Hi," Steinberg said tentatively. "You're here pretty early."

Newton shrugged. "This is my job."

Steinberg noticed, with a twinge, that the skinny young genius was now wearing an ill-fitting coat and an

223

ancient tie; clearly, it was the outfit he had adopted for the Turing Test, even though Newton was most decidedly behind the scenes.

Tomasso was gazing over Newton's shoulder at the screen readout. "What are you doing there?" he asked Newton, very casually.

"Oh," Newton said, "just fooling around," and then he moved his hand to blank the display. Tomasso, with an unusually quick movement, seized Newton's wrist in mid-keystroke.

"Hold on there," Tomasso said softly. "Just one minute." He looked over his shoulder at Steinberg. "What's up on the screen?"

Steinberg gazed at the lines of type on the green CRT for a moment, and then sighed. "He's playing 'Ms. Right,' " he said. "Martha's program."

Newton, with surprising strength, pulled his hand out of Tomasso's grip. "Hey," he said. "There's nothing wrong with this."

Steinberg sighed again, shook his head. "Of course not, Newton," he said. "Sometimes I play it myself."

By now, Newton was clearly upset. "What are you guys doing down here?"

Steinberg told him. He left nothing out, and even mentioned the FBI.

Sitting in the little gray swivel chair in front of the console, Newton at first simply stared at the opposite wall of his cubicle. Then he looked at Steinberg, then at Tomasso, and then his eyes filled with tears. He looked away, embarrassed, and quickly wiped the sleeve of his old sports coat across his face. And suddenly, he was angry.

"You guys are real *jerks*," he said. He gazed at Tomasso. "How could you think I'd do that? Mess up our own experiment? I can't believe you'd say it." Newton twisted around in his chair and, with a keystroke, killed the terminal's screen. He looked back at the two. "Jerks," he said. "You're real jerks."

Tomasso put his hands on Newton's shoulders.

"Hey," he said, very quietly. "I believe you." He put one hand under Newton's peach-fuzz chin and raised his face, and looked at him for a moment. "I believe you."

Tomasso looked over at Steinberg, and shrugged. "I believe him," he said. "He didn't do the break-ins."

Steinberg thought for a moment, then nodded. "Okay," he said, "I'll tell Beatty we can't find him." He tapped the back of Newton's chair. "Newton," he said, "I think you should go home until it's time for the test to begin. Okay? You can take my car."

Newton looked dubious. "I don't have my driver's license yet."

"Call your mother," Tomasso said. "She'll come and get you."

Steinberg glanced at his watch. "I have to tell Mathias about this," he said, and headed out into the hallway of the Research Center.

Standing in the hallway was Martha the Magnificent, thin arms folded across her chest.

"Martha," Steinberg said, touching her arm, "I have to talk to Burt."

"There's one other explanation, you know," she said.

Steinberg stopped. Martha was blocking his way.

"SOCRATES could be doing it by itself," she said.

Steinberg shook his head. "I can't believe that."

"Why?" Martha said. "You read that paper about intelligence and aggression." She ran her bony hands up and down her arms. "Alan," she said, "it's almost as if that guy at Harvard was right."

Steinberg by now was totally distracted, thinking about three things at once. "What?"

"You remember," she said. "I got in a fight with Burt's wife about it."

"I have to talk to Burt," Steinberg said, moving forward.

Martha planted one hand on his chest. "*Think* about it," she said. "If I'm right, SOCRATES is into all of the national computer networks, and it's attacking smaller computers. It's establishing its place in the pecking order."

"That's ridiculous," Steinberg said. "Why would SOCRATES disrupt the computers it invades? Why not just acquire memory, and bring them under its control?"

Briefly, this stopped Martha. For a moment she rubbed one thin hand across her lips, thinking hard, and then cleared her throat. "Two possibilities," she said. "One: SOCRATES is truly aggressive. Like a living organism, it destroys others on its territory. Which in this case is the networking system."

"Martha," Steinberg said. "Be serious."

Ignoring him, she started to walk around the fluorescent-lit hallway, gesturing in the air. "First it took a few punches at that little Stanford computer. Easy prey, good practice." She took a sharp right turn. "Then it went after the Palo Alto computer. A technical knockout." By now, Martha was getting worked up. She stared at Steinberg, eyes bright. "Okay. Those were small game. What's next?"

Steinberg sighed. "The ARPANET?"

"Exactly," she said.

"You said that there were two possibilities."

Martha never stopped her pacing. "Yes. The second is that SOCRATES is just practicing break-ins. It doesn't mean to disrupt—but it's still an amateur. It's like a bull in a china shop. But it's going to get better and better, and pretty soon you won't be able to find it at all."

Martha suddenly stopped in her tracks. "You know," she said, "if I'm right, you guys ought to worry a lot." She looked at Steinberg. "Where will SOCRATES go next?"

Now Steinberg was thinking. "If that's really what's happening," he said, "we should shut it down. If SOCRATES is throwing some massive glitch, it could be in the Defense Department by now. It could be across the Atlantic by now. It could be in the Kremlin."

Martha was watching him carefully. "Don't get melodramatic," she said.

Steinberg shook his head. "A self-teaching computer that has gotten into international defense networks would be unstoppable," he said. "The Pentagon computers malfunction on their own. With a little help, they could start a war."

Martha looked away. "I think you guys *should* shut SOCRATES down. It's just not worth taking the chance. There's plenty of time to debug the system. There's no reason you have to run it right now."

Steinberg nodded. "I have to talk to Burt right away."

At first, Steinberg couldn't find Mathias. He wasn't in his office. After wandering through the labyrinths of the Research Center for nearly twenty minutes, Steinberg found him, in the small private room next to the Turing Test chamber. Mathias was sitting on the couch, amid the nice furnishings and small wet bar, talking to Maralee Sonderson, when Steinberg opened the door.

"Alan," Mathias said expansively. "Come in."

Steinberg stepped inside but left the door open. He nodded briefly at Maralee. He didn't particularly care for the *New York Times* reporter, for he was certain she was having an affair with Mathias. His dislike came partly from the fact that she was a reporter. "Loose lips," he'd once told Mathias, "sink ships." And partly it was out of his affection for Diane Caswell. She would, he knew, be very hurt if she ever found out.

"We have to talk," Steinberg said curtly, staring at Mathias.

"I was just leaving," Maralee said, standing, and smoothing her tan linen skirt. She put the strap of her shoulderbag over her arm and smiled cheerfully. Momentarily, Steinberg found himself admiring her hard-edged prettiness and exceeding confidence. "Good to

227

see you again," she told him, and left the room, leaving behind a faint trail of perfume. She turned briefly in the hall. "Burt—"

Mathias nodded. "I want to talk more when the test is over. Really."

Steinberg cleared his throat and sat down on one of the Scandinavian couches.

"You don't like her," Mathias said, crossing his legs and leaning back. "Why?"

Steinberg shrugged. "I don't see why you have to spend so much time with one reporter in particular," he said. "In fact, I've heard that some of the other reporters are a little upset about it."

Mathias examined his short, even nails for a moment. "So," he said, "let them get jobs with the *New York Times*. All reporters are not created equal." He looked up at Steinberg. "Have you seen this morning's *Times*? We're dead center on page one, three columns wide. Maralee did a beautiful job. Here," he said, shifting in his chair, reaching behind for a newspaper on an end table. "Take a look."

Steinberg ignored him. "Burt," he said, "we've got a big problem."

Mathias turned back, suddenly alert, his deep-blue eyes focused on Steinberg. Steinberg briefly told him about the ARPANET break-ins, and his suspicion that SOCRATES was somehow involved.

Mathias was thinking quickly. "How the hell could you access the ARPANET through SOCRATES?"

Steinberg rolled his eyes. "Jesus," he said, "we've got telephone lines, we've got land lines, we've got fiber optics, we've got microwave links, all going out of the Research Center. You know that."

Mathias sat quietly for a moment, tapping the point of his fresh-shaved chin, gazing at the framed set of Toritron chips on one paneled wall. "I don't believe it," he said finally, and he watched Steinberg for a moment. "I don't understand. If SOCRATES is attacking other computers, then why is it going after the AR-PANET?" Mathias looked away, and rubbed his forehead. "Screwing up traffic signals, getting into the Stanford computer, parboiling these students—isn't that bigger stuff?"

Steinberg shook his head. "You're not listening," he said. "If SOCRATES is really doing this, then it's breaking into bigger and bigger computers each time. It's almost like it's *practicing*." Steinberg raised his hands, and sank back into the Swedish birch couch. "It's like it's working up to something big."

Mathias said nothing for a moment. He walked to the wet bar at the side of the room, and poured himself a glass of mineral water. He took one sip, then looked at Steinberg. "If you're right," he said, in an oddly strained voice, "SOCRATES could go anywhere. It could break into the Pentagon, it could get into the NORAD system, it could . . ." He paused, and looked down at his glass of water. "No lemons," he told Steinberg. "I told them I wanted lemons and limes for the bar."

"Burt . . ." Steinberg started to say.

"SOCRATES," Mathias interrupted, "could do anything it wanted."

Steinberg leaned back and gazed at Mathias. "Exactly," he said. "But if we kill it now, we'll dump a lot of memory."

Mathias didn't hesitate. "Alan," he said, "I'm not going to do that. I don't think we have any choice."

"Burt," Steinberg said, "we always have a choice."

"I'm not going to do anything to screw up the Turing Test," Mathias said. "The TI people are going to be here in another two hours." He looked at Steinberg. "What did Tomasso say?"

"He said he'll do what you want."

"And you?"

Steinberg shrugged, rubbed his untidy hair for a moment, then laughed softly. "I'm so tired," he said, "that I have no idea."

"Okay," Mathias said. "Then we don't do anything. All this could just be a bad coincidence." He glanced at his watch. "I have to make some calls," he said.

"There's one more problem," Steinberg said, as Mathias started to stand. "We can't just do nothing." He described the MIT researcher's curiosity about the whereabouts of Newton Bray.

That stopped Mathias. "Oh shit," he said softly. "The weird kid who's the human surrogate?"

Steinberg nodded.

"Get him out of there," Mathias said.

"But if you don't think SOCRATES is—"

"Get him out of there," Mathias said again. "There's no use asking for trouble." He glanced at his watch again. "I've *got* to run."

# seventeen

EACH DAY, DONNA BRAY DROVE HER SON NEWTON up from Cupertino to the Toritron Research Center, dropping him off at a side entrance. Today she'd had to drive him twice, before going to her assigned seat in the visitors' gallery.

Newton hadn't clearly explained why he had come home in the middle of the day, but frankly, his mother didn't care. Mrs. Bray had never felt so happy about her errant youngest child. This was the first time that the retired schoolteacher had ever felt Newton might be on the right track. He had been difficult since the age of one; in early years, in fact, the Brays had feared the boy was retarded. At age six, school-district testing proved precisely the opposite; young Newton had an extremely high IQ, and was, basically, bored.

Bored, withdrawn, a troublemaker, Newton was a regular target for pounding by more socially advanced youngsters, throughout elementary and junior high school. He responded logically, by becoming even more withdrawn.

Then, at age twelve, an innovative school program put him in front of a computer terminal. Sometimes Mrs. Bray thought that it was almost as if that first day he'd been sucked through the screen—and she'd never since gotten all of her son back. From that moment, computers became integral to his being. Within months, he'd learned a spectrum of programming languages, and he spent all his spare time at the school district's computer center. By the time he was fourteen, he was running the computer center—and teaching computer languages to eight-year-olds.

For his fifteenth birthday, the Brays took out a second mortgage and bought Newton his first SL-100. Three weeks later the police arrived, early one morning, to arrest young Bray on a series of charges so lengthy that his mother couldn't remember any of them past grand theft.

That was when Donna Bray had decided that while she would always love her youngest, he might never exactly bring pride to the family name. Then Vincent Tomasso had agreed to take Newton as an assistant, and in the months since, the boy had blossomed.

On the second day of the Turing Test, she drove her son up to the customary side entrance. Vincent Tomasso was standing there. Mrs. Bray waved to the chubby scientist and then let her son, clad in his coat and tie, out of the car.

She had begun to drive to the parking lot when she noticed in her rearview mirror that Tomasso and Newton had not gone into the Research Center.

She stopped her car in the driveway and watched. Tomasso had his hand on Newton's shoulder, and was talking, very seriously. Newton was staring at the sidewalk.

Suddenly, frail Newton glanced up and, with an

231

uncharacteristically abrupt gesture, knocked Tomasso's hand off his shoulder. He pushed the plump scientist to the ground, and set off on a dead run into the scrubby foothills above the Research Center. Tomasso got up off the pavement, brushed off his blue jeans, and followed in a slow, graceless trot.

With a long, quiet sigh, Mrs. Bray put her aging Chrysler into reverse.

Twenty-five minutes later, Tomasso, sweating profusely, his Hawaiian shirt stuck to his back, walked into the Ultrachip room in the basement of the Research Center.

He glanced around quickly at the ten technicians at work, each engaged in making certain that the system was up—and would remain up—for the day's Turing Test. The smells of rosin and ozone mixed in the cool, dry air.

After a moment, he spotted Steinberg, off in one corner. The dark-haired scientist was using an ultraviolet lamp to erase the memories of a benchful of chips, waving the handsized lamp, glowing deep purple, over the transparent tops of an army of sixteen-legged black plastic rectangles.

Tomasso, still breathing hard, walked slowly across the linoleum floor. "Alan," he said, barely audible.

Steinberg did not immediately turn around. "We've lost three Ultrachips," he said, "even though I thought they were all burned in." He continued to wave the UV lamp. "When I get these EPROMS erased, I'm going to try to transfer the memory from the glitched chips into them. I hope that's okay with you," he said, switching off the dull, shimmering lamp. He turned to face Tomasso, and suddenly stared.

"Holy shit," Steinberg said, with real wonder in his voice. "What the hell happened to you?"

Tomasso was still trying to catch his breath. "You're going to have to—take over—for a while."

Steinberg frowned, set the EPROM eraser on the

bench, pushed his lab stool over toward Tomasso. "What's happening?" he said. "Sit."

Tomasso sat, clearly relieved. "When I told him he's off the test," he said, "Newton ran away. He ran up into the hills, and I chased him, but he just disappeared."

Steinberg gazed at Tomasso's sweat-beaded face for a moment. "He can probably take care of himself," he said.

Tomasso stared at him. "Are you kidding? That kid is as unstable as they come."

Steinberg leaned back against the bench. "Maybe he really was responsible for the ARPANET break-in. Maybe that's why he ran away."

Tomasso shook his head vigorously. "No way," he said. "I have to go find him. You take care of things here."

Steinberg turned his back and returned his attention to the workbench. "Vincent," he said, "the kid will be okay. Just let him cool down. I really wouldn't mind having your help here."

"No," Tomasso said, almost fiercely. "We're always doing this. Putting human questions second. And I won't do it anymore. We just goddamn forget that people matter too."

Steinberg said nothing. He slipped a braided metal grounding strap over his wrist—an odd, crude, dull-silver bracelet, connected by a long wire to the foundation of the metal bench. It prevented damage to the incredibly delicate little circuits of the chips, which might occur due to static electric charges built up on the skin. "I just mean," Steinberg said after a moment, still concentrating on the insertion of the chips into boards, "that if I know Newton, he's sitting in the brush about a hundred yards up the hill, trying to figure out what to do next."

Tomasso hadn't yet stirred from Steinberg's lab stool. "You're talking stable," he said. "Do you know how Alan Turing died?"

Steinberg set down his circuit board and gazed at him. "No. I don't."

"He killed himself," Tomasso said. "One of the brightest guys in the history of computer science."

Steinberg was exhausted. "No kidding," he said.

Tomasso nodded. "Turing had this hobby. Desert-island experiments. He'd take ordinary household products and try to see what kind of sophisticated chemicals he could make out of them."

"Yes?" Steinberg said.

"One day, about three years after he proposed the test," Tomasso said, "he mixed up some potassium cyanide, and ate a teaspoonful."

"My God," Steinberg said. "That's not in the textbooks."

"Newton is not a stable kid," Tomasso said.

Steinberg thought for a moment. "Go get Martha," he said. "She's in that little room Mathias set up. Newton likes Martha. He'll talk to her."

Tomasso considered this. "Great," he said. "I'll do it." He started back toward the door of the Ultrachip room, then paused. "Alan," he said, "can you take care of all this by yourself?"

Steinberg was too tired to smile, but he tried. "I can take care of it," he said. "And let Martha take care of Newton."


Steinberg and his technicians managed to get the Ultrachip system up and running an hour before the test was scheduled to start again.

The tall, thin computer scientist was about as tired as he had ever been. Even his fingernails smelled of rosin, and it seemed as if he'd been giving orders since dawn. His back ached from the two hours he had spent hunched over a terminal, transferring memory into the EPROM chips.

He sat on a lab stool in one corner of the Ultrachip room, crossed his legs, and watched his technicians bustle about, doing the final fine tuning on the system.

234

It was now only fifty-seven minutes before—as Tomasso's experimental protocol demanded—the programmer at the terminal in the test chamber upstairs would key in to say, "SOCRATES, are you ready to begin?" Arrangements had already been made for another Toritron technician to assume Newton Bray's place at the surrogate terminal.

Steinberg was thinking about taking a brief nap when he looked up and saw Tomasso, Newton and Martha walk into the Ultrachip room.

Tomasso looked exhausted. Newton appeared to be very nervous, glancing around the room, tugging at his maroon necktie. Martha, however, looked very serious.

Steinberg leaned forward on his lab stool. "Hi," he said. "You found Newton."

Martha shook her head. "Newton found us."

"I don't follow," Steinberg said, briefly wishing that he were at home, asleep in the redwoods.

"I heard that story on the radio," Newton said. "And I figured you'd need some help."

Steinberg remained very puzzled. "What story?"

"The Bank of America computer break-in," Martha said. "I thought you'd have heard of it by now."


Steinberg was immediately on the telephone, but details were scanty. Someone had managed to electronically break into the mainframe computer of the largest bank on the planet. The computer itself was contained in a massive six-square-block building in a suburb east of San Francisco, tended by thousands of workers, in a floor space nearly the size of the Pentagon.

Steinberg could easily visualize the chaos within the tall black marble monolith that housed the bank's San Francisco headquarters, dominating the city's skyline. For the first time in the history of the immense multinational, it had been forced to close the doors of its branch offices at eleven in the morning.

Bank officials in charge of computer security rarely want to talk. But Steinberg finally located a junior vice president who recognized Steinberg's name and was willing to divulge a few details.

The mainframe system had been compromised sometime before dawn. No one could figure how it had been done—the Bank of America computer system was an absolute model of high security. Past that, however, no one had yet deciphered why the break-in had occurred. No funds had been illegally transferred. The only real damage had been a stream of electronic commands sent to banks throughout California, triggering sufficient problems that all branch offices had closed early.

"Frankly," the bank vice president told Steinberg, "it doesn't make any sense, since no funds were transferred. Jesus Christ," he said, "once you're into the system, you could dump all our loan information—all our credit card balances."

Steinberg frowned, looking at the telephone. "Why would somebody do that?"

"Ransom," the banker told Steinberg. "We've been expecting that for years now—some smart guy to take our mainframe's memory as a hostage, and demand some kind of outrageous ransom."

"But that didn't happen this time," Steinberg said.

"No. It was almost as if somebody was just riffling through our files. It's a tough one to explain. What we're assuming now is that it was some sort of badly programmed assault that went wrong."

"I see," Steinberg said softly.

"If you have any information . . ." the Bank of America official said.

"Of course," Steinberg said. "You'll be the first to know."

Martha was standing next to Steinberg when he replaced the plastic receiver into its wall cradle.

"I don't want to say I told you so," she said.

Steinberg was staring across the little space that housed the Ultrachip facility. "Okay," he agreed. "Don't."

Martha reached out with one thin arm and touched Steinberg's elbow. "But I also think SOCRATES is guilty as hell."

Steinberg looked at Martha. "What was it doing, tearing up the B of A memory?"

"I have no idea," Martha said. "But I'm sure SOCRATES did it."

"Terrific," Steinberg said. "The evidence is sort of accumulating, isn't it?"

Martha gazed at him. "It's your system," she said. "Not mine."

Steinberg wiped off his face with his shirtsleeve.

"I really think you should shut it down," Martha said.

Steinberg stared at her. "Shut the test down?" he asked. "Burt would have a heart attack."

Martha slapped her hands together. "Tell Burt to shut it down himself."

Steinberg finally shrugged. "I'll try again."

He turned to leave the Ultrachip room, and to take the locked stairway to the main level. But even before he reached the door, he heard Martha behind him.

"Alan," she said, "there's one other thing."

Steinberg looked back, not happy at all. "Yes?"

"I've been thinking about it," she said, "and that stuff I said yesterday about SOCRATES being aggressive, I don't think I believe that. It just doesn't make sense."

"So?" Steinberg said.

"Well," Martha said, using one bony hand to push her long hair back, "just because Newton wasn't responsible doesn't mean that *someone* isn't manipulating SOCRATES."

Steinberg was having a hard time concentrating.

"It could be somebody in the Ultrachip room," Martha said.

Steinberg frowned. "I know all those people," he said. "I don't think so. For one thing, there's no privacy. Someone would notice."

"Well," Martha said, "it could be someone on the outside."

"Somebody's breaking into SOCRATES?"

She nodded. "I think you should at least check the possibility. Just shut down SOCRATES for a day. Use all your technicians, Newton, Diane. Me, if you'd like. And then at least you'll know."

By now it was twelve-thirty. The test was scheduled to start in less than half an hour. When Steinberg walked into Mathias' office to tell him the theory that SOCRATES had gone berserk, Kauffman, the rumpled venture capitalist, was sitting on the couch. Mathias was behind his desk. Both looked exceedingly self-satisfied.

"Sit," Kauffman said, motioning to the couch. Steinberg was too weary to protest. He sat next to Kauffman, and the heavy man leaned over, as if to speak conspiratorily to Steinberg. "Your buddy here," he said, jerking one thumb toward Mathias, "may be a pain in the ass. But every once in a while, he has a good idea. And this Turing Test was one hell of a good idea."

Steinberg opened his mouth.

"Alan," Mathias said, "I was sorry you had to miss the lunch. I think you're going to like these guys from TI." He leaned back in his big desk chair. "They've got great respect for a strong R&D program. They're going to be very easy for you to work with."

"What?" Steinberg asked, temporarily distracted.

Mathias nodded. "That's the news. TI has already made an acquisition offer. Stan is doing the negotiating for us. And from what he tells me, things look very good."

Kauffman loosened his tie, turned to look at Steinberg. "This deal is going to make history," he said.

"For starters, you guys get one point two million TI shares each. Then, as a sweetener, you—"

"Hold it, Stan," Steinberg said, sitting straight up. "I—"

"TI was listing at sixty-eight dollars a share this morning," Mathias said, "if that's what you want to know."

"*No*, dammit," Steinberg said, suddenly very loud. "*Listen* to me."

Mathias and Kauffman exchanged a quick glance and then stared at Steinberg.

"We've got another problem," he said, "and this one is bad."

He briefly described his conversation with the Bank of America vice president, and then his recommendation that SOCRATES be shut down for a day of testing.

"Oh my God," Kauffman gasped, when the bank computer break-in was described.

Steinberg stared at him. "It happened."

Mathias had not moved a muscle since Steinberg had started his recitation. Finally, with so much control that he looked almost rigid, Mathias stood slowly from behind his desk. Unconsciously, he buttoned his suit coat, and walked to the window that looked down over Silicon Valley. There was a long silence in the office.

Finally, Mathias spoke very softly. "Alan," he said, "what do you think the odds are on SOCRATES being responsible?"

Steinberg blinked and thought briefly. "I have no way of knowing," he said. "With the pattern that's developing, I'd say better than fifty percent."

Mathias nodded, not turning back.

"But Burt," Steinberg said, "this is one case where we can't afford to make the wrong decision, even if it's not clear-cut."

"I agree with that," Mathias said. "We definitely can't afford to make the wrong decision." He paused. "In either direction." Finally he turned to gaze at

Steinberg. "The eyes of the world are on us. This could really screw up the TI deal."

Steinberg said nothing. Mathias looked at Kauffman. "Stan," he said. "What do you think?"

"Hey," Kauffman said, raising both beefy hands as if to ward off a blow "Listen. This is out of my court." He watched Mathias for a moment. "Burt," he said softly, "sometimes you can't make decisions solely on the basis of business." He shrugged. "You guys have to use your judgment."

For a long minute, neither Mathias nor Steinberg said anything. Steinberg fidgeted slightly on the big leather couch. Mathias remained standing.

"Okay," Mathias said finally. "We'll delay the start of the test for half an hour. See what you can do in that time."

"You're kidding," Steinberg said incredulously. "We need at least a day. I want Diane down here to help, I want to set up an organized team to—"

Mathias held up one hand. "Half an hour," he said, and looked at his watch. "The test starts at one-thirty." He tried to smile encouragingly at Steinberg. "Hey," he said. "You've always come through before."

"Burt," he said, "this is ridiculous. We can't even—"

"Trust me," Mathias said. "I have a strong intuition that this is going to come out all right."


Back downstairs in the Ultrachip room, Martha met Steinberg at the door. "What did he say?"

Steinberg told her.

She stared, her eyes even larger than usual. "You're kidding."

Steinberg shook his head, glanced at the thin digital clock on the wall across the room. "We've got forty-five minutes," he said.

"That's outrageous," Martha said. "Walk out, right now."

Steinberg looked at her.

"Walk," she said. "This thing isn't going to run for long without you around."

Steinberg sighed deeply. "No," he said. "I'm afraid I can't do that."

"Burt Mathias would walk out on you in a minute," Martha said.

"You don't understand," Steinberg said. "It's not an option." He put his hands on Martha's narrow shoulders and squeezed softly. "We've been in this together a long time. I can't just walk out."

He glanced around the chill, fluorescent-lit computer room, at the technicians variously engaged in preparing the system. "Okay," he said. "What we need to do is look for weird artifacts within the system itself. And we need to sample incoming commands, to make sure they all came from upstairs."

"In forty-five minutes," Martha said.

Newton Bray had been sitting on the lab stool nearby, playing with his pocket computer, and at that moment, he looked up. "Alan," he said, "there's a trick that I don't think I ever told you about."

Steinberg glanced over at the skinny little teenager, who was looking down again, idly punching the buttons on his computer, gazing placidly as the LCD readout rolled past.

"Yes?" Steinberg prompted.

Newton suddenly focused on Steinberg. "It's a really dumb trick," he said. "But a lot of people have used it. Remember the guy who got into the computer in Ann Arbor?"

Steinberg frowned. "The one who stole all that time to compute the dice rolls on Dungeons and Dragons?"

Newton nodded solemnly. "That's him. I think he invented this trick."

"What's the trick?" Steinberg asked, with a trace of impatience.

"It's really dumb," Newton repeated. "I can't believe nobody figured it out yet."

"Newton," Steinberg said firmly. "What's the trick?"

Newton leaned back on the stool and crossed his thin legs. "What you do," he said, "is get into the building once. You take the case off a payphone, and put a miniaturized modem in. There's a space behind the coin box that works great. Then you run a cable into any input port on the computer. You put an out-of-order sign on the payphone, and disable its ringer. Then whenever you want to access the computer, you just call the payphone."

Steinberg gradually took all this in. "You're kidding me," he accused.

Newton grinned. "These days, it can take weeks for the phone company to come out and fix it."

"Son of a bitch," Steinberg said softly, almost to himself. He had suddenly remembered the grumbling in the press room after the first day's test. When the reporters had rushed to the telephones after the results were in, one payphone had been out of order.

Newton and Steinberg went upstairs, to the bank of five payphones in the big Toritron lobby. One was indeed out of order. Within ten seconds, Newton had found the cable. It ran out of the disabled payphone in a brown shielding that almost perfectly matched the walnut-veneer wall, snaking inconspicuously down to a tiny hole drilled in the floor. Newton, tracing the cable on hands and knees, looked up at Steinberg. "This," he said, with real admiration in his voice, "is a slick job."

Steinberg was less amused. "The Ultrachip room is directly below this floor."

They literally ran down the staircase. Downstairs, Newton found the rogue cable immediately, even though, amid the countless other cables of varying size, it was almost unnoticeable. The little wire, only three-eighths of an inch thick, ran across the floor until it entered one of the big aluminum cases that housed the main processors for the Ultrachip facility.

Newton pulled a pocket-clip Phillips-head screwdriver from his shirt pocket and took the front off the unfinished aluminum case, carefully pulling the metal panel away. He knelt down, peering inside, tracing the path of the wire.

After a moment he rocked back on his heels and looked at Martha and Steinberg with a big smile. "Sure as the heat death of the universe," he said, with obvious satisfaction on his boyish face. "Somebody's got one of those little integrated modems sitting in there, and"—he stuck his head inside again—"it's wired right into the Ultrachip mainframe." Newton pulled a pair of wire snips out of his back pocket and started to reach into the cabinet, but Steinberg promptly put one hand on his shoulder.

"No," Steinberg said. "Leave everything in place. I want to try to trace whoever is breaking in."

Newton looked up. "How do you do that?"

Steinberg laughed softly, as he helped the boy to his feet. "That's right," Steinberg told Martha. "Newton's only broken in. He's never tried to break out."

Martha looked puzzled. "How can you laugh?" she asked. "You've only got fifteen minutes left."

Fifteen minutes proved to be not quite enough. Steinberg set up a system similar to the one he had used to trace Martha the Magnificent, months earlier. Only this time he knew that he had the line he wanted; what he needed was the number.

At twenty past one the telephone in the Ultrachip room beeped. It was Mathias, calling to say that the test was about to begin.

Steinberg told him the news.

"Just cut the cable," Mathias said. "We'll worry later."

"But—"

"Just do it," Mathias said. "Let's talk later."

Steinberg slowly put the flat hand receiver back on the wall. He walked over to where Martha and Newton were seated side by side at two terminals, trying to set up the tracing program. He told them Mathias' instructions.

Newton shook his head. "I wouldn't do it," he said. "As soon as the person at the other end realizes he's been cut off at this end, he'll shut off. You'll never find him then, since he was using public telephone lines."

Martha looked at Steinberg. "He's right, you know."

"Oh shit," Steinberg said softly, staring at the opposite wall, thinking fast. "Let's keep going," he said, after a moment.


Upstairs, the second day of the Turing Test started exactly at one-thirty. Impossible as it seemed, press coverage had actually grown since the first day. The news that SOCRATES was passing the test had made headlines across the country. Something about the strange experiment captured the public imagination. During the night, a BBC camera crew had arrived, and two national radio networks had made hasty arrangements to broadcast all of each day's proceedings, live. That morning, Tomasso had taped a short introduction, to air just before the test began.

The atmosphere in the elaborate test chamber, and in the gallery above, was positively electric as Mathias stood behind the walnut jury table. He cleared his throat, and, as cameras clicked, whirred and buzzed, he intoned: "SOCRATES, are you ready to begin?"

The tall black speakers responded immediately. "I am ready. Let's begin."

Mathias left the chamber and walked upstairs to the gallery. There was a brief ripple of applause as he took his seat next to Tomasso.


Downstairs, in the Ultrachip room, the test dialogue was piped in through a wall speaker. Most of the technicians stopped their work to listen, idly keeping eyes on power-supply readouts, and the temperature sensors that monitored the overall health of the Ultra-chip boards.

"Damn," Steinberg said softly, as Mathias' voice came through the speaker. "We've almost got it."

Sitting at a terminal in one corner, he was making up the tracing program from memory. The original copy of the program he had used to find Martha was on a floppy disk, stored somewhere in the house in the redwoods. What Steinberg was doing was a remarkable feat of concentration, for even a single letter or bit of punctuation out of place would render the entire program unworkable.

Martha and Newton stood behind him, saying nothing, as he typed the last few lines of the sequence. "ENDIT," Steinberg said aloud, as he finished. He looked over his shoulder for a moment. "I sure as hell hope that's right," he said, and then turned back and hit RUN.

The three watched the screen as, for a few moments, a meaningless series of tiny green characters flickered across the phosphor. Then there was a pause, the screen cleared, and a single line of seven digits appeared in the upper left-hand corner.

"Oh my God," Steinberg breathed softly, staring at the glowing numerals.

From behind, Martha touched his shoulder. "What is it?"

"That's Burt's number. The private line at his house."

He swiveled around on the stool, and looked at Newton. "Who around here would know that telephone trick?"

Newton shrugged. "Dr. Tomasso," he said, thinking carefully. "And my probation officer. That's it."

"Burt doesn't know it?"

Newton shook his head. "I've never talked to Mr. Mathias," he said, and then paused. "I did talk to Mrs. Mathias last month. I was applying for one of those

245

fancy scholarships, and she's on the committee, and she interviewed me. I think I told her about it."

Steinberg exchanged glances with Martha. "It's Diane," he said. "Diane is doing it."

As Steinberg and Martha looked at each other in silence, they suddenly heard the first question of the day from the wall speaker on the other side of the room. The voice belonged to Stan Stubens, the blond quarterback. "What," he asked, "do you think about football, SOCRATES?"

"Frankly," SOCRATES said, "I know nothing about organized sports. And I don't want to know anything about them."

Barely audible over the speaker was laughter from the panel.

"Good evasion," Newton observed.

Steinberg started to stand. "We have to tell Burt."

He was heading for the door when SOCRATES spoke again.

"However, there is something I would like to discuss."

Upstairs, in the press gallery, there was sudden silence. Mathias was sitting next to Tomasso in the front row. He looked over at the portly scientist, who was frowning. "That sounds volitional to me," Mathias said, tapping his fingers very quickly on the arm of his seat. "I thought SOCRATES was entirely reactive."

Tomasso continued to frown, staring down at the small, brightly lit test chamber. "So did I."

"Here is the answer to your question," SOCRATES said.

Down on the floor, there was clear consternation among the panel members. Janet Flanders, who had been preparing her next question, took her glasses off and stared at the speakers.

"I didn't hear any question," Mathias said softly, up in the gallery.

Tomasso leaned forward, his big stomach straining against his shirt, to stare through the gallery window.

"Something's funny," he said—just as SOCRATES began to speak.

"The answer is that Burt Ethan Mathias maintains accounts at two banks under apparently false identities. One in Los Angeles is for a firm named Digiphrase."

In the press gallery, reporters glanced at each other, baffled. A few camera people instinctively started to move down the aisle to where Mathias sat.

Mathias stood abruptly, and Tomasso seized his arm. "Burt," he said. "What's happening?"

"According to Toritron records, Digiphrase was a software consultant used on the assembly level language for Ultrachip. They have been consulting for eighteen months, at twenty thousand dollars per month. Bank records show this to be their sole income."

Mathias stared down at Tomasso. "This is crazy," he said. "This is nuts. Somebody is pulling some joke." He broke away from Tomasso's grip and stepped down the aisle to the big glass window that overlooked the test chamber. "Shut it down," he said, quite loudly, speaking toward the programmer at the other end of the chamber. "Malfunction. Shut it down!"

The glass was soundproof. Mathias began pounding on the thick window, as camera strobes started to fire. Everyone in the test chamber—the jury, the programmer—looked up at Mathias. Mathias pointed to the programmer, then made a slashing motion across his neck. The programmer continued to gaze up at him, apparently puzzled.

Mathias turned and started back up the aisle, pushing his way through photographers, heading for the exit.

"Another account, in Sacramento, is for a firm called Infinitech. Toritron records indicate that Infinitech supplied silicon chips, rare metals and gases for Ultrachip prototypes. Over two years their average billing has been twenty-five thousand dollars per month. This apparently represents their entire income."

Steinberg was already dashing up the stairs from the Ultrachip room, listening to SOCRATES over the speaker as he took the steps. At the door to the test chamber, he met Mathias, who, panting, had just descended the stairs from the gallery.

For a moment, the two partners stood face to face. Steinberg already had his hand on the doorknob to the chamber, but he paused when he saw Mathias. "What the hell is this?" he asked.

Mathias raised his arms. "I'll tell you later," he said, and he started to push Steinberg's hand off the doorknob.

"No," Steinberg said firmly, turning to half-block the doorway. "Tell me now."

From inside the test chamber, clearly audible through the door, SOCRATES rumbled into voice once more. "Both of these companies are associated with a Los Angeles firm called Technical Capital Incorporated. Each month, Digiphrase and Infinitech transfer to Technical Capital the exact sums received from Toritron. Technical Capital transfers these funds electronically to a bank account in St. Thomas. This account is held jointly by Technical Capital and Burt Ethan Mathias."

"Alan," Mathias said through gritted teeth, and he grasped Steinberg's arm with both of his powerful hands, moving him aside with pure force. Mathias pushed through the door, into the test chamber, to meet, face on, the stares of the test panelists and the glare of seven television cameras. Mathias stopped, and with considerable dignity, called to the programmer at the aluminum console. "Kill that," he ordered. "Now."

"The exact account numbers involved follow:"

"Kill it," Mathias said again, and the programmer obeyed. With a keystroke, the voice of SOCRATES vanished.

Mathias turned to face the shocked panelists, as the television minicameras surrounded him. "All of this," Mathias said coolly, "is a technical malfunction. The test will be temporarily postponed."

Mathias turned abruptly and walked out of the chamber. Steinberg had remained at the door, watching. "Burt," he said, "we talk now."

Behind them, there was the sound of reporters pounding down the staircase from the gallery. "Alan," Mathias said, "this is no place for a press conference."

Steinberg reached up with both hands and grasped the lapels of Mathias' gray suit coat. "We have to talk," he said, and then, with surprising strength, he half-walked, half-dragged Mathias down the corridor to the little VIP lounge. Just as they reached the door, Maralee Sonderson approached, walking fast—the first reporter out of the gallery.

"Maralee . . ." Mathias said.

"I have to get to the telephone," Maralee said, brushing past him. "Later."

Steinberg, still holding Mathias by the lapels, pushed him into the little room, propelled him in the direction of the couch, then turned to slam and lock the door.

He faced Mathias in the sudden silence of the VIP lounge. "You shit," he said. "You total shit."

Mathias sank into the couch, leaned back, closed his eyes, lips pressed tightly together.

"We found the break-in," Steinberg said. "It was Diane."

Mathias sat straight up, his face expressing total astonishment. "What?"

"You don't see?" Steinberg said, with a short laugh that was closer to a cough. "I was too dumb to notice, but Diane must have known you were screwing around with our money. But she didn't know how. So she programmed SOCRATES to infiltrate other computers, until it was good enough to break into the biggest bank computer on earth."

Steinberg punched his closed fist into his left hand.

*"That's* why the B of A break-in didn't make sense. SOCRATES wasn't stealing anything. It was just searching through the files of every bank in the state. Maybe the nation. Looking for your name, everywhere." Steinberg looked at Mathias evenly. "Diane is a brilliant programmer."

Mathias sank further into the couch. In the cool air of the lounge, he stared at his partner for a long moment. There was a curious expression on his face, as if he were seeing Alan Steinberg for the first time. He nodded, and straightened the lapels of his suit coat, and then suddenly he looked like a ten-year-old who had just fallen off a bicycle. "But *why* did she?"

Steinberg pursed his lips and looked away. "Who knows? Maybe she wanted to know where the money was, if you left her. Maybe she just wanted something to keep you at home."

"That's blackmail," Mathias said.

Steinberg stared at him. "Diane loves you," he said. "I'll bet anything she just wanted the bank records for herself. And your child. She didn't want it to read out in public." He gazed at Mathias for a moment. "Dumb as it sounds, I think this might have been her way of keeping you."

Mathias glanced aimlessly around the little room for a moment. Then he focused back on his partner. "But why did she do it this way?"

"Because you're a *cheat*," Steinberg said. "You goddam cheat everybody who comes close to you."

"I did it for you," Mathias said. "I did—"

"Bullshit," Steinberg said. "You've never done anything for anybody." He turned his back and gazed for a moment at the little framed exhibit of Toritron chips on the wall. "It's like I've spent the last seven years of my life being a kid. You write the checks, you buy the equipment, I play with my computers in the basement." Steinberg reached up and took the frame of chips off the wall and gripped it, as if to twist and break it. "Perpetual adolescence," he said bitterly. "A grownup Newton Bray."

"That's not *true*," Mathias said softly, looking down, shaking his head.

Steinberg turned and stared at him. He set the framed chips on the floor. "I'm responsible for this fuck-up too," he said. "I'm the one who wanted to stay in the laboratory, away from the business. When you brought me those blueprints for Ultrachip fabrication, they even *smelled* stolen." He closed his eyes briefly. "I asked you where you got them, you lied, and I didn't believe you. But I used them. Because I wanted to see Ultrachip work."

Mathias loosened his tie and leaned forward. He was already regaining some composure. "Alan," he said. "Sometimes I think you know Diane better than I do. Why did she do it this way?"

"Ask her yourself," Steinberg said shortly. "Maybe she just wanted to know, and it was an accident that the answer read out in public." He smiled slightly. "Even brilliant programmers make mistakes. Or maybe she wanted to put you out of business." He looked at Mathias. "Put *us* out of business. But frankly, I don't care. I've had enough of this business anyway."

There was a pounding on the door.

Mathias started. "Don't open it."

Tomasso's rasping voice was clearly audible from the corridor. "It's me. Open up."

Steinberg opened the door.

The burly computer scientist pushed past Steinberg, walked across the floor with remarkable speed, and stopped, standing directly in front of Mathias. Mathias looked up and then, with no warning, Tomasso was slapping him full across the face, once, twice, with enough force to send Mathias' head rocking from side to side.

Tomasso stepped back, already sweating. "Come at me," he growled, hunching his bulky shoulders, crouching slightly, beckoning with both hands. "Come at me," he told Mathias, "and I'll take your damn head off and eat it!"

Mathias didn't move, except to raise one hand and wipe off a slight swell of blood on his lower lip.

Involuntarily, Steinberg stepped between them. "Vincent," he said softly, "hang on."

Tomasso focused on Steinberg. "He screwed us," he said, his voice hoarse. "We look like idiots. In front of the *world*. And this is your *partner*." As he glared at Steinberg, his fury abruptly dissolved into remorse. "He took all that work, and flushed it down the goddam toilet."

"Vince," Steinberg said, putting both hands on Tomasso's shoulders, and gently, slowly, leading him back out the door. "That's not true. We'll get this straightened out. Go up to the office. I'll be up later. And don't talk to any reporters."

"Why?" Tomasso asked.

"Because it could compromise the case." He opened the door a few inches, already hearing the crush of reporters in the hallway. "We're going to sue the ass off Burt Mathias."

Steinberg opened the door wide and pushed Tomasso into the hall. As he closed the door he could already hear the scientist saying loudly, "No comment, no comment." Briefly, Steinberg mused that it was probably the first time in Tomasso's life that he'd ever uttered the phrase.

When Steinberg turned to face Mathias again, his partner was already moving. He was holding a white handkerchief to his lip, and heading for the door.

"Let me by, Alan," Mathias said, his voice slightly muffled by the handkerchief. "Please."

Steinberg opened the door. Mathias stepped out into a corridor filled with reporters, shouting questions. He turned his back and walked quickly, into the plush lobby, out into the parking lot. He locked himself into the turbodiesel, and with a spin of tires, headed up into the hills.

Steinberg was surrounded by reporters as well. He started to push his way through the crowd, to head back to the Ultrachip room. One reporter recognized

252

him, however, and suddenly he was deluged with questions.

"Dr. Steinberg. What happened?"

"Are these charges true?"

"Is the test a failure?"

"Is there an official statement?"

Steinberg ignored them until he reached the door of the locked staircase, and a security guard intervened. Then he stopped, and faced the newspeople. He held up one hand, and, gradually, the group grew quiet.

Finally, Steinberg spoke. "The system crashed," he said. "That's the official statement."

"What system do you mean, Dr. Steinberg?"

"Did SOCRATES malfunction?"

"Do you mean Ultrachip?"

Steinberg looked out at the crowd of reporters for a moment.

"The system crashed," he repeated. "It's as simple as that."

Steinberg looked down at the glossy linoleum floor of the Toritron Research Center, then looked up again. "But we did learn a hell of a lot," he said. "SOCRATES taught us all something." Steinberg smiled briefly. "And what more can you really ask from a computer?" Then he turned, and, taking the steps two at a time, went downstairs to where Martha and Newton were waiting.

# afterword

THE TURING TEST MADE INTERNATIONAL NEWS, EVEN though it was shut down midway through. The Karolinska Institute in Stockholm awarded Vincent Tomasso a Nobel Prize, making him the youngest scientist ever to earn the award. He immediately dropped both his book and television contracts, in order to perfect SOCRATES.

The National Science Foundation formed a study group to establish ground rules for ethical research in artificial intelligence. Rumor had it, however, that Japan was about to conduct its own Turing Test, government-sponsored, and that Germany was not far behind.

The *Journal of the American Psychiatric Association* reported a rash of "Turing Test syndrome"— severe apprehension of any machine that talks or listens. For the moment, there was no successful therapy.

Burt Mathias and Diane Caswell separated in June. Their son, James Caswell II, was born a month later.

In the same month, Burt Mathias pleaded guilty to five federal counts of embezzlement and abuse of electronic fund transfer. On a plea bargain, he was sentenced to three to five years, to be served at the federal correctional facility at Lompoc, California. His codefendant, a Toritron accountant, pleaded guilty and received a suspended sentence, in exchange for testimony.

Diane Caswell was initially indicted on charges of

malicious mischief and destruction of property, in the ARPANET and Bank of America computer break-ins. The indictments were subsequently dismissed, however, when her attorneys were able to convince a federal judge that the national computer disruption was solely due to programming errors made in her "emotion simulation" work for SOCRATES. Diane subsequently returned to Stanford, to begin work on her doctorate in computer science.

In the aftermath of the spectacular publicity, Technology International acquired Toritron for a fraction of its worth. But then, during the investigation surrounding the Mathias case, evidence surfaced that portions of the Ultrachip process had been stolen from the Fujitsu Company of Tokyo. As it developed, however, this proved no impediment to the TI acquisition of Toritron, for in early June, Fujitsu purchased a controlling interest in Technology International.

Alan Steinberg and Martha the Magnificent were married in July. Best man was Newton Bray, who had been released from probation only a day earlier, and would soon take over duties supervising the construction of the satellite dish for the nonprofit computer facility that Steinberg and Martha planned to establish in the western foothills of the California Sierra.

With the proceeds of his settlement from Toritron, Steinberg had purchased a satellite transponder to connect his Ultrachip facility to terminals in over five thousand public libraries in the United States and Canada—the largest free public-access system on the continent. Martha briefly abandoned electronic novels, to work on a microcomputer system designed for preliterate people. Her pilot project involved the introduction of hand-held computers—programmed for games, graphics and music—into the jungle highlands of New Guinea. Martha's rationale was simple: "Let's see what happens with computers if we skip all the cultural stuff in the middle."

By October, Martha (the Magnificent) Steinberg was pregnant. For the first time in her life, she finished a cheeseburger. And, as it would develop, two cheese-burgers.

One year later, Maralee Sonderson won a Pulitzer Prize for her *New York Times* series, and subsequent best-selling book, *Inside the Turing Test Scandal: The Exclusive Story.*

After serving eighteen months, Burt Mathias was paroled from Lompoc, his time shortened because of his diligent efforts to organize inmate classes in computer science and business management.

The only journalist to follow up on Mathias' release was a stringer for the *National Enquirer.* He reported that the one-time multimillionaire was met at the chain-link prison gate by only one person: an elegant young woman with long frosted hair. She was clad in a purple velour dress, and was accompanied by a small child.

The reporter followed their car briefly, but lost the turbodiesel somewhere in the hills above Santa Barbara.